PENGUIN BOOKS

PEARL HARBOR

Randall Wallace was born in Tennessee. He is the author of five previous novels, including *The Russian Rose*, *So Late into the Night* and *Braveheart*. The *Washington Post* said of him, 'The reader is held. Wallace knows how to shift scenes, how to build plot and subplot and tie them together, how to create suspense with teasing foreshadowings of hidden pasts and untold histories.'

PEARL HARBOR

RANDALL WALLACE

PENGUIN BOOKS

PENGUIN BOOKS

Published by the Penguin Group
Penguin Books Ltd, 27 Wrights Lane, London W8 5TZ, England
Penguin Putnam Inc., 375 Hudson Street, New York, New York 10014, USA
Penguin Books Australia Ltd, Ringwood, Victoria, Australia
Penguin Books Canada Ltd, 10 Alcorn Avenue, Toronto, Ontario, Canada M4V 3B2
Penguin Books India (P) Ltd, 11 Community Centre, Panchsheel Park,
New Delhi – 110 017, India
Penguin Books (NZ) Ltd, Cnr Rosedale and Airborne Roads,
Albany, Auckland, New Zealand
Penguin Books (South Africa) (Pty) Ltd, 5 Watkins Street, Denver Ext 4,
Johannesburg 2094, South Africa

Penguin Books Ltd, Registered Offices: Harmondsworth, Middlesex, England

Published in Penguin Books 2001
6

This film and TV tie-in edition published 2001

The moral right of the author has been asserted

Printed in England by Clays Ltd, St Ives plc

To my sons

Andrew & Cullen

with the fervent hope that neither they
nor anyone else's children
will know war

Book One

INNOCENCE

1

Danny Walker could still smell the sweet scent of the pine wood where Rafe McCawley had bored two holes through the nail keg and run a rope between them, to tie around their waists like a seat belt. The two boys sat on that keg, its top barely bigger than a slop bucket but large enough for the narrow butts of two ten-year-olds living on the farm scraps of America's Great Depression.

But they had their own airplane.

It was a biplane, one of the first crop dusters anywhere in the South. Rafe's father had bought it after the spine of its fuselage had cracked and its engine was thought to be too worn to be much use to anybody. He had cannibalized it for spare parts. Now its wings were jagged stumps of splintered wood, ripped fabric and rusted wire; its propeller was a two-by-four Rafe had found on the farm, and its windshield sheltered a sparrow's nest. But it had once flown in the Tennessee air, and now it flew farther and faster than any airship had ever flown, in the minds of two farm boys.

"They're coming in from the left!" Rafe screamed,

and threw his shoulder against Danny. Rafe had lean ropey arms, a tall frame and the quick eyes of a pilot. Even at the age of eleven, Danny had noticed this quality of his friend's eyes: not nervous, not twitchy, just quick.

"I see 'em!" Danny called back above the imaginary roar of their plane's engine and the buzz Rafe was making with his lips as he jerked the broken broomstick that controlled the maneuvers he was making through the sky in his mind.

"Get 'em, Danny!"

"I got 'em, Rafe!" And his tongue tickled his teeth, unleashing a thrashing pulse of machine-gun fire. Danny loved it when Rafe called him by name, called to him like a brother. Rafe was the only one in life who called him Danny. His mother had called him Daniel, but she had died when Danny was four. The best thing his father ever called him was Boy.

Danny's hair was light brown, like his mother's had been, and he had her green eyes. At least he hoped his eyes had come from her. An image of the softness of her eyes as she once had looked at him, gazing at him in quiet love, blazed in his memory whenever he thought of her. But her life seemed so distant now, and he had begun to wonder if his memories were only the projections of his fantasies, and he saw her as Rafe saw their plane, soaring in the sky.

"He's behind us! Behind us! See him?"

"I see him, Rafe!" Danny hollered, and twisted in his seat to fire toward the ruptured tail section of their craft. But in truth Danny saw nothing but the barn and the plowed fields beyond, though they glowed for him in the pure joy of togetherness. Rafe, he was sure, could see the Red Baron's biplane arcing down toward them. Rafe could see everything, could really see anything he could imagine. It was the most remarkable thing about being with Rafe. With Rafe, there was the world everyone else could see, and then there was the world that he could see, a world where old wrecks flew, and boys were pilots, and they were brave.

The only thing Rafe couldn't see was how to spell words. On the plank dashboard he'd rigged up for the plane's controls, he'd chalked the letters RUDR. Danny, winner of the Beaver Bottom Elementary School spelling bee the last three years running, had never been able to hear a word spoken without seeing exactly how to spell it in his mind. And Danny didn't just see words, he heard them sing and play with each other, he heard them rhyme or clash as they bounced around in his head. Still, Danny would've traded all his visionary gifts for Rafe's. In games like Dodgeball Rafe saw the ball's flight before anyone else—where it was bouncing, where it was heading; it was almost as if he could look into the future of the flight of a ricocheting ball. This made Rafe the better athlete when it came to things like batting or catching; and he had speed too, in his legs and hands as well as his eyes. Danny's big advantage on the playground was that he could fight. When he got punched in the nose, he never cried; he hit back, and always harder than he was hit. It was because of this that their friendship was sealed.

It happened one cold November, when the sky was slate gray and the mood of their teacher was just as dark. She'd given them the assignment of writing a page about the meaning of Thanksgiving, and had then told the students to exchange papers with the classmate sitting next to them. It was a routine of hers. "Check each other's spellin'!" she'd call out, and the pages would rustle across the aisles. Danny had always sat beside Rafe; they would draw pictures of World War I air battles and whisper and snicker, and it was that very noise-making that had gotten them separated. So now it was Calvin Pearson sitting beside Rafe, and when Danny saw the papers exchange, he already felt cold in his stomach.

Danny made his new deskmate's corrections quickly—there was only one mispunctuation, and Danny picked it up instantly—then looked in sick fear at Rafe's face. Rafe had no idea what was wrong or right with Calvin's paper, but that was not the problem. Calvin frowned down at Rafe's paper, then smiled, and began drawing circles around words with his red crayon, and then before Danny or anybody else could do anything about it, Calvin held the paper up high and laughed and called to the class, "Lookey here at how smart Rafe is!" The paper was covered in red—but it was not as red as the humiliation on Rafe's face.

The teacher said sharply, "Give that back to Rafe, Calvin!" and left it at that.

But Danny didn't. At recess he raced out of the schoolhouse door, ran like a bullet at Calvin, slammed his forehead into Calvin's nose, then fell across his chest and punched him until they pulled him off, though Danny broke away twice to punch and kick him again.

That fight marked Danny's public life in a way noth-

ing had before. He and Rafe were more than friends;
they were brothers.

The boys both paused in their game as the engine
sounds of the real plane above them grew louder and
higher in pitch as the plane descended over a field lush
with young plants. In the cockpit was Rafe's father, a
Baptist deacon who raised his own crops, fixed anything devised by man, and turned other people's junk
into useful machinery. The plane he was diving earth-
ward in at that very moment was a crop duster he had
assembled from parts culled from a dump outside a
nearby military base, combined with those he had
stripped from the wreck Rafe and Danny played in. He
had painted the plane a ruby red, and its wings and
spinning propeller flashed sunlight as it rushed a few
feet above the plowed ground, released a trail of crop
spray and climbed again, up into a crystalline blue sky.

Danny watched and thought how beautiful it was.
Like heaven were the words that came into his mind.
Then, for some reason he did not yet understand, *Volunteer State* sang after them. It would be years before he
would write the line, in describing his home: ". . .
Maybe it's not heaven; it's just Tennessee. But for as
long as there's been an America, men have fought and
died for this place—as volunteers." Then he would
comprehend where the urge to express himself on paper
had come from; now he looked at life, and peace, and
felt its joy.

Rafe, pressed beside him on the same nail keg seat,
watched the plane dip again, release a blossoming trail

of soft spray, then pop higher as his father pushed the foot control and the elevator flaps on the tail section bit the air, and Rafe felt it. Rafe felt everything. To Rafe McCawley, the world was an endless source of living stimulus, and he lived connected to it through the sensations of his heart. Movement, sound, sight, smell—all affected his emotions.

He was not thought of as an emotional boy; feeling early on that most people did not experience life as vividly as he did, he learned to keep his intensity to himself. Most people thought of him as quiet and inward. But to the ones with whom Rafe felt a real kinship—the ones whose spirit had a glow, a scent like fresh bread, a taste like cool springwater—Rafe was a volcano of life.

Rafe's heart locked onto those people, and stayed.

He knew he and Danny would be friends for life. Their differences, like Danny's ability with words, were not barriers; Rafe saw beyond the fact that written words made sense to Danny and were so confusing to him. And Danny was always ready to enter the world of imagination that two Tennessee boys could find on a spring day.

"Bandits at two o'clock!" Rafe yelled.

"Power dive!" Danny responded. And together they buzzed their lips in a flying noise and worked the controls, Rafe's bare feet on one pedal, Danny's on the other. The barn beside them, unpainted except for the hand lettering that said MCCAWLEY CROP DUSTING, remained firmly in its place, so the boys had to stare at the control cages chalked on their makeshift dashboard to see the world spin and dip around them. In their minds their overalls had become flight jackets, and their bowl-cut hair was covered with leather helmets, the very gear for wearing when saving America from the aggression of the German Kaiser. Danny held his fists in front of his face and spat machine-gun sounds, then blew an explosion through his cheeks.

"Good shooting, Danny!"

"Good flying, Rafe!"

"Land of the free . . ." Rafe said, in holy conviction.

"Home of the brave!" Danny returned, as if he had said *Amen*.

But before they could turn their dreams to confront another challenge against the safety of democracy, a man's hand closed around the straps of Danny's overalls and snatched him from the cockpit.

Surprised as Danny was, he knew it before he saw: it was his father's hand, strong, battered and dirty, the way the hand of a man with but a single arm so quickly becomes. Cole Walker, Danny's daddy, was a veteran of World War I and had left one of his arms in the Argonne Forest and brought back lungs scorched with mustard gas, so he was not a man inclined to be sensitive to the concerns of those whose bodies were whole. He dropped Danny on his feet and let him go just long enough to spin him around and snatch him by the front of the shirt, lifting him half off his feet again and shaking him.

"You no-count boy! Johnson come lookin', said he'd pay a dime for you to shovel his pig shed, and I can't find you no place. I done told you, you spend time playin' with this stupid boy can't even read, you ain't never gonna 'mount to nothin'!"

With all the shame and fear that burned in Danny at

that moment, what came from his mouth was, "He's not stupid, Da—"

Before he could finish the word *Daddy*, his father slapped him off his feet.

Rafe, who had been smacked on the bottom by his father's hand and had even been switched once for swearing, had never seen a grown man slap a child in the face, much less hit him so hard as to knock him to the ground. He was so horrified he couldn't get a sound out.

Danny was not even surprised—but when his father snatched him up again, twisting the overall straps so tight they choked him, he struggled. It did no good; his father began marching across the plowed field, dragging Danny as he went.

"Da—" Danny gasped. "Daddy—"

But Cole Walker's fury made him blind to what he was doing—until something hard cracked across his back with such force that his arm went limp and he fell with his face between the furrows. He'd been hit at the top of the spine, where the neck and shoulders meet in back, and the impact had caused his mind to flash white for a moment and then go black. The world swayed like a porch swing, and then Walker pitched over, turning belly up, and his eyes found what had hit him—the two-by-four propeller, in the hands of Rafe McCawley.

Rafe held the board like a baseball bat, cocked, ready to swing again. "Let him alone!" he shouted.

Walker's eyes bulged in rage; he staggered to his feet. And Danny was screaming, "Rafe . . . Daddy . . . No!"

Danny's father had not shaved since the last time Danny had seen him, which was three days before. There were scratches on his face, the blood dried over, like he'd stumbled into a barbed-wire fence sometime during his absence. His eyes were bloodshot, he stank of vomit, and he looked murderous. None of that scared Rafe, if he really saw it at all. All Rafe really seemed aware of at the moment was Danny's vulnerability and the plank in his own hands. He drew the plank back further and hissed, like an oath, "I'll bust you open, you . . . German!"

The words touched something deep in Cole Walker's broken brain. He froze. He blinked like a calf. And then he began to cough, in sick ugly convulsions, an old soldier broken by trench warfare, stress, cigarettes and booze—ruined lungs and a ruined life. He finally gasped enough breath to choke out, "I *fought* the Germans."

His eyes found his son, and they registered what he had just done. His mouth moved a moment, then formed words. "Danny, I . . ."

The words ran out on him. He turned and staggered away. Danny looked at Rafe with a communication deeper than blood, then ran off after his father. "Daddy! Daddy! Wait."

Danny caught him, took his father's hand, and walked away with him, gripping his fingers in forgiveness.

Behind Rafe, Jake McCawley rolled his plane to a stop and shut down the engine. Rafe heard the silence more than he had heard the motor's sound, and only then glanced back to see his father frowning at Danny and Cole Walker receding across his field. "What's goin' on, son?" Rafe's daddy said.

"Nothing," Rafe answered. "Danny's dad just come to get him." Rafe turned back to the ramshackle plane and replaced the two-by-four propeller. But his daddy was still looking toward Danny and his father, walking away. After a moment, Jake McCawley spoke. "Hey, boy," he said, "you wanna go up?"

Rafe's eyes lightened in delight, and he ran to the plane, hopping up onto the wing and scrambling into his father's lap. "Hey, Daddy," he said, as his father clipped the seat belt around them both, "will you take Danny up sometime?"

"Sure will, son."

As his father restarted the hot engine and pressed the plane forward in a rolling turn, Rafe looked out toward Danny's receding back and understood with absolute clarity that for as long as he lived, nothing would ever hurt Danny Walker unless it went through Rafe first.

2

Twelve years later, over a U.S. Army airfield in New Jersey, a squadron of planes sang in unison through the sky. Rafe was in the lead plane, and Danny flew the plane just off his right wing. They were fighter planes, but America was not at war. It was January of 1941.

The world had changed a great deal in those twelve years, though most of the changes seemed to have taken place across the oceans. A man named Adolf Hitler had taken control of Germany, and many people around the world, including the great American aviator Charles Lindbergh, looked across the Atlantic and saw the changes as good. Hitler reorganized his country after the chaos of the "Great War," the War to End All Wars, as the newspapers had called it, and now Germany was full of energy and motivation. Some people—a majority in non-German Europe, a minority in America—found themselves troubled about where those motivations were aimed, especially as Hitler raised great armies and launched the production of massive supplies of new weapons.

Hitler was not the only one to do so. Across the Pacific, as far from America as it was possible to get on the surface of the planet Earth, the Japanese had begun building their own empire, encroaching on their neighbors.

Instead of opposing the efforts of Japan and Germany to build up their ability to make war, America had, in general, assisted them. Japan could not function without oil, and the United States remained its prime supplier. For years Japan had bought every piece of scrap metal it could find, and again America, hungry for cash in the years of the Great Depression, had been its best source. In rural communities one of the simplest methods of raising spending money was to collect the discarded pieces of broken equipment that seemed to be lying around every farm and haul them to scrap yards in town, where somebody was always ready to buy. Rafe and Danny had even gone into that business themselves for a while. They had stopped it after the day they'd returned to Rafe's family's farm, where Danny now lived too, and had shown Rafe's grandfather the hard money they'd just received. His grandfather had sat in silence rocking on the front porch, listening to them exult with the success of their private enterprise and the plans of what they might buy with the first discretionary money of their lives; finally Grandpa McCawley spat a long stream of tobacco juice and said, "Boys, when they turn that metal into shrapnel and them plow tips start whistlin' by your ears, you ain't gonna be so happy you made that money."

Danny's father, dead now, had lost his arm to shrapnel, and after Grandpa McCawley's comments the boys knew they'd either have to find another way to make spending money or do without it, and since there was no other way, they did without.

But only for a while. They found something else that paid them, something they loved so much they would have paid to do it: crop dusting. With the help of Rafe's father they had scavenged an entire set of parts and built a second plane for the family business, and the only fights they ever had were over whose turn it was to fly.

Then they discovered the United States Army Air Corps, and life took on a new significance. Now it was Lieutenant Rafe McCawley and Lieutenant Daniel Walker in the cockpits of the two planes at the head of the squadron cutting through the sky over the New Jersey airbase, as Captain Connor, the training captain, radioed instructions from the ground: "McCawley, Walker, loosen up that formation!"

"You said tighten up," McCawley's voice came back to him, and even over the tinniness of the radio it had its distinctive quality; when McCawley was in the air, he always sounded like he was laughing. "Didn't he say tighten up, Danny?"

"He said tighten up," came Walker's voice, and the training captain would've sworn the tips of their two planes, already less than a yard apart, moved to within a foot of each other.

"Not that tight!" he barked. Captain Connor loved

those two guys; there was nothing like brimming confidence in a pilot, as long as he could back it up with skill, and these two Tennessee boys had shown up on the first day of cadet school with as much flying skill and far more natural potential than any of the instructors who were supposed to be teaching them. If the Army Air Corps had been training more young pilots—and there weren't too many older ones with nothing else to do—the two runny-nosed hotshots would've been instructors themselves. The training captain had rank, but on an airbase for fighter pilots nothing gives a man more power than his courage and skill, especially if it's a base run by Colonel Jimmy Doolittle. Still Captain Connor liked the two young bucks. Cocky as they were, they retained the inherent politeness of Tennessee boys.

McCawley, in the point plane, led the squadron in a fast turn, and Connor watched the maneuver in admiration and noticed the other eight pilots in the group following with more skill and assurance than ever. It was as if McCawley and Walker cut grooves through the air for them, trailing excitement in their wake, and the other young guys sucked it into their intakes and poured it out through their own exhaust manifolds. "That'll do," he radioed. "Let's bring 'em in."

The P-40s, the Army Air Corps' best fighters, began landing in tight order. They taxied off the runway right beside where the training captain stood, shut down their engines, slid back their canopies with a flourish and hopped out full of life and adrenaline. *If I had half their energy*, Captain Connor thought, *I'd own the world*. Then he noticed the planes had stopped landing, but they were two P-40s short. He didn't have to check off

faces to know which two they were. "Where are Mc-
Cawley and Walker?" he said.

Then he saw the two planes still in the air; they'd cir-
cled to opposite ends of the airfield and were now heading directly at each other, like two bullets playing
chicken.

"Aw no . . ." Connor muttered, as all the young pilots looked skyward.

Inside the cockpits Rafe and Danny steadily pressed
the throttles forward and felt the steady surge in speed as
their two planes closed on each other at double the rate
they could fly. The rushing excitement was awesome.

The pilots on the ground watched speechlessly as the
P-40s hurtled at each other. Billy—Billy the Kid, because
he was the most boyish-faced of the pilots—looked in
rising panic at his best friends; as the planes drew so
close they couldn't possibly get out of each other's way,
Billy screamed to drown out the sound of the collision.

Twenty feet above their heads, the planes came together, and at the last instant—when it seemed to the
onlookers that the planes had already hit—the two
P-40s snapped a quarter turn so that their wings were
vertical and shot past each other, belly to belly. The
wind blasted the clothes of the men on the ground, blew
their hats from their heads, as if they stood in the vortex
of a passing hurricane.

In the cockpits Rafe and Danny exploded in laughter,
their planes racing away from each other as fast as
they'd closed, their hearts sharing the same thrill, the
timeless pleasure of living totally in the present. Danny
let his plane soar on its own, rising like a hawk resting
on the wind; Rafe celebrated his excitement by spinning

his plane like a corkscrew before jerking his stick straight up, as if to punch through the gravity of earth and sail unfettered toward the stars.

On the ground, the other pilots laughed and congratulated each other, as if they too were in those cockpits.

The training captain let his cap land on the ground near his feet before he said anything. Then all he could mutter was, "Dammit! Those guys are a menace to national security."

Anthony, a slender Italian from a Brooklyn neighborhood, picked up the captain's hat and handed it to him, smiling. "You know what they say, Captain. You can take the crop duster out of the country—but don't put him in a P-40."

Danny landed and taxied his plane over to join the others, shutting down the engine before he stopped rolling. He slid back his cockpit cover and raked the leather helmet off his head, his chestnut hair popping up full and youthful, his teeth movie-star luminous as he grinned at his friends. He'd unbuckled his seatbelt and was halfway out of the cockpit when he looked around and said, "Where's Rafe?"

Red, so named because of the bright hair topping his skinny body like flame on a flagpole, tipped his chin toward the sky, where Rafe's plane was climbing in a slow, deliberate spiral, up and up.

"I said get down here, McCawley!" the training captain barked into the radio.

But he was answered by a burst of static and the suspiciously garbled words, ". . . can't hear you. Repeat?"

Danny swore beneath his breath and bounced back into his seat; he was starting to refasten his harness when Captain Connor snapped, "You're down, Walker! That's an order!"

"What about him?" Danny said, climbing out and following the spiral of Rafe's plane, up and up.

"He's not taking my orders anymore," Connor said, almost to himself.

Danny was about to ask him what the hell he meant by that, when he noticed Rafe leveling off and setting the plane into a firm and engine-steadying speed, like a rider gathering a horse before a dangerous jump. "He's gonna do it," Danny said.

"Do what?" Billy said.

"*It.*" Rafe's plane was a speck above them, and for a moment it seemed to pause in the air.

"What *it?*" Billy asked, with Red and Anthony frowning the same question at Danny.

"The outside loop." For years it had been the holy grail of aviation, a stunt attempted by test pilots and barnstormers alike, leaving splattered remains inciner-ated in burning fuel. It had been first achieved but a few years before—by the very Colonel Jimmy Doolittle who now commanded this airbase. Since then, others had tried it. A few had even succeeded. The others had died.

In a normal or "inside" loop, the pilot simply pulled back on the control stick and let the nose of the plane rise until the whole aircraft fell over like a kid doing a backflip off a boat dock. The plane's momentum and in-herent aerodynamics made the maneuver feel natural and almost self-correcting; it had been done for decades and was commonplace. The outside loop was another story. Once a pilot pushed a plane into its maximum dive and then tried to complete a circle from bottom to top and back again, with the cockpit of the plane on the outside rather than the inside of the loop, he could not see the ground rushing up and had to trust his life to his instincts and skill at a time when everything worked against him; it was death or glory, with no in between.

"Oh no," Captain Connor said. "Oh no. Oh no . . ."

Anthony and Billy joined in, chanting with him, as they felt their insides congeal like cold piss around their hearts, "Oh no. Oh no. Oh no . . ."

Rafe, in his cockpit, took a deep slow breath and found that place within himself where he had learned to go in times of stress and danger; it was very near that inner place he had always gone to when he felt isolated, scorned for being different, persecuted for his errors in the classroom—the same spot he'd withdrawn to when Calvin Pearson had held up his paper for ridicule. This place of calm and commitment had pain nearby, and anger and determination as well as a dragon's breath of fear, blasting like a blowtorch. When at the center of his spirit, Rafe could draw the energy from those emotions, but they did not pollute the purity of his instincts or the clarity of his goals. *Do it* were the only words involved in the experience, and they were subliminal, like the echo of a dream, rather than a sound in his mind. Once he'd made the decision to do something—and he had envisioned what he was about to do long before this moment—his body began to move without his mind needing to send it verbal instructions. As now, when his left hand moved to the throttles and pushed them steadily forward, as his right hand shifted the stick toward the nose of the plane and the horizon rose and the earth loomed before him.

Power dive.

The P-40 screamed toward the ground, picking up speed. Hurtling down under full power, he was going faster than the plane was designed to go, and an orchestra of physical forces began to vibrate and then shake the plane. The buffeting could slow him down, and he needed every shred of speed possible; he backed the throttles just enough to ease the shuddering of his fuselage, and kept dropping, faster and faster.

Down on the ground, Danny whispered like a prayer, "You can do it, Rafe. You can do it."

The P-40, hurtling toward the ground at nauseating speed, snapped into a half roll, streaking upside down over the runway. Rafe, experiencing more g-forces than the human body was designed to take, hung inverted in his harness, the asphalt of the runway shooting past, ten feet below his head. None of the men on the runway had ever seen any object travel that fast before. Bullets were swifter, but those you couldn't see; the P-40 was a screaming flash of engine and wind.

Rafe pushed the plane into a climb, his cockpit on the outside of the circle, and it shot skyward again, propelled by its enormous speed. But it quickly slowed; propeller-driven planes rapidly lose the battle with gravity when moving vertically. Danny and his friends watched without breath or noticeable heartbeat as the plane reached the top of its arc and almost stalled; if it lost enough airspeed then all of the mystical lifting power of moving air would be gone and it would drop to earth without control, like the hunk of lifeless metal it truly was.

Like it truly was . . . if not in the hands of a pilot. Rafe feathered the throttles and nosed the plane over toward the earth again. Only this time he had very little altitude. And that was the whole problem with the outside loop. The outside loop seemed against nature; it suggested the Icarus of Greek mythology, so drunk with the thrill of flying that he flew too high and destroyed himself.

To Danny, to Billy, Red and Anthony, to Captain Connor and the squadron's other pilots on the ground, it seemed Rafe didn't have enough altitude to make it. His plane had almost stopped dead at the top of the arc; he'd milked the upward speed to its absolute limit, to get every inch of altitude possible, but still, he was so low!

The truth be told, it seemed that way to Rafe too. That quiet place within himself, the place of facing danger, was not completely silent now; it vibrated with the sucking feeling of a voice about to scream, and a sudden chill bit his insides.

But he was going. He pushed the throttles to their limit.

He could not just ram forward his other controls and expect to survive. To live he had to gather speed and pick exactly the right instant—if such an instant existed in the physics of wind lift and air density on that particular day—to make the plane's controls convert velocity into turning power.

The plane raced down, still with its belly on the inside of the curve. . . .

And made it full circle, with barely a foot to spare.

His friends—all except Danny and Captain Connor—burst into cheers.

Rafe, in his cockpit, permitted himself a smile.

The hearts of those on the runway were still thumping in their chests as Rafe's P-40 touched down and rolled toward them. The squadron pilots ran out to meet him; Captain Connor just stood there shaking his head.

Danny got to the plane first, jumping onto the wing as Rafe came to a full stop and slid back his canopy. Danny grabbed him by the harness and shook Rafe so hard that his body banged around in the seat. "You could'a killed yourself, you stupid bastard!" Danny shouted. Then he dived into the cockpit and hugged Rafe, his feet in the air as the other pilots crowded in yelling congratulations. Danny said into Rafe's ear, "That was the most beautiful thing I ever saw."

3

Colonel Jimmy Doolittle was one of those men who, in his mid-forties, was even tougher than he had been in his twenties. There was no way to prove this, of course; he could not go back and take on the younger version of himself in a bar fight, but Doolittle had sometimes imagined that very thing, and he was pretty sure the older version of himself, though possessing aches and pains and stiffness and no longer having the absolute physical resilience he had known in his youth, still could've prevailed, on will alone. And experience, of course. When he was a young hotshot pilot, he was bursting with that brash bravery necessary to fly a fighter plane. But the other kinds of courage, like the will to persevere in the maddening world of military bureaucracy, the determination to see things through to the end and make them come out right for the Army he loved and the men he both served and commanded— those kinds of courage he had developed later.

But still from time to time he pondered that fantasy question of just how tough he would have to be now to dominate his younger self. He thought about it because he trained young pilots, and he knew he could never do his job right unless he believed—and they believed too—that he was still better than they were.

Making them believe this had never seemed to be a problem. Every cadet he ever saw revered him. They snapped their spines to rigidity when in his presence; most of those he called into his office, even those brought in for commendation, actually trembled.

Doolittle liked the respect, the rigid spines. He did not like the trembling.

Rafe McCawley was not trembling.

But he was damn sure standing at attention.

Doolittle sat at his desk, watching him. "There are some people," Doolittle said, in a slow voice meant to sound ominous, "who think the outside loop is reckless and irresponsible."

"How could it be irresponsible, sir," McCawley began, with the Tennessee accent that had softened a good deal since he'd been living with the mix of men in the Army, "if you were the first man in the world to do it?"

"Don't get smart with me, son."

"Never, sir. I just meant it's dangerous only for the kind of pilot who wants to show off, rather than inspire the other pilots in his unit. And after all you've done for me, sir, working out the transfer, I did it to say thanks. To honor you, sir. What the French call an *homage*."

"That's bullshit, son. But it's really good bullshit."

"Thank you, sir."

"I've thrown a lot of men out of my outfits, McCawley, but never had one volunteer to leave." Doolittle paused and pondered that fact for a moment, and Rafe stood there wondering if he had finally pushed things too far, as everyone had seemed to be telling him that he was going to, throughout his life. Doolittle stared out the window before looking back at him and going on, "I've never seen America so determined to sit on its hands while all of Europe's at war, either. When Air Commander Fenton told me the Brits were creating the Eagle Squadron to give American volunteers a chance to help them fight the Germans, I had two thoughts: a lot of Americans are gonna die . . . and I wish I could go myself."

Doolittle stood, moved around his desk, and shook Rafe's hand. "I admire your courage, McCawley," he said. "Good luck over there."

In the barracks where Rafe's squadron slept, his buddies were getting slicked up for a night on the town. Danny stood at the mirrors above the sinks hung on the latrine wall and splashed Old Spice into his palm, smacked it onto his face and neck, and admired his reflection.

It was not himself he was so proud of. He took pride in what he had already done in his life and what it had taken to do it; but Danny was not the kind of man to stand back and adore himself. He knew the power of symbols, he felt what they meant; and there was no symbol in his life greater than the uniform he wore. It was one of equality, and one of merit. Rich men's sons, even in America, might still be able to use the power of wealth to wrangle cushy positions in the Army, but no one could buy those pilot's wings. The men around him, they had earned their wings as Danny had earned his,

and Danny respected them all, even if they lacked skills
that some others had. They had fulfilled requirements that
were unforgiving, and they lived in a profession that
sent its failures as well as many of its successes to the
grave. Danny loved the substance of their commitment
to this profession. As for his own skills, he would accept the superiority of no one, even Rafe. To Danny,
now as it had been throughout his life, an edge that
anyone held over him was only temporary. Danny was
climbing, learning, improving, and he would never
stop. He had truly become, already, an officer and a
gentleman.

To Danny's right stood Anthony and Billy, combing
Vitalis through their hair. Anthony, with his rich black
Italian hair and his years of practice for summer nights
in Brooklyn, had achieved the perfect patent leather
look on either side of a razor sharp part. Billy, however,
was from Kansas—the state, not the city—and combing his dense yellow hair, even with oily lubricant, was
like trying to rake a cornfield. Still, Billy was not dis-
couraged. The softest and gentlest guy in the unit, with
the most boyish face, he seemed to care about everybody and to care what they thought about him—and
since everyone liked him, he was perpetually happy.
That Anthony, with his New York edge and attitude,
would accept him not just as a buddy but as a best
friend gave Billy an almost giddy love of life. Enthusi-
asm brimmed from him as he checked himself in the
mirror and burst out, "You good-lookin' sumbitch . . .
don't you *ever* die!"

"That's your line for tonight, ya know," Anthony

said, patting his hair with the middle joints of his fingers, as if his combing job was too perfect to help in any other way.

"What? Good-lookin' sumbitch?" Billy wondered.

"No, numbnuts, *die*. You get your nurse alone, you look her in the eye, and you say, 'Baby, they're training me for war, and I don't know what'll happen. But if I die tomorrow, I wanna know that we lived all we could tonight.' I've never known it to fail."

Red, on the other side of Danny, finished brushing his teeth and spat into the sink. Red had a stutter when he was excited or nervous, even with his friends. Tonight his stutter was especially pronounced. "He's n-never known it to w-work, either," Red said.

Laughing and shoving each other, they moved to the door of the barracks, toward the night beyond and the base bus into Manhattan, and the nurses they would be meeting there. As they stepped out the door, they ran into Rafe coming in. "There you are!" Danny said. "I thought I was gonna have to miss the nurses, and you know how disappointed they would'a been."

Rafe smiled but there was something clouded in his eyes. Danny thought Doolittle must have dealt him some harsh discipline and tried to add an optimistic light to Rafe's perspective by adding, "So Doolittle didn't kill you! Attaboy!" He threw his arm around Rafe's shoulder and started to walk with him toward the buses.

Rafe patted Danny on the back in a paternal way Danny had never felt from his own father but had sometimes felt from Rafe's dad. "Danny, there's something I gotta tell you."

"Yeah . . . ?"

But Rafe didn't want to say it right there among the
other guys. "Ya'll go ahead," he told them. "We'll
catch up."

So as the others moved toward the bus, Danny and
Rafe lagged back, and moved to a patch of ground at
the edge of the parking lot, beneath a dim street light. It
was a mild night as New Jersey winters go; the ground
was not frozen but it was grassless and hard, swept
clean by winds and policed of every cigarette butt and
scrap of gum wrapper, as the ground on Army bases always was. It was a bare place for a heart-to-heart talk,
and from Rafe's demeanor Danny already knew that's
what they were about to have.

The guys in the bus were excited. Their training was almost over, and rumors had started weeks before about
where they would be sent next. Most of them had traveled little in their short lifetimes; there was not a man
among them who had been farther from home as a civilian than the Army had already sent them in their various training postings on their way to becoming pilots,
so almost any possibility for the future sounded like an
adventure—as long as there were women. Being cooped
up with other young guys pulsing testosterone just
sharpened their appetites for the fairer sex, and previous
evenings on the town had already taught them that
leather flight jackets, silk scarves and pilots wings were
a potent aphrodisiac. Nurses weren't as easily impressed
as civilian girls were, but that was just part of the night's
challenge, and the pilots were anxious to get on with it.
"Let's go!" Anthony shouted to the bus driver.

"We've gotta wait for Danny and Rafe," Billy said.

"Wh-what are they doin'?" Red wondered. And all three looked toward Rafe and Danny, at the edge of the darkness. They seemed to be arguing about something. Danny had taken a step back, and was rubbing his palm into his chin, like he didn't know whether to shout or to fight. Billy, Red and Anthony had seen them argue before; they did it like brothers. But this looked different, like something was really . . . wrong.

"How could you do this?" Danny was saying.

"The colonel helped me work it out."

"I don't mean how'd you do the paperwork, I mean how the hell did you do it without letting me in on it?"

"I'm sorry, Danny, but they're only accepting the best pilots." Rafe offered him a smile, but it wasn't his best one, the one that just popped onto his face and made you celebrate with him. This one was the kind of smile a kid wore when taken to a tent revival.

"Don't make this a joke, Rafe. You're talking about war, and I know what war does to people. It's people dying. And it's the wrong people, the ones who don't profit. I read somewhere that war is a farmer's son from Kansas trying to kill a factory worker's son from Berlin, with neither of them knowing why."

"Maybe if I could'a read that, I'd be smart enough not to volunteer."

"Dammit, Rafe—" Danny tried to hold his emotions back; they just built up and boiled over. "It's no joke, and it's no game! It's war—where the losers die, and there aren't any winners, just guys who turn into broken-down wrecks like my father."

"I know that's how you feel, and that's why you should stay. But I feel different. I feel like it's my duty to go."

"Don't preach to me about duty! I wear the same uniform you do! If trouble wants me, I'm ready—but why go look for it?"

"Because it's looking for me."

Dammit! Danny thought to himself, for a guy who thinks of himself as inarticulate, Rafe always hits you right in the heart. Danny stood there simmering, trying to come up with something to say; and once again, Rafe beat him to it.

"I know you're right, Danny. War's not fun, it's not a game like it was back when we were boys. We're men now—and we live in a world where somebody strong is hurting somebody who's weak. And never in my life have I been able to just stand by and watch that happen."

And now Danny stopped simmering and just stood there in the flat, true silence that Rafe always brought him to, sooner or later.

From the window of the bus they heard Billy holler, "The nurses are waiting!" The driver added punctuation with the sharp *whoosh* of his airbrakes releasing.

Danny didn't move. "Let's go," Rafe said.

"Some other time. I don't feel like a party."

Rafe could find no words to keep Danny from walking away. Rafe just stood there on the bare ground beneath the street lamp and watched him stride off into the darkness, and as angry and as hurt as he knew

Danny was, Rafe never doubted for a moment that he would get over it. There was nothing in the world that could break the bond between them.

Over at the bus, Red was holding the driver around the neck with one arm and was honking the horn with the other. Rafe glanced back at Danny once more and wished he could stay with him and drink a beer and talk.

But Rafe had someone else he had to see that night.

Red honked the horn again, and Rafe turned and ran for the bus, hopping into its doorway just as it began to move.

4

The trains of 1941 had their own beauty, and this one had felt seats the color of chocolate and compartments paneled in shellacked wood, with little electric lamps framing the windows and throwing a glow over everything. Empty of passengers, the cars smelled of the wood and the scent of the oil that seeped up from the iron wheels; but the train was not empty now. It was full of passengers on their way into Manhattan from upstate New York, and the ten Navy nurses gathered in the rear of the car spilled talk and laughter and life and the scent of their own floral fragrance through the interior and out into the flickering countryside.

Evelyn Stewart sat quietly in the glow, gazing at the countryside as it shot past. Like the others in her group, she wore the dark blue uniform of her profession, with its distinctive white trimmed hat pinned into her light brown hair. She was the rarest of individuals, a leader who never sought attention. When people first met her and noticed her inwardness, her apparent lack of any hunger for approval, they found it easy to conclude that her air of self-sufficiency was a natural consequence of her beauty; anyone with such natural physical elegance had approval shoveled at them. But the few who truly got to know her realized Evelyn was neither as calm as she appeared on the outside nor as indifferent to approval. She was driven, she was focused on whatever obsessed her, and excellence at her job was one of her passions. She did seek approval, but the approval she was most hungry for was her own. Her father had been a military officer; her mother, the daughter of a South Dakota doctor, had dreamed of being a doctor herself but had followed her husband's nomadic life instead. Somewhere along that ride Evelyn had concluded that no one's opinion would ever shape her life as much as would her own opinion of herself.

The other nurses with her worked in her unit at the naval hospital. Two shared her rank, but even they recognized Evelyn's abilities and deferred to her, especially during emergencies. But that was at the hospital. Now they were on a train to meet pilots, and they were content to let Evelyn stare out the window as they celebrated. For them the party had already started.

They were all pretty and ripe—perhaps a bit too ripe, their lips painted bright red, their faces powdered, their spirits high. Unafraid of ever growing fat and unconcerned about ever growing old, they smoked cigarettes, swigged Cokes and munched on Moon Pies. To Evelyn, the talking of her friends at this moment was just background noise, so deeply was she lost in her own thoughts; and yet, like every nurse who could focus on a task and still be attuned to significant noises or the lack of them, another level of Evelyn's brain monitored the sounds around her. She heard Barbara, a sultry brunette with a whiskey voice and the oldest of their group, lecturing two of the youngest nurses about their coming evening with the pilots.

"Now listen to me," Barbara was saying. "Here's how it happens with pilots. I mean it's true of all men but *especially* with pilots. First they look at you when they think you're not looking at them, and their eyes jump out of their head and they make faces at their buddies as if the damn fools think we see them only if we're looking right at them. A man completely forgets, if it ever occurred to him in the first place, that a woman can see out the back of her head, and even around walls."

"Especially if there's a man there," giggled Sandra, a green-eyed girl from Chicago.

Barbara gave her a nod and went on; the other girls had laughed but shut up quickly, anxious to hear the voice of experience. "You've got to think of them as fish. A man has just about the same brain power as a river bass, and if you really look at them, their mouths move almost exactly the same way. Their eyes dart around, they spot the bait. . . ." At this point Barbara inhaled, pressed her shoulders back, and cocked her head at a sultry angle, drawing whoops and applause from her audience; she took a movie-star pull from a cigarette, and went on, "and they stroll over, drunk with their own desire. Of course I'm talking about when you meet them for the first time. The ones you already know, they'll walk over with their eyes dancing, like they haven't thought of anything but you since the last time you met. And the truth is, maybe they haven't. Their little fish brains are that small."

Betty, a little blue-eyed blonde bombshell from Texas who barely looked old enough to have finished high school, said, "Gaw lee, you thank that's true?"

Barbara just looked at her, and the other girls laughed until Betty did too.

"But sooner or later," Barbara said, "and I mean tonight, if any of you girls have turned into minnow-brains on me, they'll hit you with their line. Every soldier will do it sooner or later, and every pilot will do it, *tonight*. They'll buy you dinner, they'll give you wine, maybe even champagne, they'll dance with you and press themselves up against you, and the next chance they get, they'll put their lips beside your ear—" Here Barbara formed her own lips into a fish mouth that made her eager friends explode in laughter. "—And then . . . and then they'll say, 'Baby, I never thought it could be this good with anybody. You're special, Baby. You're the *one*! I wish this night could last forever but we both know it can't. I'm going away, and . . . and I may never come back again. . . . ' Then he'll look right into your eyes and say, 'So we have to make this night last forever in our hearts, Baby. We have to make it a night we'll never forget.' "

Barbara stopped and took another drag on her cigarette. The train rumbled along the track. For a moment the nurses were all silent. Then Sandra said, "I tell you what. If one of those cocky flyboys tries a line like that on me? . . ."

Betty looked at her with doe eyes. Even Evelyn, feeling the pause, glanced to her from the window.

". . . I'm gonna give him anything he wants."

The nurses cackled like a coven of witches.

Evelyn was laughing with them; but when the talk turned to speculation about their next posting, she began looking out the window again.

"I can't wait to see the world!" Betty said with a dreamy drawl. "Where do you think they'll send us?"

"I hope it's somewhere warm," Sandra said.

"You and me both," Barbara said. "I want someplace in the Pacific, where all you need is a good party dress and a bathing suit."

"I don't want a good party dress," Betty shot back. "I want a good man."

"Then you better talk to Evelyn," Barbara answered. "She's got the best man in the Army."

Evelyn tried not to react, but she felt the eyes of all her friends on her.

"Come on, Evelyn," Barbara sang. "Tell us how to find one like Rafe."

And without turning from the window, Evelyn let her thoughts drift back two months before, to the military medical center in New York City. . . .

Because of the cutbacks made in the U.S. Armed Services throughout the Depression years of the 1930s and the further strain brought about by Washington's efforts to supply Great Britain and Russia with defensive resources as they fought for survival against the Nazis, the branches of the U.S. military were making do as best they could, and with a shortage of doctors as well as everything else, they were sharing some of their checkup facilities. So it was that Evelyn and her group of U.S. Navy nurses had found themselves in a scene of controlled chaos, with young pilots, both Army as well as

Navy, stripped to their underwear and holding paper-work, being herded through the ordeal of inoculations and medical monitoring.

The endless cycle of booster injections and confirmations of the top-range physical function required for all fliers meant mind-numbing repetition for the nurses, and it was certainly no less trying for the pilots. Evelyn had decided to perk up the process by rotating her staff between stations. Following her leadership policy of personally accepting the worst jobs first, she had assigned herself the visual acuity station. It was the dullest checkup of all; in two years of active duty, she had never known or heard of any pilot—all of them fit males in their early twenties—to have passed the dozens of eye checks required to gain entry into flying school, and then suddenly develop near- or farsightedness. But regulations were regulations, so Evelyn did her job, finding diversion only in listening to the exchanges coming from Betty's inoculation table next to her desk.

"Come on, honey, look do you really have to do this?" a guy with slick black hair was saying. Evelyn would later discover his name to be Anthony. Even without knowing him, though, she knew he was a pilot; they oozed an attitude of cocky independence.

"No," Evelyn heard Betty say, "if you'd rather, she can do it." Betty nodded toward the next table, where a huge nurse with massive forearms stabbed a soldier's pale butt. And before the pilot could give her an answer, Betty gave him an injection.

"OW! What, you already dull that needle on every ass in the Army?"

"We're Navy nurses." Betty smiled, like an angel. "Next station, please."

"I'm just saying I've been inoculated a thousand times already! Is this necessary?"

"The government says stick 'em . . . we stick 'em! NEXT!"

Evelyn managed not to smile. She admired Betty's spunk. But she worried about her flirtatiousness, too. The men would be all over her, and the prospect of that clearly did not trouble Betty. Evelyn figured she'd never had her heart broken. The other nurses had enough experience to know that men could be wonderful, but none of them were always that way.

Then an argument broke out across the room, and its urgency cut through the clatter of the syringes on the metal trays and the chatter of the men around them. A pilot was pleading with a doctor, and what he seemed to be begging for was his life. "Doc, listen, I've passed a dozen medical checks! You write that, you take my wings away!" the young man was saying.

The words caught the ears of every pilot in the room. They tried not to hear, but they couldn't keep talking enough to keep from it. They tried to look away, to occupy their minds with other thoughts; that's when Evelyn first noticed the two pilots standing in the middle of her line. One was tall, so lean and hard his muscles looked like they were made of ropes. The other was not quite so long limbed, but equally fit. Evelyn could not help noticing that the taller one was worried about something, and his friend was whispering rapidly and nodding his head in some kind of reassurance. The taller one was looking at the eye chart on the wall twenty feet behind her, and he was not squinting, as a man worried about nearsightedness might; his eyes were wide and darting, as if he were trying to memorize the chart but couldn't stay mentally focused on it long enough to do so. The conversation going on beside him was only making matters worse, as the words rattled every pilot in the room. "Doc, please . . . hang on a minute. I don't have a murmur, there's some mistake . . . !"

Still the doctor wrote, not looking up. "If it clears up," he said, "we can retest you." He said it knowing that never happened; so many men wanted to be pilots, and there were so few instructors and planes to train them in that any washouts found themselves as personnel officers or air traffic controllers. The doctor grabbed a rubber stamp and slapped MEDICAL REJECTION onto the heartbroken flyer's paperwork. Evelyn saw the tall pilot in her line jump at the sound as if he'd heard a gunshot.

All the way up to the front of the line, the two flyers kept whispering. When the man in front of them finished rattling off the lines she told him to read and Evelyn stamped APPROVED on his papers, the tall flyer jumped forward, sliding his paper onto the desk in front of her downturned face. Too quickly he spouted, "J—L—M—K—P—O! Eyes like an eagle, ma'am."

She kept her eyes down on his file, and saw that his name was Rafe McCawley. Still without looking up she said, "Slow down, soldier. And instead of the bottom line, read the very top one."

He froze. "But . . . that's . . . they're so big, how's that gonna . . ."

"Please read the top," she said.

The second pilot, standing close behind his friend, coughed loudly, but Evelyn did not look up and remained so silent that he had to know she was listening, and would hear any help he tried to give.

"Uh . . . ," the tall pilot said, "R . . . J . . . C . . . no, no, J, C, Q, W. I mean W, Q."

Evelyn, who knew the chart backwards and forwards, was intrigued by this. Weak vision caused mistaking a letter for a similar one—turning "Q" into "O" or "R" into "P," for example. This guy was *reordering* letters—on the biggest, most legible line of the chart.

Evelyn flipped open his file and scanned his test summaries; his math and spatial reasoning scores were both 99, extraordinary. But his language usage score was 68. She thumbed quickly to the rear of the file, where his initial application for the Air Corps, the only handwritten section of his entire service record, lay; there she saw the same reversing of letters, and the literal phonetic spelling of certain words, giving his sentences a confused, almost childish appearance. But what he said in those sentences was clear and forceful, even heartfelt. He had written at the very bottom, "I love to fly. In the sky, I smel the breth of God." To think something so simple and beautiful, yet spell it incorrectly . . . this was not ignorance, she realized, it was dyslexia, the condition in which the brain jumbles letters. She had read about it. Science did not understand the cause; it seemed to have something to do with the structure of the particular brain, and a great many people who exhibited the condition were gifted, even brilliant. Dyslexia was little known, widely misunderstood and difficult to identify

because it was variable and inconsistent; the dyslexic
could read a word correctly once, then see the same
word incorrectly a moment later. Army rules, however,
were not variable or inconsistent: any man identified as
dyslexic was disqualified from being a pilot.

"The bottom line again, please," Evelyn said. "But
read it right to left . . . and every other letter."

Rafe McCawley struggled again, to do what she had
asked. "Uh . . . E . . . X . . ." he read.

His friend behind him coughed again, covered his
mouth with his hand, and whispered something. Then
Rafe said, more confidently, "X, E, J, U—"

Evelyn looked up suddenly and caught Rafe in her
stare. His eyes locked onto hers and his heart went right
into them, and Evelyn had a feeling she wouldn't try to
understand until much later, when she wondered if his
eyes couldn't soak in the dry incidentals of life, like the
sequence of letters, because they were so busy pouring
so much heart out of them. But at the moment, her
mind didn't struggle with such thoughts; she just looked
at the half-naked young man standing in front of her,
with so much feeling in his eyes.

She shifted her gaze to the other young man behind
him, and her heart broke for him too. He was frozen,
mortified in the knowledge that he'd been caught; and
yet it was clear in the way he glanced at her—a repre-
sentative of enough military authority to have him de-
moted for an honors violation—with no worry for what
she might do to him, but with an absolute concern for
the feelings and future of his friend, that this man had
somehow, long ago, learned to stare down any fear for
his own fate.

She shifted her eyes back to Rafe. She saw the sweat pop out on his forehead and slide down his cheeks as she looked back to his paperwork.

A voice inside her told her not to do what she wanted to do, which was to pass him anyway. Her responsibility was to follow regulations; the manual sat right there on her desk, as a reminder. The trouble was, the U.S. military didn't make distinctions about what caused men to fail an eye chart test. If the point was to assure they had sharp vision, this man had passed. As for his reading, he'd gotten by in flight school—that was obvious from his file. Right there in front of her it said: FLYING SKILLS, CLASS RANK: #1.

That was impressive. But still she had that voice inside her, the one that said it wasn't just her duty to the military she had to obey, but her duty to protect these men who did such dangerous jobs. If their physical abilities let them down in critical situations, they could die—and then whose fault would that be, if she had passed him, knowing he had a problem?

She reached for the medical rejection stamp on her desk.

He caught her hand.

He glanced nervously at the medical supervisor two desks away and said softly, urgently, "I can read, I just have trouble with it sometimes, I jumble the letters, I'm slow at reading manuals. But you don't fly with manuals, and you don't dogfight with gauges. You feel speed and position, and I'm the best pilot in this room. This manual says a guy who's a slow reader can't be a good pilot. That file says different. Which one are you gonna believe?"

He stood frozen in front of her. He stared deep into her eyes, pleading from his soul, and then whispered, like a prayer, "Please don't take my wings."

She stared back into his eyes, then reached for one of the two stamps on her desk: APPROVED and REJECTED. Her hand reached as if it had a will of its own, hovered, grabbed one . . . and stamped APPROVED on his paperwork.

So Lieutenant Rafe McCawley moved away, having passed the last eye chart he'd have to read before his squadron received its first deployment, where picky medical checks were less frequent and more casual. When the shooting started, doctors became less concerned about testing the healthy and more occupied with patching up the wounded.

Evelyn did not watch Rafe go. She tried to put all thoughts of battlefield wounds out of her mind, and reached out to accept the next file, from Lieutenant Daniel Walker.

"Okay, Lieutenant," she said, glancing at his file. His said: FLYING SKILLS, CLASS RANK: #2.

She looked up at Danny Walker. He too was handsome, his hair light brown and full, his eyes green. In those eyes was appreciation for all she had just done. Something about his eyes made her a touch uncomfortable; he seemed to see her as better than she believed she was.

She flipped through his file for a moment and saw his math and spacial reasoning scores in the 80s; but his verbal scores were 99. Then she understood just how close Danny and Rafe were. She had no doubt whatsoever that Rafe had passed every previous eye chart test by having Danny behind him, whispering help whenever he got into trouble.

"So, Lieutenant Daniel Walker, how about you?" she said.

"How about me?" he answered, and gave her his best flirting grin.

"Listen, Romeo, just read the chart," she said.

When she left the east side Army medical center that night, walking out with her friends, she saw two men waiting across the street, silhouetted in the light of the street lamp behind them. They were Army aviators, in leather jackets and peaked caps, and Evelyn knew instantly they were Rafe and Danny. She paused for a moment, and that was just enough time for Rafe to move forward, weaving through the New York traffic, leaving Danny standing under the lamp like a soldier standing guard over the rest of his life.

"I'll catch up with you," Evelyn said to Betty, who, as soon as she saw Rafe coming, smiled and drifted away. Evelyn watched Rafe as he moved up and stopped. In those tailored pants the Army gave its pilots and the leather jacket snug at the waist and broad at the shoulders, he almost made her swear. *Why does the Army have to make these pilots so damn handsome?* she found herself thinking.

"I just wanted to thank you," he said. "For saving my career."

"I didn't save your career," she said.

"You didn't?" he said. "That's how it looked to me."

"You did the work. You did the training. You passed all the other tests. I thought you deserved to pass this one."

"Deserve is one thing," he said, and for the first time she saw his grin, flashing across his face like lightning on a summer sky. "Regulations are another."

She didn't have a response for that, she just looked at him, and he looked at her in a way most men didn't. Evelyn was aware that men found her attractive—what beautiful woman doesn't know that? But the look most men gave her was one of desire, of wanting to possess, like they'd look at a new Pontiac or a steak they were hungry to devour. Rafe looked at her like he saw something magical and wonderful inside her, something he recognized because it was inside him too.

"I was just wondering," he said, "why you did it. It wasn't my charm, was it?"

"What charm?"

He laughed. Across the street, Danny ran a hand across his own mouth, like a big brother, hearing the laughter and hoping it meant the encounter was going well.

"Okay," Rafe said. "But I still want to know why you did it."

"My father was a flyer," she said. "I know what it means to a pilot, when someone takes away his wings."

Rafe nodded, his smile gone, but that penetrating look still in his eyes, the blue and red neon sign of the pub window behind her reflecting in his irises. "My father was a pilot too." He hesitated for a moment. "Look, I . . . I don't want to be forward. But I do want to thank you. Would you let me buy you a cup of coffee sometime? If you'll just tell me how to find you."

In the train, Evelyn turned from the window and looked back at her nurse friends. She realized Betty was saying, "Evelyn? Yoo-hoo! Ev-e-lyn!" It brought her mind back to the present.

"So tell us!" Sandra said. "How do we meet the man of our dreams?"

"Just ignore the surface," Evelyn said, "no matter how good it looks. And pay close attention to his application."

5

Rafe stood on the platform with the other pilots and waited for the train. He'd bought flowers from a cart outside the station, and the other pilots looked at him and seemed to be wondering whether he already had a lover among the girls on the train, or had figured out a better strategy for getting one. As they waited, a couple of the guys darted outside to find the flower vendor themselves, and rushed back to the platform with their newly bought bouquets; nobody wanted to be last in line when the nurses arrived.

The platform grew quiet for a moment, as if it knew the train was coming; porters and switchmen and the others who run a railroad materialized on the long finger of concrete that pointed out toward the twenty lanes of curving track, and in rolled a locomotive, sighing steam. It shuddered to a stop, and clouds of hot vapor jetted onto the platform and gave the moment, for Rafe, a dreamlike haze.

Evelyn is the world to me. Those were the words that came to his mind, as he felt the romance of the setting and tried to make sense of it. He wasn't a poet like Danny, he couldn't come up with ways to describe something as no one had ever described it before. But he needed to make sense of his decision to leave, and try to understand it himself so that maybe he could explain it to this woman who was to him what no other woman had ever been.

He hid the flowers behind his back as the train doors opened and the porters pushed steps into place. The train car seemed to hold its breath, and then it began to exhale nurses.

Evelyn was the eighth one through the door. Her eyes found Rafe easily, his head above most of the crowd. His smile fed off hers, each of them brightening as they saw the joy on the other's face.

The girlish blonde beside Evelyn had to be Betty. Rafe had never met her; his dates with Evelyn since their encounter at the medical center had all been private events, starting with a rendezvous in a coffee shop that turned into a four-hour exchange of life stories and laughter followed by a day-long picnic and a Sunday drive through the upstate hill country in a car Rafe borrowed from the rich uncle of one of the guys in his squadron. They had meant to view the autumn leaves, and had strolled a forest path and held hands, kicking cascades of red, yellow and gold in front of them as they walked. Mostly, it seemed, they had looked at each other. It was the first time they had kissed.

Evelyn had told Rafe about Betty and the other nurses, and Rafe had told her about Danny, of course, but he had felt no need to explain his life to her. She seemed to know already what was important to him.

Having waited so eagerly for the nurses, the other pilots pretended to barely notice their arrival now, strolling with forced detachment toward the young women they'd already met or picking one out and walking through a crowd of her friends to strike up a conversation. The unattached girls pretended to have planned an evening solely in the company of their fellow nurses, and that the notion of altering those plans to include male companionship was an entirely new concept.

Rafe had no such pretense. He pushed his way through the crowd, took Evelyn into his arms, and pressed a kiss onto her cheek. Then he let her go and smiled at her. "Hello, Lieutenant," he said. "Good to see you."

"You too, Lieutenant," she said.

Betty, beside her, cleared her throat loudly.

"Rafe, this is Betty," Evelyn said.

"Hi, Betty." He drew a rose from the bouquet he held, then handed the rest of the flowers to Betty. The single rose he gave to Evelyn.

She blushed and glowed. She looked at Betty. "Told ya," she said.

"Thank you." Betty giggled.

"Danny would'a brought 'em," Rafe said. "But he couldn't make it tonight."

"He's not coming?" Evelyn said, as Rafe took her elbow in one arm and Betty's in the other, escorting them both along the platform.

"No, he got some news . . ." Rafe said, not looking at her. "He'll be okay, he just didn't feel like coming tonight. We'll find Betty a substitute."

"Evelyn and I will just share you. Won't we Evelyn?" Betty said.

"At ease, Betty," Evelyn said, and squeezed Rafe's arm as they walked out of the station and onto the streets of Manhattan.

Rafe loved music. He'd heard plenty of music in rural Tennessee, most of it sung in church by reedy-voiced farm families straining to hit the high notes, abetted by the accompaniment of an off-key piano played by an arthritic widow, and even then he'd heard the passion and the longing of the songs. He'd also stood in a pine thicket on a warm afternoon, listening to the soul songs of the grandchildren of slaves as they mourned a lost loved one through the whole of a summer day. There was nothing like music that came from the heart.

Rafe wasn't sure about swing. It was exuberant, even exhilarating; it was far more complex than a hymn but still it felt impulsive. Rafe liked all that about it. But it was trendy, too, and for that he distrusted it. The eye-catching dance steps, the fingers wagging in the air—all that struck Rafe as affectation, and he harbored the native Tennessean revulsion for all things that were put-on.

But the barrel-chested Negroes blowing saxophones for the crowd of pilots, nurses and other military officers gathered in the jazz club seemed to love nothing better than the music they were playing, and to crave nothing more than the present moment.

Rafe, Evelyn, and their party of friends sat at a round table, half booth and half chairs, in one corner of the smoke-filled room. The women were drinking Cokes; the men had already moved to beer. Anthony had paired up with Sandra, and Billy with Barbara. Betty, to Rafe's right, had found Red sitting on the other side of her.

"I hear they may send us all to Hawaii," Sandra was saying.

Anthony popped the beer bottle from his mouth in mid-swig and said, "Sounds good to me! I'll be glad to help you pick out a bathing suit!" He lowered his lustrous eyebrows and said, "It'll help you promote your suntan."

"I'd prefer to advance my career," Sandra said.

"Can't help you with that. But I can advance your love life." The other pilots laughed; Billy applauded.

"Flyboy, you can't even get off the ground." The nurses laughed louder than the men had, and threw napkins at Anthony.

Red seized the moment, leaning closer to Betty. "H-Hi," he stammered, "I'm R-Red. Red Strange."

Evelyn and Rafe both were listening as Betty blinked at Red and said, "Your last name is Strange?"

"N-No," Red said, "it's W-Winkle. But you know the football player, Red G-Grange? Well, the guys call me R-Red, cause you know, I'm red . . . and they think I'm strange, so, you know, Red G-Grange, Red Str-Strange."

Betty, who had never heard of Red Grange, the "Galloping Ghost," blinked again and said, "I don't get it. Was Red Grange strange?"

"H-How would I know?" Red said, shrugging nervously, his shoulders twitching just as his tongue did when he stuttered. Doing his best to keep eye contact with Betty, he groped for his beer. Billy had just dumped catsup onto a plate of fries and shoved the open bottle back onto the table. Red grabbed that instead and tried to swig from it. Rafe and Evelyn saw him do it; Betty did too. And when Red returned the bottle to the table as if nothing had happened, they said nothing.

Red still held onto the catsup bottle.

"Do you always stutter?" Betty asked him.

"Only when I'm n-n-n-"

"Nervous?" she helped.

"Yeah. But if I have to get something out, I c-can always s-s-s-" and then, in a bell-clear baritone, he sang out, "—*siiing*!"

Betty reached for the catsup bottle, took it from Red's fingers, and covered his hand with her own. "Don't be nervous," she said.

Red looked at Betty with love in his eyes.

Under the table, Rafe and Evelyn's hands found each other too. After a moment Evelyn said quietly, "They're shipping us out. Pearl Harbor."

"As far from the fighting as you can be. That's good."

"Well," she said, wanting everyone to be cheerful tonight, "at least America's not fighting." Rafe said nothing. Sometimes he answered with silence, and it was always loud. At those times she could feel him thinking, though she could not always read his mind. She went on, "The rumors say the Navy's worried about Japan, so they're shifting everything they can from the West Coast over to Hawaii. Maybe the Army will post you guys there too—or is that wishful thinking?"

Rafe looked out toward the dance floor for a moment, but his eyes didn't follow the jitterbugging; then his eyes shifted back to Evelyn. She could feel him about to say something, when he was distracted by what Billy was just then telling Barbara, in a somber voice uncharacteristic of him. "I just . . . need you to know," Billy was saying, "that you're a very, very special woman. And . . . they're training me to be a warrior, to go to battle wherever my country needs me . . ."

Anthony, opposite Billy, was listening too, and giving Billy a big-eyed stare that said *Don't overdo it.*

"But the point . . ." Billy said to Barbara, who sat there listening, motionless and unblinking, "the point is that nobody knows what the future is, after tonight. So we have to make tonight . . . special. As special as you are."

Anthony liked the last little phrase; that was evident from the way he pursed his lips, like a Sicilian approving a sweet melon.

Barbara raised an elegant hand and stroked her chin with long red fingernails. Rafe noticed that the other nurses around the table were listening too. Finally Barbara nodded and said, "I think that's the best I've ever heard that line delivered." For a moment Billy went pale; and the way Anthony's lips began to dance, it seemed the sweet melon had gone sour. But Barbara wasn't finished. "I hope you can back that up, flyboy— 'cause you're not ever gonna forget tonight." With that she planted a smoldering kiss on Billy's lips, as his whole spine went rigid.

Evelyn drew Rafe to his feet and pulled him away from the table, far enough from the table for them to have their own private talk, sheltered by the surrounding swirl of party goers. "What's wrong?" he asked, close to her ear, through the noise.

"Nothing," she said back to him in the same way. "I

don't want to be with a crowd tonight. I just want to be with you."

At that moment, in tune with the magic that all her moments with Rafe seemed to possess, the band began to play a slow dance. Rafe reached for her—maybe because she was already reaching for him—and they drifted around the floor with the other dancers. She put her head against his chest and he squeezed her. But she could still feel his silence, the build-up of something unsaid. She looked up into his face.

He stopped dancing. "Let's go outside," he said.

Several couples were already out on the dinner club's glassed-in veranda; none of them were paying any attention at all to the view outside. Rafe led Evelyn to a far corner. The tall bright squares of Manhattan gleamed to their left, and New York harbor lay in front of them, shimmering and black.

They stood there together. He wanted to kiss her—she could feel it—but still he said nothing.

She looked at him—and now neither of them saw anything except each other. He leaned toward her; she closed her eyes and waited for his kiss.

But it didn't come. When she opened her eyes again, he was looking down, and holding tightly to her hand.

"Whatever you've been trying to tell me," Evelyn said, "it can't be all good—or it wouldn't be so hard to say."

"I'm going away."

"We're all going away." She brushed her lips to his, meaning to do it soft as breath; but as soon as they touched, their desire for each other drew them hard together, one small space of warmth against the cold night.

Again Rafe had to force himself to pause. "Yeah, but . . . I'm going to the war. I'm flying in the Eagle Squadron, an outfit the British have started for American pilots."

"I don't understand."

"Hitler's taken over Poland and Czechoslovakia and a lot of other countries guys from Tennessee can't pronounce, and every time, he says that's all he wants— then he takes something else. I don't understand politics but I understand bullies, and I know this one has to be faced up to."

"But you're in the U.S. Army, how could they order you to go?"

"They didn't," he said, looking away from her. "I volunteered."

Emotions battled within her. She wanted to hold him, she wanted to scream, to shake him. She sat there looking away from him, and for a moment she felt panic; not the outer, trembling, running panic, but the inner kind, when the heart knots in fear and screams that all the other guardians of the soul—hope, faith, dreams, memory and anticipation—are lying, and the troubles they sense must surely not be happening at all. Yet there was Rafe before her, his eyes turned toward the harbor and the Statue of Liberty at its center, its tall golden form actually reflecting in his eyes. Romantic as the moment could've been, Evelyn knew that not every man who went to war came back alive, and she loved Rafe so much, wanted him so much, that the old superstitions of her childhood whispered that God would never let her keep anything she loved like she loved Rafe.

"Rafe . . ." she began slowly, "I'm a nurse. I do what

has to be done. Not what I want, what *has* to be done—"

"This has to be done," he said, more in argument with himself than with her. "I'm just the only one who sees that."

She understood then that Danny must've opposed this decision too. "And the future of the world is all up to you?" she said. She felt badly for the way that sounded, but she didn't take it back.

"It's up to me to be who I am," he said.

Now anger began to rise above her affection. "I passed you," she said bitterly. "I let you through. And now you volunteer for the most dangerous place you could go."

"You're not responsible for that, Evelyn . . . any more than you're responsible for the fact that I love you." He paused. "Evelyn . . . I've always thought you knew how I feel about you. Maybe I made it up, maybe it happened too soon to be real, maybe . . . maybe, maybe. All I can tell you now is what is. And tonight I have to tell you, I love you. So I can't tell you what most of the other pilots are telling their girlfriends tonight, about making this night special. This night's already special for me, because you're here and I know how I feel about you. I'm going away, and however you feel about that or about me, I don't know how to change. But I'm gonna come back. I will come back. And when I do, we'll get a chance to know if what I feel tonight— what I hope you feel—is something that lasted. Something that's real."

When she looked back at him there were tears in her eyes, and nothing else but love.

Servicemen and nurses shared steamy kisses on the sidewalk before entering the revolving doors into the hotel. Other couples headed straight through to the lobby and moved to the elevators without pausing for any preliminaries. Rafe and Evelyn, warm from their long walk from the jazz club, stood beside the revolving doors, in each other's arms, kissing. The fact that other couples around the hotel entrance did the same, even dressed in identical uniforms, each pair looking like a carbon copy of the next, did not for a moment make Evelyn and Rafe feel less unique. Rafe pulled back and looked into her eyes, finding himself tempted to forget all of his resolve and wipe out all the lofty aspirations of his love, so tempted that he had to tell her, "This is already the most beautiful night of my life, and I don't want to ruin it."

She kissed him softly on the lips and said, "You couldn't ruin it."

"Not now. But if I don't come back, I don't want to leave you with sadness and regret."

"I don't know if you can choose that, Rafe." She said this looking down toward the sidewalk, stained by old chewing gum and spilled drinks and the street grime of New York's decades. Then she lifted her face toward him, and the light from the street glanced off her hair. "And if I had just one more night to live," she said, "I'd want to spend it with you."

"I'm not trying to be noble. I'm afraid. And the idea of having more love than I've ever had—and knowing I might never have it again—that scares me worse than anything."

She lowered her head against his neck.

He whispered to her, "I will come back. Whatever happens, I'll find a way."

They kissed again. Their hands touched a final time, and then they both forced themselves to let go.

She moved into the revolving door, alone. When she was halfway through, he stopped the door, and she turned to look at him through the glass.

Rafe mouthed the words: *I love you.*

Evelyn returned the words, all mouth and no voice: *I love you.*

He released the door, stepping back away from it, and she pushed the rest of the way around and moved inside. She walked to the front desk and retrieved her room key, then looked back through the broad front window and the street beyond, where he stood waiting. He lifted his hand in a last wave, and walked away.

It was not until he was gone that she realized she still held the rose he had given her at the train station.

6

At that same train station, the next morning, Rafe and Danny stood in the dawn chill, the sunlight a milky yellow on the deserted tracks. The platform itself was nearly vacant; all the other military personnel in the area would be receiving their traveling orders later that afternoon, and not one of them was being sent north—to Canada, for attachment with the Royal Air Force, then across the North Atlantic, to Great Britain.

Rafe hadn't told the rest of his buddies in the squadron where he was going; he'd left that to Danny. Explaining Rafe's decision to them might help Danny feel better himself about what Rafe had done, but Rafe hadn't planned it that way; he just hated parting from people he cared about, and softened the blow of the separation by telling himself that it wasn't really a goodbye, since he'd see them all again and would carry them with him anyway.

Evelyn, of course, was a different matter. About her, he felt exposed, and his sense of comfort careened from the serene solidity he felt when he was with her to the sickening doubts he felt when he was not. Ever since he'd left her at the hotel he had despised himself for not staying, if just to hold her or stay up with her until dawn; and he had told himself that she would be an idiot to care about a man so unconnected to the actual world of common sense.

Rafe's gear, his entire personal kit for going off to war, was packed in a duffel bag at his feet. When a conductor's voice sang out, "All aboard," he lifted the bag and slung it over his shoulder, then glanced once more toward the revolving doors that led onto the platform from the station.

Danny caught the look. "Didn't you say you told her not to come?"

"Yeah," Rafe admitted.

"Then why are you looking for her?"

"It's a test," Rafe said. "If I tell her not to come, and she comes . . . then I know she loves me."

"ALL ABOARD!" the conductor shouted again.

"You're still a kid, you know that?" Danny said.

"Always will be. Danny . . . if anything happens to me, I want you to be the one to tell her."

"Well, make sure nothing does happen to you."

"You too." Rafe stuck his hand out to Danny. Danny knocked it away, and hugged him.

The train waited beside them, looking empty and cold. Rafe stepped onto it and found a seat beside a window, opposite Danny on the platform. The trainmen shut the doors and the trains groaned forward as the couplings between the cars felt the pull of the locomotive.

Danny smiled and waved, as Rafe lifted a hand to him.

Under his smile, Danny whispered, "Give 'em hell, Rafe."

And then Rafe was gone.

Evelyn ran down the corridor that led from the central station, her eyes searching the numbers above the doors that led out to the maze of platforms. She had told herself that she wouldn't come; Rafe had asked her not to, it was what he wanted . . . wasn't it? She had gone to bed, refusing to set the alarm, hoping to wake well past the time for changing her mind. As if she would've slept; she tossed throughout the night, decided to set the clock as a trick to help her sleep, and was still awake when she shut off the alarm a half hour before it would've gone off.

Still she had told herself she wouldn't come. They had already said good-bye. Why make it harder on them both?

She was aware of no moment when she had decided; she'd just grabbed her coat and headed to the station in a rush. Now she couldn't find the platform, the numbers didn't seem to follow each other the way they should. She ran past a man mopping the corridor floor, then almost collided with a porter who had just stepped through the swinging doors out onto a platform. "Please!" Evelyn said breathlessly. "Is this the platform for the 6:27?"

"Yes'm," he said, "but it just pulled out."

She banged through the doors.

She didn't see Danny passing through at that very

moment, two doors down, moving from the platform back into the corridor.

Evelyn stood on the concrete, damp with the chill air of morning, and watched the last cars of the train round the long curve toward the main track, and disappear.

She had never felt more alone.

———

Four days later, Rafe stood on the deck of a Canadian freighter loaded with wheat, diesel fuel, ball bearings, steel for making machine-gun muzzles, and one American pilot bound for the Eagle Squadron. Rafe had come up on deck in search of relief from the motion sickness and claustrophobia of the inner compartments. He found the open deck helped with the claustrophobia, but did nothing for his tossing stomach.

He could see five other vessels pushing through the waves alongside the freighter he was on. He knew there were twelve other ships besides those in their convoy.

Before them lay a sky bruised with angry clouds. They were sailing into a storm.

Rafe closed his eyes and thought of Evelyn.

As Rafe headed east, Evelyn journeyed west.

She and the other nurses in her naval medical unit received orders that put them on a train that crossed the Mississippi at St. Louis, rumbled through the plains, traversed the desert states and the Rockies and reached San Diego, where they boarded a ship that sailed into the blue Pacific, and golden sunsets, toward the island paradise of Hawaii.

———

Danny and the rest of his squadron did not travel by train. They flew their fighters overland, to bases where cranes lifted the aircraft onto ships, which then transported both planes and pilots to their ultimate destination, as far from the Atlantic storm clouds and the war in Europe as it was possible then to imagine—a place called Pearl Harbor.

7

In the eternal dusk of the British Isles, every object, natural, mechanical, or human, looked cold and gray, bled of its colors. Rain seemed to hang in all directions, not pooled into clouds but rather spread through every molecule of air, so that the entire atmosphere was soaked and ready to squeeze cold dampness into everything it touched.

The runways of Bassingborne Airfield were wet and barely distinguishable from the dark earth around them. Near the squat, ancient hangars, British fighter planes—Spitfires and Hurricanes—sat surrounded by mechanics hurriedly ripping off bullet-riddled fuselage panels and digging into overworked aircraft engines. Rafe walked across the tarmac, still carrying his duffel bag. He moved up behind a slim, pale British officer, Air Commander Peter Richard Tubbs, who was bent over, surveying engine damage on one of the Spitfires. Rafe waited for the officer to stand upright and then said, "McCawley, sir," saluting.

It was not until then that Rafe realized Air Commander Tubbs had no right arm.

Tubbs said, "We'll get you situated in some quarters, and then introduce you to the equipment you'll be flying."

"If you're patching up bullet holes right here on the runway," Rafe said, "maybe we should skip the housekeeping and get right to the planes."

Tubbs turned and led Rafe across the tarmac. Though Tubbs was missing an arm, his walk was balanced and crisp; he had the spirit of a commando, and Rafe was sure the air commander continued to do physical conditioning exercises, even without a right arm. He was clearly a tough, strong leader; but he was not of the same mold as Doolittle, who conveyed the inherent American sense of connection with his men. Tubbs was a British officer, with the aloofness that came from a class-conscious society.

Halfway across the tarmac he said to Rafe, "Are all the Yanks as anxious as you to get themselves killed, Lieutenant?" He pronounced it *Leftenant*, the first time Rafe had ever heard it said that way.

"Not anxious to die, sir, anxious to matter."

Air Commander Tubbs pursed his lips and nodded, without looking at Rafe again.

They rounded the side of a hangar, and the first thing Rafe saw was the tail of a Spitfire, adorned with the emblem of the Eagle Squadron, a fierce bird screaming in attack. The tail looked good; but as more and more of the plane came into view, that impression changed. A trail of bullet holes moved up the fuselage, chunks of material had been shot out of the wing skin. But most striking of all was the blood still splattered over the inside of the cockpit. "Good lad," Tubbs said. "Didn't die till he'd landed and shut down his engine." He paused for a moment, let Rafe take that in, and said, "Welcome to the war, Lieutenant."

Tubbs walked away, leaving Rafe to stare at the bloody cockpit.

8

Captain Jesse Thurman was a U.S. naval intelligence officer. He had dark hair so thick and wavy it concealed the size of his head. He wore a seven and seven-eighths hat size, and when the other guys in his section at the Pentagon heard that they'd said, *So that explains it*. That was the only excuse they could come up with for why he always seemed so much smarter than everybody else.

And they'd needed an excuse, because otherwise it was so hard for them to live with the fact that he got to solutions quicker, invented new ways around old problems, took leaps over the mental morass they were always creating with their discussions of logic and probability. He didn't have an Ivy League education like most of the others, didn't come from a big city—Thurman's mother had been a schoolteacher in the rural Midwest, and the first eight years of his formal education had come solely from her. He seemed to enjoy reading, he went to church, he had a pretty, quiet wife who was the only woman he ever looked at and two young children. Most people found him likeable—until they got in his way, refusing to see the conclusions that were so clear to him. Then he lost all his patience; he became short-tempered and sarcastic. These were not traits designed for quick promotion within the military.

But Captain Thurman was not without his political instincts. One of his uncles—he'd been raised without a father, his own having died when he was an infant—had once told him that a man did not advance in life by making those higher on the ladder of success look worse, but rather by making them look better, and Thurman had understood that advice. The admirals above him in the Pentagon's chain of command figured out quickly that if they wanted to look perceptive and instinctive, they'd better have regular discussions with the quiet captain who worked mostly alone in a corner office next to their War Room.

But they had never brought him along to the White House—not until today.

Thurman sat two seats away from the far end of a long mahogany table that reflected the brass bars and the bright ribbons of the uniformed men who gathered round it. The presidential cabinetmembers wore their own uniforms: the starched white colors, muted ties, polished cuff links. Thurman felt out of place but not uncomfortable; he knew he would be expected to say nothing. He also understood that he'd been invited because his bosses in the Navy were finding these meetings in the White House to be confusing, and they found danger in such uncertainty.

Captain Thurman didn't have much time to ponder the atmosphere around the table. As soon as the last advisor was seated, the latches on the broad doors at the opposite end of the room clattered in oiled precision, and both doors swung open together, pulled by a tall, wide-shouldered Negro, George, the personal valet of President Franklin Delano Roosevelt.

The president sat in a wheelchair, his head lifted, his jaw jutted forward. His shoulders were as wide as the valet's, and spread beyond the rattan back of the wheelchair. His shirt was starched and luminously white, his tie silken, his hair combed back, lustrous. Roosevelt's hands relaxed upon the arm supports of the wheelchair and appeared powerful; Thurman had heard the stories of Roosevelt's athletic prowess before the polio had struck, the fever hitting him after a full day of swimming and running with his children and leaving him, barely twenty-four hours later, paralyzed from the waist down. Now, it was whispered around Washington, Roosevelt still insisted on exercising his torso to keep himself looking robust. Thurman saw the biceps and deltoids bulging beneath the tailored suit and knew those rumors were true. He also saw the president's legs, shriveled beneath the cloth of his pinstripe trousers, and braced with the iron supports that attached to his shoes.

George, the valet, moved silently to the handles at the rear of the wheelchair, and rolled Roosevelt into the room.

Everyone stood.

Deposited at the head of the table, and with George backing out and closing the doors as quietly as he had opened them, the president said, "Sit, gentlemen."

Even before they'd settled back into their chairs, Roosevelt was speaking again. "I'm afraid I'm in a bad mood. Churchill and Stalin are asking me what I'm asking you: How long is America going to pretend the world is not at war?"

General George C. Marshall was the president's most trusted military advisor. The legends said that Roosevelt, notorious for expecting his opinions to be accepted as fact and his wishes to be instantly obeyed, had first noticed Marshall—truly noticed him—when the general was but one of the many bureaucrats brought into the White House to supply the president with the information he was constantly demanding. At one meeting, not unlike the one they were currently attending, Roosevelt had confidently expressed a plan and everyone at the table had nodded their instant assent—everyone except Marshall, who had cleared his throat and then said firmly, "Mr. President, I believe that is a terrible idea." Roosevelt, so the story went, had stared at Marshall in stunned silence, while all the others at the table had paled. Whatever the truth of that story—and Thurman doubted the truth of every story—when Roosevelt was looking for a new chairman of his Joint Chiefs of Staff, he had reached far down the list of possible choices and had appointed Marshall.

Now General Marshall spoke up and said, "We've increased food and oil supply shipments to them, Mr. President, and—"

Roosevelt cut him off. "What they really need are tanks, planes, bullets, bombs—and men to fight! But our people think Hitler and his Nazi thugs are Europe's problem." Roosevelt shook his head and his lips moved in what Thurman felt certain was silent profanity. And he knew that if the president was interrupting General

Marshall, there was no·use in anyone else trying to speak. Sometimes the Boss only wants to hear himself. Thurman understood that. He was that way himself.

"We have to do it again," Roosevelt said. "Send the Brits and Russians more of our ships and anti-aircraft weapons."

One of the admirals asked, "And keep cannibalizing the Pacific Fleet?"

Roosevelt turned his face toward the window. His spectacles reflected the gray light of the late winter. "What choice do I have?" he asked himself. "We're building refrigerators while our enemies build bombs."

As Captain Thurman left the White House, ignored by the other officers with him, he reflected that all the rumors he'd heard about Roosevelt seemed to be true.

He also reminded himself that any intelligence officer who believed every rumor had no intelligence at all.

———

On the other side of the planet from Washington, D.C., and at almost the same moment, Admiral Isoroku Yamamoto entered a windowless room in Tokyo, where the Japanese War Council was gathered. They too surrounded a table, but this one was barely a foot high, and they sat upon cushions on the floor. Yamamoto removed his cap and bowed as he entered, his head dropping enough to show respect but not so much as to show fear of these aggressive warriors, who had wrested all practical power from the emperor. Yamamoto took his seat, accepted the tea that was the symbol of welcome, and breathed a long, slow lungful of the air. He noticed it smelled of sweat. These men, though they glowered and glared, were anxious. They tried to exude power because they were afraid of the consequences of not having any. Yamamoto knew they were dangerous.

He also knew they needed him, and feared him too, because of his knowledge. Yamamoto had been educated in America, at Harvard. He was acknowledged high and low as the finest military mind in their country; Japan had no other like him. His planning for their recent campaigns had been flawless; relentlessly Japan had been expanding throughout Asia, grabbing islands from Russia, terrorizing the Chinese mainland, gobbling territory in Indochina. Their successes had confirmed their every belief in the superiority of the Japanese character. Yamamoto knew they were drunk with it. He had tried to remind them that no nation, especially one so lacking in essential raw materials as Japan, could live long without diplomacy, but the warlords considered negotiations to be but one of the shadowy and deceptive faces in the art of war. Many members of the Council had expressed the opinion that Yamamoto's stressing of caution was the result of cowardice, and Yamamoto's few friends within the Council had warned him to take precautions against assassination.

Yamamoto, though educated in America, was no less Japanese than any of the others. He was not afraid to die.

But he was a realist, too. He knew he could dream and wish and contemplate any vision that suited his soul, while meditating in his garden. But he would face the facts. In this he was not unlike an American military leader whose character he admired, Robert E. Lee, who fervently wished to avoid war, but who accepted that if it must come, it must be fought both wisely and furiously.

Yamamoto got right to the point.

"War is inevitable," he said. "To hide from this fact is death. We send troops into China, the Americans cut off the oil that is our lifeline . . . we have no choice but war."

Yamamoto gave his listeners a chance to absorb this. His endorsement of their aggressive policy was everything they wanted, and yet it was unexpected.

"And if we must fight the Americans," Yamamoto went on, "there is only one way. A massive, sudden strike, before they can prepare. Deal them a blow that will cripple them for years. In that time we can conquer all of the Pacific, and they will be forced to ask for peace."

One of the Council, Nishikura, the very member whom Yamamoto's friends had identified as the one most intent on having him killed, said, "You see us as capable of such a blow?"

"The Americans themselves have made it possible. We will annihilate them in a single attack—at Pearl Harbor. Here," Yamamoto said, "let me show you how." He began to push aside the pots and teacups, so that the entire lacquered surface of the tabletop became a smooth and gleaming Pacific Ocean.

9

Pearl Harbor was a jewel even more regal than the oyster gems that gave it its name.

It was an emerald of calm water, surrounded by the island of Oahu, in the center of the lush and fragrant chunks of volcanic overflow that compose Hawaii. The Pacific Ocean takes up roughly half of the planet Earth, and Hawaii, lying near the Pacific's center, is farther away from any other significant land mass than anyplace else in our world. And for anything bound to cross the greatest of oceans, Pearl was not simply a welcoming paradise, it was a near necessity.

Ford Island was a low, sandy stretch of high ground in the middle of the harbor that provided not only additional shelter for ships to anchor but also a perfect military position for anyone choosing to control that privilege. In mid-1941, more than sixty warships—aircraft carriers, battleships, destroyers, submarines and all the attendant vessels, the heart of America's Pacific Fleet—surrounded Ford Island.

Evelyn saw those ships in every direction, as she and

her friends arrived in military Jeeps at the main gate of the Ford Island naval installation, and the warships were so thick around the perimeter that she could not at first see the water beyond them. For a moment she was disoriented, and she wanted to ask one of the Marines who was guarding the gate to point out the main harbor to her, but before she could, he grinned and said, "A-lo-HA!"

The nurses in the Jeeps looked at each other, as the driver signed in, then smirked back at the Marines and pulled away. "You know the ratio of men to women on this island?" Barbara said. "Four-thousand . . . to one."

Betty took from her purse the new pair of sunglasses with plastic palm trees glued on the sides that she had bought from a vendor's booth as soon as they'd stepped off the ship. She slid the glasses onto her face and yelled back at the Marines, "See ya on the beach, boys!"

Evelyn did not linger at the nurses' quarters. She found her room—a cubicle she shared with Betty—and left her bag unpacked at the foot of the bunk, to go off alone in search of the base hospital where they would work.

What she found was an immaculately clean facility of empty beds, white sheets glowing luminous beside the windows lining both long walls. Soft air, scented with the sweet fragrance of island plumeria, drifted across every pillow, and carried away the chemical smell of the bleach used to scrub down the hardwood floors. Evelyn thought it was the cleanest place she had ever been.

She found a corpsman tidying up a supply cabinet and asked why the hospital was so empty. He told her the worst injuries they'd had to treat since he'd been there were two sprained ankles and a half dozen cases of sunburn.

Evelyn walked back to the nurses' quarters, certain that in coming to Pearl Harbor she had found herself as far from war as possible.

Except that Rafe was in the war. And that made battle and all its horrors as close to her as her own heart.

———

Tracer bullets marking the trail of fire from the wing guns of a German fighter cut through the air outside Rafe's cockpit, and he pulled back on the stick, pressed forward on the throttle and worked the control pedals, easing back on one foot and pressing forward with the other, sending the Spitfire into a climbing turn. He did it instinctively; he had become intimate with the plane. He liked it; he thought of Spitfires as feisty, like mongrel dogs. They were responsive; they were fast. The dark green Messerschmitts and Focke-Wulfs they fought against were heavier and more powerful, and carried steel shielding for their pilots; with a Spitfire, the plane's own lightness, with its consequent speed and maneuverability, was its principle protection; but after endless hours of combat and constant patchwork, the planes began to feel flimsy. As Rafe forced the fuselage into the stresses of a hard turn, he felt it shudder. He could not think about that now. If the plane came apart on him, then he would die; but if he hesitated and doubted his plane as the Messerschmitts were bearing down on him, he would die anyway.

Driving his plane all the way through the turn, he doubled back on the attackers and ambushed the pilots who were trying to ambush him. His finger pressed the gun trigger and he watched as his own tracers bit their way into the tail section of the German fighter.

Rafe did not hear the bullets, nor did he hear the rattling of his own plane. In combat, he was not attuned to sounds; vision was everything. He watched as the stream of bullets he fired moved up the fuselage of the Messerschmitt and smashed their way into the cockpit; he saw blood fly from the body of a German pilot who could not have been much older than himself. As he flew through the airborne trail of smoke and oil and the German spiraled down toward the North Sea, Rafe wondered, for a fleeting moment, if the other pilot had been a farm boy too.

That night he wrote a letter, composing it in a single pass, then using a borrowed dictionary to check the spelling before redrafting it carefully by hand.

> *Dear Evelyn,*
> *It is cold here. So cold, it goes deep into your bones. It's not easy making friends. Two nights ago I drank a beer with a couple of the R.A.F. pilots—beer's the only thing here that isn't cold—and yesterday both of them got killed . . .*

Evelyn read the letter while sitting under a palm tree from whose lee she could watch the sky turn pink with the sunset over the Pacific. "There is one place I can go to find warmth," Rafe wrote, "and that is to think of you."

She did not write back just then. There would be no pickup of letters until Monday, and she needed the time to let the swelling of her heart go down enough to write him something that would sound strong for him, worthy of him.

On Sunday afternoon, she showered at the nurses' quarters, let her hair dry in the sea breeze that always rose after midday, and put on a light cotton dress. Her legs and arms were already growing brown from the sun, and her hair had lightened a few shades. Betty and the other girls were putting on makeup, but Evelyn wore only lipstick, out of habit; she was going out to be alone.

She walked to the beach and found a spot on a rock smooth enough to sit upon. She kicked off her shoes and propped her writing pad on her knees, then took the fountain pen her father had given her when she had joined the Navy, and began to write.

The Germans had come early that night, and the Spitfires and Hurricanes met them readily. It was a melee, planes everywhere, in and out of clouds, and with visibility so limited Rafe thought collision might be more likely than death by bullets. Then a shout from another R.A.F. pilot cut through the engine noise and the static of his radio. "Get them off me! Someone get them off me!"

Rafe scanned the air between the broken clouds; down and to his right he saw a Messerschmitt with guns blazing; ahead of it was a British Hurricane, already smoking. "I'm on him!" Rafe answered, and slammed his control stick hard right, throwing his Spitfire into a power dive, straight at the topside of Messerschmitts. Rafe's bullets chewed up its cockpit and the German plane spun into a fast corkscrew spiral. Rafe followed it all the way down, seeing it impact the water; instantly he climbed again.

The pilot of the mortally wounded Hurricane, in the moment of safety Rafe had bought him, slid back his ruptured canopy and bailed out, his chute blossoming and carrying him toward the water. Rafe swung his plane toward two more German fighters and made a high-speed pass right between them, firing as he went; as they banked left and right he found the clouds, then dropped as quickly as he could to try to find the British pilot's chute in the water.

Through luck he could barely believe, he saw it, still half-inflated in the water, and the British pilot with it. Rafe slid back his canopy and dropped a buoyant smoke marker, radioing the position to Air-Sea Rescue before he climbed to face the Germans again.

Rafe could think of nothing more horrible than death alone, in cold dark water.

At Bassingborne Airfield, Rafe brought his battered Spitfire down onto the tarmac, and then he did feel the straining of the fuselage, and heard the crying of the metal, like the whining of an old dog. And he was grateful for life, grateful to the old dog of a plane, and patted it like he would a loyal hound, worn and tired and home from the hunt.

Thirty minutes later he was sitting on a chair he had located below a lantern behind the blackout curtains, reading a letter he had found on his bunk. Evelyn's handwriting was without elegance, there were no unnecessary loops or curves; it was plain, as straightforward as Evelyn.

Dear Rafe,

It's strange to be so far from you. But you should know this: Every night I look at the sunset and try to draw its last ounce of heat into my heart, and send it from my heart to yours. . . .

Rafe sat for a long time with the letter in his hands, feeling what she had felt, touching what she had touched. His whole body was warm.

Rafe jerked, startled to see Air Commander Tubbs standing beside him. When had he come up? Rafe started to stand but Tubbs quickly said, "No, no, please keep your seat. I just wanted to let you know, they found Nigel."

"Nigel, Commander?"

"The pilot that went down today, the one you risked your life to help. Air-Sea Rescue picked him up. They say it will take him a few days to feel warm again. But he's alive, and he'll be back with us."

Rafe nodded, glad to hear the news. Commander Tubbs started to walk away, then turned back and said, "Some of us look down on the Yanks for not yet joining this war. I'd just like to say that if there are many more back home like you, God help anyone who goes to war against America." Tubbs smiled, and then saluted.

He was already walking away again when Rafe saluted back, and then called, "Thank you, Commander."

"No," Tubbs said, over his shoulder. "Thank you."

10

Danny and the rest of his squadron were flown to Hawaii on a four-prop transport plane with fuel bladders crowding the inside of the fuselage. No one got airsick, though it did happen, even to pilots. They'd picked up five hours on the time zones from San Francisco, three more from the East Coast, and when they landed it seemed strangely early in the day.

A drab green Army bus took them to the base and dropped them with their duffel bags in front of a wooden barracks. It was just before noon, local time. They looked around at the palm trees, the rich green saw grass, the bushes with flowering blooms. "Hawaii!" Anthony said. "It's paradise!"

"Yeah, right," Danny said, and picked up his duffel. "We protect boats and sunbathers."

Anthony, Red and Billy exchanged looks as they followed him up the barracks steps. Danny had been in a foul mood the whole trip; ever since Rafe had left, he had been itching to know when he could get into the ac-

tion, and paradise in the Pacific was not where he figured he'd find it.

They entered the barracks and Danny stopped suddenly; the others, their heads lowered with the weight of
their duffel bags, piled into his back like runaway
freight cars. What had brought Danny up short was the
sight of sleeping pilots, still in their bunks.

"You believe this?" Billy said. "They're all asleep!"

"They're all d-drunk," Red said. And he had to be
right; the pilots in the bunks were wearing Hawaiian
shirts, still stinking of beer from the night before.

Danny paused for a moment, then barked out,
"Drop your cocks and grab your socks! The terrors of
the skies are here!"

A couple of the sleeping pilots groaned and covered
their heads with their pillows. Then the one nearest the
door sat up, his hair pointing every direction of the com-
pass, his tongue working as if to wipe a terrible taste
from his mouth. Danny and the new arrivals watched as
he shifted and dangled his feet over the side of the bunk.
As his feet touched the floor, a sensation seemed to reach
his sotted brain; he raised one foot to look at its bottom,
and found a new tattoo on the sole of his foot; he
blinked as if trying to remember how it got there.

"Hey. You. Mr. Coma."

"Where's that lizard?" the near-comatose pilot wondered.

"What lizard?"

"The one that slept in my mouth last night."

"This is an air base?" Danny said, to nobody in
particular.

But Coma answered. "We got a saying here. A-lo-HA!"

The shrill sound of a naval whistle and a sharp command from the deck officer announced the arrival of Admiral H. E. Kimmel, commander of the American Pacific Fleet, onto the deck of the battleship *West Virginia*. The *West Virginia*, like her sister ships *Tennessee*, *Nevada*, *Missouri*, and *Arizona*, was only a few feet shorter than the *Titanic* had been, and weighed more. Each of the battlewagons had main guns capable of hurling high explosive shells over twenty miles. The destructive power of any single one of the ships was awesome; together they were a terrific fighting force. But they were not all that Admiral Kimmel had. The newest naval theories said that aircraft carriers, not battleships, would be the central sea-based weapon of the future. Through the planes they carried, they projected a power radius over hundreds of miles; they could attack land targets as well as ships, they could bomb, torpedo, strafe. Kimmel had two carriers under his command; they both lay at anchor at Pearl Harbor.

Carriers were ugly contraptions in the eyes of many sailors. Call a battleship a dinosaur if you wanted to; think of it as no more than a modern frigate. But a frigate was a beautiful thing to a sailor. And there was no admiral on earth who could walk onto a battleship like the *West Virginia*—with its perfect symmetry and its powerful sweep from tapered stern to pointed bow, with its enormous guns spread and bristling—and not feel its majesty.

"Admiral aboard!" the officers sang, and a line of sailors in pristine whites all snapped to attention, saluting in unison as Kimmel stepped down from the crossing platform and returned their salute. No man could make admiral without an appreciation of tradition, but Kimmel was not inordinately enamored of fanfare. Yet he saw in the crisp execution of the rituals a pride of the men for their ships, and he knew that men who took such pride would pay attention to the basic tasks—the greasing of bearings, the suppression of rust, the stacking of shells, the calibration of gunsights—that made and kept a naval vessel an effective weapon.

Admiral Kimmel walked with the ship's captain down the line of sailors and spoke quietly with him as they moved. "I like the way you've got them looking. The false alarms we've gotten from Washington could make us lose our edge; I'm determined not to let that happen."

The captain nodded; there was nothing he could say. Kimmel had kept the captains of his major vessels informed of every alert he'd received from the War Department, and they had dutifully responded to each. But the warnings were frequent and contradictory; the Japanese were making war on their neighbors, everybody knew that, it had been happening for years. The Japanese were capable of attacking American targets all over the Pacific. But the Pacific was a huge ocean, and what did it mean to be ready, to stay alert? If warnings come constantly, then doesn't *alert* come to mean routine?

Kimmel's inspection was interrupted by the arrival of one of his aides, carrying a message in his right hand.

He handed the folded paper to Kimmel and said, "From Washington, Admiral."

Admiral Kimmel stopped midway through his inspection, and read. Messages from Washington important enough to be hand-delivered deserved immediate attention. The message was brief and left him frustrated. He handed the paper back to his aide, suppressed the urge to show his anger, and said quietly, "Get on with it." Then he turned and moved on with his inspection. His chief strategic advisor, a rear admiral on his staff, remained with him, walking at his opposite side, across from the captain.

Farther down the line of sailors, Kimmel said to his chief strategist, "I'm supposed to cover half the globe with this fleet, and they keep pulling our ships. Now I'm ordered to transfer twelve more destroyers to the Atlantic Fleet, and all the available anti-aircraft weaponry. Don't they know what we're facing out here?"

His strategist responded, "I've studied the war game analysis they've sent us of the likely outcome of a Japanese attack against each of our major bases in the Pacific. In each case, we lose."

Kimmel nodded. "They know that, and still they take our ships?"

"Apparently they feel Europe is the greater danger."

"These risk assessments—do they include Hawaii?"

"They say Pearl Harbor's too shallow for an aerial torpedo attack. And we're surrounded by sub nets. All we have to worry about here is sabotage, so we've bunched our planes together to make them easier to protect. But from the air Pearl's safe; it's everywhere else that we're vulnerable."

They reached the end of the deck. Kimmel nodded to the captain, who passed the order for the sailors to stand down. Kimmel looked out over the waters of Pearl Harbor. After a moment he said, "A smart enemy hits you exactly where you think you're safe. Step up surveillance of Japanese communications. Make sure Washington's doing the same."

With its stupendous natural beauty and large population of ethnic Japanese, the Hawaiian Islands have always attracted visitors from mainland Japan who tour energetically and take pleasure in recording their travels with cameras. In 1941 one of these tourists hiked through the verdant hills of Oahu. Stopping at an overlook on the trail, he withdrew from his picnic basket a superb camera, equipped with a professional lens. He turned toward Pearl Harbor, and began shooting pictures.

All around Pearl Harbor, other tourists were similarly engaged. One had even booked an hour flight with a private plane to see and photograph the beauty of Pearl Harbor from the air.

It was a week before the new photographs reached the remote Japanese island that sheltered a harbor remarkably similar in shape and depth to Pearl, and they created a stir among Admiral Yamamoto's planners, who had already constructed a scale model of the American installation so large that Japanese technicians were wading around in water up to their knees in order to adjust the mock-up ships and place them in positions that matched the latest spy intelligence. It was those positions that created excitement among Yamamoto's staff, who were gathered on a shaded platform beside the mock-ups. But it was the photographs they were staring at now.

"Look at the ships, all grouped!" Genda said breathlessly. "Perfect targets!"

"And the planes!" another officer said. "They are—what is that American expression? Sitting geese?"

"Sitting ducks," Yamamoto said quietly. "Air Commander Genda, you've arranged a demonstration?" He had told Genda to reduce the obstacles they would face to their fundamentals. Yamamoto, like military minds from Genghis Khan to Robert E. Lee, understood that battle plans succeeded or failed not because of nuance, but because of their basic common sense; though Yamamoto knew that his officers, being Japanese, would obey their orders without question, he wanted them to act with an assurance that could come only with the certainty that their daring plan was going to succeed.

Genda unveiled a water-depth illustration so simple a child could have drawn it: white sky, blue water, yellow sand, showing the distance between the sea surface and the bottom of Pearl Harbor. "We have fixed our torpedoes to allow for the shallow depth of Pearl Harbor," he said.

On a long table next to the water-depth illustration lay an actual Japanese torpedo. Genda lifted a set of wooden fins attached to a circular metallic band and slid them onto the torpedo. "Our engineers developed a modification—these wooden fins. Attaching them this way makes the torpedoes travel in the shallow harbor."

Coming out of the blustery skies at the end of another day, a squadron of Spitfires chirped in for landings. The planes were shot up and battered. Rafe was the last pilot to land; his fuselage now bore seven swastika victory symbols.

He taxied to a stop and was met by Ian MacFarlane, the Scottish mechanic who had been keeping Rafe's plane airworthy in spite of constant combat. Ian had seen much in the months he maintained the Yank's Spitfire, but the condition of the plane now as Rafe shut down the engine caused Ian to simply mutter, "Leapin' Jesus!"

Climbing out of the cockpit, Rafe said, "The struts are loose, the hydraulics are leaking, and the electrical system's shorting out in the cockpit."

Mating the fuel hose with the Spitfire's tank, Ian shook his head and asked, "Which of those three ya want fixed?"

"All of 'em."

Rafe started away, and Ian called to his back, "If ye'd wanted a bloody Cadillac, ye should'a stayed in the bloody States!"

"Right," Rafe said. "And if you don't give me a plane that can handle combat, you better start learning to speak German."

"Fook ya!" Ian said, trying not to smile. Unlike the Englishmen in the unit, who didn't much like Yanks, Ian instinctively enjoyed them.

"Learn English, then!" Rafe shot back.

"Fook ya dooble!"

Rafe moved to the barracks, as Ian got the fuel flowing and moved to help the armorers reload the guns. Fuel and ammo—first things first.

Rafe reached his cot and dropped exhausted onto his

back, trying to stretch his neck and shoulder muscles from the hours of confinement in the cramped cockpit. In the cots next to him some of the other pilots had already fallen asleep. Rafe knew he needed to do the same. He wondered if he should write Evelyn first. He had not heard back from her since his last letter; there had not been time for the mail to make a round trip, but he wanted to write her anyway, to say . . . what? *I love you, I miss you, you are the last thought in my mind as I drift off to sleep each night. . . .*

The siren blew, the Germans were coming. Rafe jumped from his cot along with the others, everybody running.

"Bloody Krauts!" he heard someone say. "Night raid!"

Rafe reached his Spitfire just as Ian was removing the fueling hose. He shook his head at Rafe and said, "I have'na been able ta—"

"Crank her!"

"But—"

"Crank her!"

Ian gave the prop a spin, and the engine caught instantly, its roar steady and powerful. Rafe scanned his gauges and found all his fluids full, all his temperatures warm and in the safe zone. He pushed his throttle and the prop pulled him onto the runway.

Ian watched him go. "God speed ya, laddie," he whispered, his own private prayer.

The squadron of Spitfires tightened into battle formation as soon as they were airborne and in less than five minutes were out over the Channel.

The night sky was made darker by mounds of nimbus clouds, cut by the white flash and slash of lightning, the way artillery looked when fired on the ground. Rafe took his position just right of the squadron leader and watched the clouds ahead.

He did not have to wait long. He was scanning the distance, using the visual technique of focusing a hundred yards ahead of his propeller, then running his attention toward infinity and then back again, when he saw a German fighter, a Focke-Wulf, breaking through the clouds off to their left. "Here they come! Ten o'clock high!" he called over his radio.

The thundering clouds seemed to crack open, spilling a huge attack formation, fighters and bombers, coming straight at them.

In Rafe's radio he heard his squadron leader's voice: "Alpha group, on the bombers! Beta group, take the fighters." Experienced and disciplined, the R.A.F. pilots peeled off in tight formations.

It happened without conscious thought: Rafe and the British squadron leader rushed side by side at the bomber at the head of the German phalanx, both Spitfires blasting away with their guns. In a moment they had shot past, in a long ducking arc, trying to avoid the return fire of the bombers; but Rafe was sure he had seen the lead bomber wobble. "We've got him!" he called over his radio. "Stay on him!"

He threw his plane into an ultra-tight high-speed turn, coming up right between the tails of the lead German group and the noses of the second. His turn was so tight that his Spitfire groaned with the g-force.

Coming out of the turn and straightening, Rafe

stitched a trail of bullets from the tail to the nose of the lead bomber, and it began to smoke. Still holding altitude, but wounded. The front bomber, the leading crew, the best bombardier . . . if he could take out that plane, he might disrupt the entire group, spread them out, give the other Spitfires a chance to race in among them rather than nibble along the edges—maybe even deflect the whole mission. Thousands of tons of enemy bombs that would not fall onto a city. Rafe hurled his plane into another tight turn, to come around and finish the bomber.

The g-force pressed him into his seat, it flexed the fuselage . . . and popped an oil line inside Rafe's cockpit. Hot, pressurized oil was suddenly spraying everywhere—all over Rafe, his controls, and, worst of all, over the inside of his cockpit glass.

He wiped at the oil with his hands and that just smeared it and made it worse. He could see nothing, not the German bombers, not the German fighters, not even his own wingman. His gauges were obscured; there was even hot oil in his eyes.

The British squadron leader saw Rafe's plane veering away from the bombers. And he saw the German fighters moving up to pounce on him. "McCawley!" he yelled into his radio. "Get to the clouds! Get to the clouds!"

"I can't see the clouds!" Rafe called back. "I'm flying blind!"

But he was not flying in a panic. He could hear the strength of the engine and feel the bite of the propeller through the sky; he knew he had airspeed and altitude, and he had never needed gauges to fly. And he knew he had comrades who would fight for him as he had fought to protect them. He steadied the Spitfire's altitude, pinched the control stick with his knees to keep it still, found the oil line and pinched off the break with one hand, and with the other pulled off the silk flying scarf that protected his neck from chafing. He had just begun using the scarf to clean off the cockpit glass when the second disaster struck.

The hot oil was dripping all through his cockpit, and when it reached the old plane's corroded electrical wiring the fluid caused an arc . . . a spark . . . and suddenly flames were spreading through Rafe's plane.

He snatched the fire extinguisher from its mount beside him inside the cockpit and triggered a cloud that snuffed the fire but filled the entire cockpit with choking smoke; between that and the smeared fluid on his glass, he was blinded once again.

That was when the first of the Messerschmitts struck him, its bullets ripping the front of his fuselage on the first pass. Miraculously the engine was still turning; he had power, he might still maneuver a little; but where? He tried to open his cockpit cover to clear the smoke, but it was jammed.

He pulled out the .45 pistol he carried and pointed it straight at the cockpit glass, shielding his eyes. He pulled the trigger three times, the pistol barking and bucking in arc, the overhead canopy fragmenting and tearing away with the blasts. The outside wind tearing by the plane cleared the smoke enough for him to take a breath and try to see. He fought the stick, but the plane had stopped responding.

The Messerschmitts swarmed in and raked him

again, bullets riddling his engine. It locked up immediately; Rafe tore at the controls to free the prop's drag and keep up enough air speed to have glide control.

"Get out of there, McCawley!" the squadron leader's voice rang in his radio. "Get out of there!" Rafe's plane descended, dropping into clouds and momentary safety, then passing through them, exposing him to the German fighters again.

The squadron leader tried to chase and cover him, but Rafe's Spitfire was dropping faster and faster, and he still wasn't out of the plane as the Germans dived on him again. They had been close enough to see the line of swastikas painted on Rafe's fuselage. Had he been able to bail out they might have spared him; for pilots on both sides were still observing the aerial chivalry of the first world war and were not shooting pilots in parachutes; that would come later. But the young German pilots in their Messerschmitts and Focke-Wulfs were not going to let an ace pilot save his plane and escape them.

Rafe's Spitfire hit the broken fog over the water, and for a moment the squadron leader lost sight of it; then he saw the plane emerge from a patch of fog, do a half roll, and hit on its top, splashing and ripping apart all at once.

There was no chance whatsoever that anyone could have survived the crash.

The squadron leader winced, paused in pain, and reported on his radio, "McCawley down. No sign of any parachute."

11

The punch cut deep into his ribs, driven upward toward his heart like the thrust of a knife. Dorie Miller winced and brought his left elbow down to cover the spot, still keeping his gloved hand at the side of his face. His opponent double hooked him with his right hand—Damn those left-handed boxers!—just under Dorie's left elbow, and the pain shot right into his spine. For the first time in his boxing career, Dorie felt his legs go numb.

And it hadn't been that long a career.

The Navy liked to breed loyalty to a ship; it was the tangible symbol of the Navy as home. Whatever you sail in, even if it's a plywood patrol boat, try to make it the best damn patrol boat in the fleet, and fight any man that says different. Pride breeds skill, and competition builds excellence; so men have always justified their desire to show their dominance. At Pearl Harbor, with the great battleships of the Pacific Fleet lined up side by side, it was more than natural that there would be contests within and among the ships; it was imperative.

Dorie Miller was heavyweight boxing champion of

the battleship *West Virginia*. And that gave him notoriety, a notoriety he had never had before in his life or in the Navy, because he was a Southerner, and shy, and a kitchen helper, and a Negro. None of those things mattered, though, when you laced on the boxing gloves and met another man in the center of a makeshift ring, strung together on the deck of a warship.

On his way to winning the championship of the *West Virginia*, Dorie had never felt the encouragement of his shipmates, almost all of whom were white, like the other sailors who fought him. None of the other black men aboard ship—the cooks, the valets, the men who carried shells from the magazine to the gundecks, or who mopped the officers' floors or shined the officers' shoes—would oppose Dorie in the ring. There were one or two of them who might even have beaten him, especially after Dorie had taught them to duck and move and shorten up their punches, but Dorie had been the first one of their group to volunteer to fight in the "smokers" that determined the boxing rankings within the ship, so the other colored sailors took their place at the perimeter of every crowd and rooted for him, cheering even louder in their hearts than in their throats. The white sailors, even the ones who bet on him, always seemed to hope that another white man would knock him down.

That was until Dorie became the *West Virginia*'s champion. From that moment on, his shipmates—a white, black, or purple polka dot—were going to bet their money on him and cheer with all their might, no matter who Dorie fought. This white boy from the battleship *Nevada*, with his left-handed style and rat-

tlesnake speed, was scaring all of them, except Dorie—
who at that moment was hurting too much to be scared.

Dorie, his legs feeling lifeless beneath him, threw a
right-hand lead that *Nevada*'s champ, enjoying the
cheers of his shipmates on the deck of their own ship,
caught with his gloves. Most of the men Dorie had
fought were not nearly so polished in their skills—these
battles were usually more toughness than technique—
and it flashed through his mind for the first time, *Dorie,
you're gonna lose*. But as the guy danced forward again
Dorie dropped his left into an uppercut that caught him
just below the sternum, and the guy grunted, clinched,
and said, "You hit pretty hard—for a cook."

Dorie wanted to hurt him for that; he struggled his
way out of the clinch and threw a right-hand haymaker,
too angry, too long, too out of balance. It was just what
his opponent expected; he beat Dorie to the punch with
a short right counterpunch that cracked into Dorie like
a piston. Dorie saw a dull flash of light, he felt the cut
over his left eye, he saw the blood spatter and flow.

The blood didn't bother him, nor was there much
pain, not during the fight itself. But Dorie's knees wob-
bled, he couldn't control them, and that did trouble him.

Dorie heard the sailors screaming outside the loose
rope square around him. For a fleeting moment he was
aware of the sunshine pouring down, and the high
white clouds above them and the bleached and scrubbed
wood of the deck below his feet; of the mountains in the
distance, and the ships all around, pressed up against
the piers like logs drifted onto a riverbank. Dorie
seemed to see it all from someplace far above himself, as
if the punch had momentarily knocked his mind free

from his brain. Time slowed down. He saw his opponent pausing, like a cat ready to leap, knowing Dorie was stiff and ready to be finished. He saw the guy stepping in, saw his punch coming . . . and without even thinking, Dorie threw his own.

He heard the sharp crack of a punch landing, and his opponent just went, fell down and did not move.

As the sailors went wild with yelling, Dorie touched the back of his glove to the gash on his forehead. The glove came back smeared and wet. And his only thought was, *But it's Sunday.*

———

Evelyn and six of her nurse friends had walked to a church just outside the base for services that morning. It was a Congregational church, the Congregationalists having come from New England a century before to specialize in the conversion of Polynesia. The Congregational missionaries, with their intelligence, sincerity, and Yankee practicality, had established business enterprises as well as churches, and many of the largest and best land tracts in Hawaii were owned by the descendants of these missionaries. The saying around the islands was that the Congregationalists had come to Hawaii to do good, and had ended up doing damn good.

Their services were thoughtful and dignified. Evelyn found comfort in the simplicity of the sanctuary and the honesty of the traditional hymns. It did not give her peace but it brought her hope, and that was plenty.

As Evelyn and her friends walked back toward their quarters, the base was quiet. Some were sleeping in; others were enjoying a duty-free day by getting off the base in any way and every way possible, visiting the beaches, picnicking in the mountains, playing sports, strolling through Honolulu. In Hawaii, everybody seemed to love life, and think of work as just another four-letter word.

"Let's find a bar and some officers," Barbara said.

"Right after church?" Martha wondered.

"You've gotta sin some, to get forgiveness!" The others smiled at Barbara's sassiness—all but Evelyn. "Come with us, Evelyn, you definitely need some sinning."

"I've got to inventory the supplies."

"Inventory supplies. On a Sunday?" Barbara wondered. She loved to play, but if there was work to be done, Barbara wouldn't let anybody do it alone.

"She wants to write Rafe," Betty said.

"You girls have fun," Evelyn said, and smiled—softly and a bit sadly, Betty thought—and walked toward the base hospital, appearing to be lost in her own thoughts.

The other nurses watched her go, and Sandra, plainest of the group, said, "Ten thousand men on this island who would worship at her feet, and she's stuck on a guy on the other side of the planet. I wish she could forget him."

"You don't forget love, honey," Barbara said. "Not ever."

As Evelyn approached the hospital she saw the tall, broad-shouldered black man with his face pressed to the glass panel of the front door, his hands cupped around his eyes to shield the glare so he could peer inside. He wore a T-shirt and Navy-issue pants. The door, she knew, was always unlocked; why was he so shy that he wouldn't enter without knowing someone was there? Evelyn moved up behind him. "Can I help you, sailor?"

When he spun around she saw the gash on his head, closed only with a Band-Aid. The wound had wept blood down his T-shirt; it was still wet enough to be red. " 'Scuse me, ma'am," he said. "All the ship's doctors is golfing, and I couldn't find nobody to look at this."

"Our doctor's gone too," Evelyn said. "But I can call one for you."

"Sorry to trouble you," he said, and started to move away.

"Wait, let me look at that." He stopped and let her fingers pull back the Band-Aid, then gently press open the cut to see its depth. Then she stepped back and looked at his face. "What's your name?"

"Dorie Miller, ma'am."

"I'm Lieutenant Stewart. And I'm just a nurse. But I'm not playing golf, and that cut needs sewing, or else it's gonna make a big scar. Whatta ya say?"

Inside the hospital, in a room otherwise vacant of patients on this quiet weekend morning, Evelyn sat him on a stool and stitched the wound. Dorie's eyes were rolled up as if he could watch from inside his skull.

"How'd you get this?" she asked him.

"Boxin'."

"Win?"

"Yes ma'am."

"What do you get for winning?"

"Respect."

Evelyn clipped the last stitch and handed him a mirror. He studied her work. The stitches were close, tight and even, the ragged edges of the cut fitted carefully together so that there was an even seam of skin. Dorie, who had been cut before and bore the scars of many battles, knew this one would barely show.

"No doctor would have done that any better," he said.

Evelyn walked him to the door. He stopped there and half nodded, half bowed. "Thank you, ma'am."

"Tell me something, Dorie. A man as big as you, you still have to fight with your fists to get respect?"

He glanced up at her once, then looked far away. "I left my mother and joined the Navy to be a man," he said. "They made me a cook . . . not even that . . . I clean up after the other sailors eat. In two years, they've never even let me fire a gun."

"You take care, Dorie."

"You too, ma'am."

She worked through the day, busying herself with sorting, counting, rearranging. The supplies had been stored neatly, tucked out of the way; but they weren't where they needed to be in case of emergency. Evelyn's father had often told her, "Accidents are exactly that— something that's not supposed to happen. So be ready for them." Evelyn had no particular premonition of disaster at Pearl Harbor; years later, there were those who would report a strange sense of coming danger, but Evelyn's concerns were more personal and immediate. Rafe was at war, and it helped her feel closer to him to be preparing the medical cabinets, just in case a sudden need should arise.

At dinnertime she decided to head back to the nurses' quarters, and as she stepped from the hospital door and out onto the low wooden steps, she thought again of Dorie Miller waiting there that day, a boxing champion, a sailor, who hesitated before entering a naval hospital, in doubt that he would be welcome. She thought of how far the world had yet to go.

And then she caught sight of something that held her transfixed: a man, silhouetted by the light of the setting sun, moving slowly down the long palm-lined walk between the hospital and the harbor. She could not yet make out his face, but he was wearing a pilot's dress uniform and walking toward her. Her heart slammed against her ribs; her head went weightless, and without meaning to she whispered, "Rafe . . ."

She moved forward, and he drew nearer. *Why is he moving so slowly?* sang a voice inside her, soaring with joy, as her heart welled up within her. He's back, he's here, he's real! And then she saw his face.

It was Danny. His face was sad as death itself.

And even before he told her, she knew.

12

Evelyn and Danny sat on the bench beside a massive Banyan tree where Evelyn had watched so many sunsets. Evelyn was numb. Danny was struggling. "I . . . lived with Rafe's family after my father died. Rafe taught me how to fly. I never thought there was anything that could hurt him in the air."

Evelyn looked toward the dying colors of the day and said, "He told me you're the only one he ever saw who was better in the air than him."

". . . He said that?" Danny paused and stared up at the clouds, edged up orange, softly fading. "Up there, he was always pushing me to fly better and faster."

He looked back to Evelyn. She was still staring away from him. The sight of her, so lost, like he was, without a man they had both loved, pierced Danny; he looked away, struggling to keep the emotions from pulling him completely under. He said, "Look, uh . . . Rafe's dad . . . he wrote me with the news, and it took me a couple of hours to work up the guts to come here and tell you. But if there's anything I can ever do to help—you let me know, okay?" Still she stared into the distance.

He stood and put his hand on top of hers, as much for his comfort as for hers. "I understand why Rafe loved you," he said. "You're as strong as he was."

Still she said nothing, and he had nothing more to say. Her hand was limp and lifeless beneath his, and he felt he could do nothing better now than to leave her alone. So he patted her hand twice, in farewell, and moved away.

When he reached the turn in the path, he looked back and saw her figure in the gathering darkness. She had begun to break down; as he watched, her whole body started convulsing, and she doubled over in grief.

Without thinking, he moved back to her and placed a hand on her shoulder. He sat beside her again, and suddenly she turned to him and sobbed upon his shoulder. Danny wrapped her gently in his arms, and then he too broke down, having found the first place where he could truly grieve.

———

The next day they gathered in the officers' club, a low wooden building between the hangars and the barracks. In the pilot's corner of the bar, all of Rafe's pilot buddies gathered around a shelf of shot glasses, one for each man in the squadron. Above it was a smaller shelf, a few glasses on it upside down.

It was so quiet the fans turning slowly on their grease-packed ball bearings from their mounts in the ceiling were the loudest noise.

Evelyn and her nurse friends were there too. Tears slid down several faces, but Evelyn had cried herself dry.

Each person in the room held a splash of whiskey in a shot glass. Danny lifted his. "To Rafe McCawley. The best pilot and best man I ever knew, or will ever know."

All the rest of them answered, "To Rafe."

They tossed down the liquor. Danny turned, reached to the high small shelf, and set the glass he had drunk from upside down upon it, behind a hand-lettered marker. The markers by all the other glasses on the top shelf listed names along with the explanation TRAINING CRASH. But Rafe's said, "Rafe McCawley, KILLED IN ACTION."

Danny stared at the row of downturned glasses—and it became too much for him. He kept his back to the room—when it became clear that he could say nothing else and could not turn and face them, everyone else filed quietly away.

Everyone except Evelyn. She stood for a long moment at the doorway, watching Danny's back as he sobbed, wanting to find some way to comfort him as he had comforted her.

But she had nothing to give. She left, closing the door gently behind her.

13

Admiral Yamamoto walked along the docks beside Genda and watched as the harbor crews prepared his aircraft carriers for voyage. His secrecy was complete, his efforts to create an atmosphere of normalcy were extreme. He had even divided his forces so that the entire battle group would not leave together, but rather would rendezvous in the hidden wastes of the ocean. His precautions seemed to have paid off; the dockhands loading supplies onto the carriers were relaxed, even casual. They seemed to view the coming mission as nothing more than a normal training sortie.

But the pilots moving up and across the gangways were different. There was a crispness to their movements, their uniforms were immaculately pressed, they had dressed for victory—or for death. They had been practicing relentlessly with torpedo and bombing runs against the island lagoon whose resemblance to Pearl Harbor was unmistakable. They knew.

Yamamoto turned to Genda and said, "You've

trained the pilots well, but no one has ever shot at them."

"If we achieve surprise," Genda answered, "the Americans will offer little resistance." Genda was enthusiastic and wanted to say more, but he saw the look on Yamamoto's face that told him the admiral was searching his mind, demanding that it ask of itself, one more time, what could go wrong, and how any mistake could be prevented.

At last Yamamoto said, "Set up teams of radio operators to send out messages the Americans will intercept, concerning every potential target in the Pacific. Include Hawaii—the clutter will be more confusing that way."

Genda understood, and smiled. "Brilliant, Admiral."

"A brilliant man," Yamamoto answered, "would find a way not to fight a war."

———

Hawaii lay beneath a blanket of stars, majestic and peaceful.

In the nurses' quarters of Ford Island, Betty lay with her eyes closed in the two-bunk cubicle she shared with Evelyn. Betty was not asleep, but she stayed motionless and pretended to be, for over in Evelyn's bunk, life was not beautiful or at peace. Evelyn lay with her face turned to the wall, her shoulders heaving with her sobs, as she grieved in silence for Rafe.

Downtown Oahu, early on a Saturday evening, was alive with soldiers and sailors and women, and with locals happy to be taking their money. Bars served tropical drinks and played live music; restaurants featured fresh fish cooked with pineapple and macadamia nuts.

On the main drag of Oahu stood a moviehouse, whose sparkling marquee announced a Charlie Chaplin film.

Inside the moviehouse Danny Walker settled into a seat, alone and off to one side. The theater was not quite full, but it would be later, when more dating couples had finished dinner. Still, the atmosphere was festive. Army buddies called to one another; the young men showed off, the young women laughed. All of them found it exciting to be in a movie theater, to enjoy the excitement of motion pictures.

The subdued houselights dimmed into darkness and the audience grew quiet. The screen flickered to life with the pre-feature newsreels. The first was about all the positive signs that America was emerging from the Great Depression; it showed happy workers returning to their factory jobs, and the narrator gushed with optimism. The audience watched this with interest—any kind of film was a marvel to them, and they were accustomed to civic cheerleading of the current events coverage. Then came a segment about the war in Europe. It began with footage of British civil defense workers putting up patriotic propaganda billboards bearing Churchill's image with his words emblazoned above him: GIVE US THE TOOLS AND WE WILL FINISH THE JOB! In an edgy, excited voice, the newsreel narrator repeated the words and added, "So Churchill declared, and in this case America has given more than supplies: the Eagle Squadron, American volunteers in the Battle of Britain!" Suddenly the screen in front of Danny was full of images of pilots running to their Spitfires and taking off.

Danny sat motionless, riveted as the narrator went on: "They are fighting bravely and holding back the Germans, to the frustration of Hitler and the rest of his bullying mob!" There was no mention of the losses among the pilots of the Eagle Squadron, no mention of Rafe McCawley, his friend, the lifelong soulmate who had taught him to fly, who had sat beside him on a nail keg crate and . . .

It was too much for Danny. He stood and made his way to the aisle even as Charlie Chaplin began his pigeon walk across the screen.

He stepped through the aisle door into the lobby and was heading toward the main doorway when he ran into Evelyn, emerging from the other side of the theater. "Ev—" he stammered in surprise. "Evelyn."

"Hi, Danny," she said. And it was suddenly obvious to both of them that they'd come to the theater, and were now leaving it, for exactly the same reason. They stood there in an awkward silence. Visible through the theater doors was a diner, glowing on the other side of the street. Danny looked at it, then looked back to her. "Want a cup of coffee?" he said.

Two minutes later they were sitting at a booth in the diner, the theater now on the other side of the street, its marquee glowing and still drawing latecomers. A Samoan waitress poured two cups of coffee and left them with menus that neither of them looked at.

Evelyn sipped from her cup, then set it down and said, "Nothing like a comedy for picking up your spirits, huh?"

"Yeah. That was a lot of laughs."

"Even after three months, I never seem to smile," she said, then tried to contradict herself, lifting the sides of her mouth, trying not to look so sad. And maybe it was working; she felt better, sitting there with Danny. "How are you doing?"

"About the same as you, I guess. And even now, it's not just the loss, it's . . . the guilt."

"You mean about helping him hide his reading problem, to save his wings?"

"I don't think he would've even finished high school if I hadn't cleaned up his assignments for him," Danny said, realizing he hadn't yet touched his coffee. He stirred in some cream along with a heavy dose of sugar. "After that, it was just natural. When we joined the Air Corps, I helped him hide his problem jumbling letters, and never even thought about what I was doing."

"So now . . . you're telling yourself that if you hadn't helped him he'd still be alive?" said Evelyn.

Danny nodded and half laughed at Evelyn's insight. Or maybe it wasn't insight; maybe she was going through the same thing.

As if in answer to his thoughts she said, "Well . . . how about me? I passed him. When I should've failed him. And he'd be alive."

"And why did you pass him? I always wondered that."

"My father was one of the pilots who taught Colonel Doolittle. So many of his friends just dried up and died when they were told they were too old to fly anymore." She took a longer sip of her coffee. "When I start thinking like this, like we both are, I try to tell myself that when you take away what a person loves, you've already killed them."

She set her cup down so quickly it rattled in the saucer. She'd just realized those words might be true for her too; Rafe was gone, and she felt she had died herself.

Danny didn't seem to read that thought; he seemed comforted by what she'd just said. "You're right," he told her, nodding, his eyes distant. "Rafe—what made him Rafe—would've been dead the minute you took away his wings. He had to prove himself, to those people that called him a dummy."

"It's so . . . strange. It's as if . . . the flaw that made him suffer was the gift that made him great."

Danny looked at her and their gazes stuck, the two of them connecting in a moment of grace, believing for one moment that maybe light really does spring from darkness.

The waitress interrupted, refilling both their cups from a steaming coffee pot.

"Weird, ain't it . . ." Danny said. "Rafe made people find something in themselves. Reading to Rafe is what started me loving books—wanting to write, to be another Hemingway. Weird dream, for a kid from Tennessee. But Rafe made me dream, he saw what I could hope to be, and helped me hope it. He did that to everyone he knew—especially the ones he knew the best. And I guess nobody knew him like you and me."

Out on the streets of Oahu, every woman who wanted company had a date, and Billy and Red were happy men, doubly happy in double dating. Billy and Barbara were walking down the street arm in arm; close behind them were Red and Betty, not touching each other but keeping close, as Red stammered, "I . . . I . . ."

"Why are you nervous tonight?" Betty asked him.

"W-well," Red said, "It's b-because . . . because I w-want to tell you something. I . . . I . . ."

Billy had stopped talking with Barbara for a moment and was listening to Red, silently urging him on. As Red struggled, it became too much for Billy, and he turned around and said, "Sing it to her, Red."

Red came to a dead stop on the sidewalk; the idea of singing what he wanted to say dominated his entire being, so that the world around him shrank to the circle of himself and Betty; he became unaware of Billy and Barbara standing so close, watching, or of the other pedestrians passing by. In full voice he sang, "I just want to tell you, Betty, I LIKE YOOOU! I almost . . . almost . . . love you . . . !"

Betty stood looking up at him with her blue doll's eyes, blinking for what was a long moment to Billy and seemed an eternity to Red. Then she said, "Well Red, I almost, almost love you too." She kissed him on the lips, just a peck, and Red turned the color of the stoplight dangling above the street.

"So," Billy said. "Dinner first? Or a movie and then—"

It was then that he spotted Evelyn and Danny in the diner. They were less than ten feet from him, lit up like mannequins in a shop window, and just as oblivious of everyone around them. Barbara saw them too, as did Red and Betty. For all the world they seemed as lost in each other as Red had been in his song to Betty.

———

Inside the diner, Evelyn found herself smiling. The release, the comfort of getting to talk about Rafe with someone who loved him as deeply in his own way as she had in hers, made her feel she could breathe easily for the first time since she'd learned of his death. She sat back in her chair, toyed with her coffee cup, and said, "Rafe made me feel that life could be bigger and better . . . and he wouldn't let the world make him feel small."

Danny nodded and smiled as she had; that was the Rafe he knew, too.

Evelyn was growing talkative. "I mean," she said, leaning forward again, "growing up in a military family, I moved every year—new apartments, new schools, new people . . . no attachments. It came naturally to be a nurse—try to help the pain, just don't let yourself care too much. I'm a nurse who never saw blood . . . or ever knew love, until I knew Rafe—"

Evelyn stopped short, seeing Billy and Barbara staring at her through the window.

Danny turned to see what had stopped her so suddenly, had drained the smile from her face, and saw his friends out on the sidewalk. Billy was already trying to look blank, which made him seem even more embarrassed; Red frowned in confusion. But the face that really spoke was Betty's: her face went from amazement to satisfaction to worry, all in the space of a moment.

They all waved to each other, trying to be casual, and the four outside moved across the street to the theater. Evelyn and Danny found themselves sitting in self-conscious silence.

"Should I walk you home?" Danny said finally.

"No, I'll be fine," she replied. "Thanks for the coffee. Thanks for everything."

She stood before he had time to react, laid her face upon the top of his head as if kissing him there with her cheek, crossed the floor quickly and stepped out into the night, leaving Danny alone with his coffee, and the scent of her still in the air.

———

Captain Thurman sat in his corner of the War Department basement and watched as the teletype machine, wired directly to the encryption/decryption section upstairs, punched out a decoded message. The machine left spaces wherever there were words or phrases in the intercepted Japanese transmission that Washington's spooks could not decipher. As the typed pages rolled slowly from the machine, Thurman saw more blank area than printed words. But his eyes—deeply intelligent, cat green eyes behind thick horn-rimmed glasses—snatched the words and bored into the empty spaces between them. He was quiet for a long time, and then he said to a tired lieutenant he had assigned to pore over previously transmitted sheets of decryption, "None of this makes sense."

"Well, uh . . . of course not, sir," the lieutenant said carefully. "It's only partially decoded."

"Was your previous boss an idiot?" Thurman demanded.

"Sir?"

"You heard me."

"He . . . uh . . . was not difficult to keep up with on an intellectual basis, sir."

"Do me a favor, Lieutenant. Give me a straight answer when I ask you a question. He was an idiot, right?"

"He was an idiot, sir."

"Good. So that's your excuse for treating me like one. Just force of habit, correct?"

"I'm sorry, sir."

"Don't be sorry, be aware. Aware of the fact that you no longer work for an idiot. I know the decoding is partial, otherwise, why did I have them send you to me?" Thurman had pulled every string he had to gain a certain kind of intelligence help; the lieutenant, mystified at a sudden transfer from the public affairs section, had been dispatched to join Captain Thurman in the basement. Thurman had told him he had been chosen for his imagination, and he gave the lieutenant the mostly empty transmissions to struggle through.

"I mean the part that we understand doesn't make sense," Thurman said. "The Japanese are sending military instructions all over the Pacific, but there's no logical pattern."

The lieutenant, still baffled, said, "Sir, I don't . . ."

"They're trying to confuse us!" Thurman interrupted. He stared at the transmission in front of him, stared at it for a long time. Finally he said, "You know, I hate it when somebody tries to bullshit me."

14

To familiarize the new nurses with the hospital, Evelyn had devised a plan whereby each nurse would go through a sequence of locating everything necessary to treat patients, so that the gathering of antiseptic, sutures, bandages, towels, pillows and bedpans would be second nature and so diminish confusion and mistakes, some of which could be fatal; a suffering patient, for example, given an overdose of morphine by two different nurses too busy or distracted to check his chart, could die. So the nurses ran their drills and scurried about the hospital enjoying the feeling that they knew their jobs and were good at them. Each of them carried a basket of items off their checklist; it was like a medical scavenger hunt.

"Hey!" Betty said, calling from the supply cabinet, "has anybody seen the tourniquet straps?"

Evelyn, who served as the drill's official judge, moved over and said, "We're low on them. I've ordered more—they go there on the second shelf. Give yourself a check and go on to the next item."

"Check," Betty said.

Evelyn lowered her voice and said, "It wasn't like it looked."

"I know that," Betty answered softly. "The only thing that worries me is that you feel you had to say so."

"What do you mean?"

"It's been months. You've already grieved enough for a lifetime. Now you've got to move on."

"I'm moving," Evelyn said, a bit louder.

Betty lowered her voice even more, to a near whisper. "I'm your roommate," she said. "I hear you crying when you think I'm asleep."

Evelyn sucked in a deep, silent breath, as if she could take back the grief she had revealed. She had wanted to keep her problems private, especially from young Betty, whom she had tried to protect like she would a younger sister. But like most younger sisters, Betty had noticed far more than even those closest to her would assume.

"Evelyn," she said, "I lied about my age so I could get away from home. My father never let me date, my brothers chased off any boys that ever looked at me. Now I just want to live, you know? And I see you and I want to be like you, so full of life. And now . . ." Betty shook her head, her blonde curls bouncing over her blue eyes. "Would Rafe have wanted you to die, just because he did? He arranged for his best friend to be the one to tell you because he wanted you to be okay, to let go. And that's what you have to do."

Evelyn put a hand to her mouth as if that would stop the tears. Betty hugged her, and Evelyn wept quietly on her shoulder, but for only a moment. Evelyn let go quickly, brushed away her tears, and both she and Betty went on with their work as if nothing had happened.

That evening Evelyn opened the trunk at the foot of her bed. From among her pressed civilian clothes and other personal belongings, she dug out her diary and carried it back to the bed, where she sat down and opened it to the rose pressed inside, the one Rafe had given her on their last night together.

Evelyn stood on the volcanic rocks jutting out into the gentle waters of the harbor. She cradled the rose carefully in both hands. Its petals were dry, fragile as ashes. The rose was now a flat misshapen thing, but that did not matter to her; in her heart it would always be what it had once been: alive and fresh and full of promise, like life itself. Whatever that rose had meant, it could always stay in her heart, couldn't it? This is just a relic, she told herself.

Evelyn forced herself to hold the dried, flat rose over the water, but couldn't let go. Then she took it in her hand, made a fist around it, and ordered her fingers to crush it. Her fingers trembled.

But they would not obey.

As the setting sun poured a layer of orange sheen upon the surface of the runway, Danny sat in the cockpit of his P-40 and fired a short burst from his wing guns. Oak blocks jacked up under the plane supported the fuselage and kept it perfectly steady; a wooden target hundreds of yards away absorbed the bullets. Billy, standing outside the right wing tip, observed the target through binoculars and said, "Nope, they're still not converging." Red and Anthony, bent beneath the wings, adjusted the cannons with screwdrivers, and when Danny fired another burst Billy reported, "Bang. Right on target." He pulled the strap over his head and wound up the binoculars. "Let's get going, I'm thirsty. Coma's got some Navy pilots coming over to the bar; we're gonna soften 'em up with Mai-Tai's and then fleece 'em in poker."

"I'm in," Anthony said, tossing his screwdriver into the tool box that Red was already closing.

"You guys go ahead," Danny said. "I'm gonna stay and check the gauges."

"The mechanics have done that!" Anthony told him. "Come on, we're pilots!"

"I want to check 'em again."

"I'll stay and help you," Red volunteered.

"That's okay, thanks, I got it."

Red was about to protest but Billy put a hand on his shoulder to silence him and then asked Danny, "You okay?"

"Yeah!" Danny said quickly. Then after hesitating he said, "No." Danny had to take a deep breath. He looked around the circle of his best buddies. "I've fallen in love with Rafe's woman."

"I saw this coming," Billy sighed.

"I didn't. I tried to stop it from happening . . . but it has."

For a moment there was silence around the circle. Then Red spoke up. "Sooner or later she'll be with somebody, Danny. Rafe asked you to take care of her. He's probably lookin' down from heaven right now, hoping you'll be the one."

"Bullshit!" Anthony barked, seemingly angrier at Red than at Danny. "Even if you're dead you don't want somebody doin' your girl—especially your best friend!"

Red surprised everybody with the strength of his comeback. "Danny's being more of a friend by taking care of her himself!"

"Yeah?"

"Yeah!"

"Tell that to somebody who ain't from Brooklyn!"

"Knock it off, you guys!" Billy broke in, "this arguing isn't helping."

Danny nodded, as if in agreement with them all. "I know it's wrong," he said. "I just don't know what to do."

None of them had any response to that. They all stared down at their shoes upon the tarmac. Then Billy said, "I can't give you any advice, buddy. Except . . . except maybe this. Whatever happens between you and Evelyn, whether you go with what you're obviously feeling or you walk away from it—whichever you do, don't let it be because of Rafe. Let it be because of you."

Billy led Red and Anthony away. Danny, left alone in the stillness of the evening, found himself with a sudden peace that he could not explain. His friends had caught him in a crossfire of advice that had reflected their own character more than Danny's situation; but each was right in his own way, for the conflicting feelings all existed inside Danny, and the acceptance of that truth—that Danny was a torn man, full of grief and hope and pain and desire—released the death-grip around his soul, a soul he now realized was not the rough and rigid ice he had felt it to be, but now was more a fluid pool of spirit, lying quiet and at peace.

He was still lost in the silence of that feeling when a voice from behind him said, "Danny . . ."

Startled, he spun round and found Evelyn, having approached from the grass and stopped ten feet away, still off the runway. "I'm sorry," she said, "I didn't mean to interrupt you."

"No, not at all," he said. She stood there looking beautiful in the gathering dusk, her smile both soft and sad. "What can I do for you?"

"I just . . . I'd like the address of Rafe's parents. I thought maybe if I could write them . . ." She trailed off, then tried again. "I'm . . . having a hard time letting go of the past." She seemed to want to say more, but couldn't find the words.

Danny nodded, understanding all she said and didn't say. "I've tried to do that by focusing on the future," he told her, smiling at his own failure, "but that hasn't worked either. It's just reminded me more that whatever I faced, any trouble I ever got into, I knew Rafe would come after me and I wouldn't be in it alone. Now . . . it's not that way anymore."

He found a pencil and a slip of paper in his pocket and scribbled the address for her. He crossed the space between them and put the paper into her hand.

"I hope it helps," he said. "I've written three times myself—but it hasn't helped me."

She slipped the paper neatly into her purse and snapped it shut. But she couldn't move. She looked away, toward the last light of the day, just a gray line at the edge of blackening sky. She looked back to Danny. "Rafe told me he didn't want to leave me with a lifetime of regret. So we held back. And now regret is all I have," she said.

This stabbed him; he didn't know what to say. Clearly she didn't either. He looked toward the horizon too. Then up at the stars. Then, more quickly, back at his plane. "Hey," he said. "Have you ever seen Pearl Harbor at night?"

"Well . . . sure," she said.

"From the air?"

The takeoff was smoother than Danny expected, and rougher than Evelyn hoped. She had worried about her added weight in the plane, though he had assured her she was far lighter than a full load of fuel and ammunition would have been. But the cockpit felt so cramped, with her wedged onto Danny's lap and the seat belts strapping her in so tightly that she felt useless and clumsy and had kept insisting, before they took off, that they would never get airborne, even though she had grown ever more excited and hopeful that they would. Her bulk in the cockpit apparently presented no problem to him, though he had to reach around her waist to hold the control stick and could only watch the gauges by looking over her shoulder; it seemed to her that he flew the plane with something other than his hands and his eyes, through some other connection to it that flowed from his whole body. She felt both thrilled and completely safe.

The pull of the engine was smooth and powerful; she felt its steady surge pushing his chest into her back, thrusting her off the ground and into the air.

The sky above them was startlingly clear; the brightest planets glowed steadily, the soloists of a heavenly symphony, as the chorus of stars danced around a full moon. "So beautiful!" she said.

"Hang on."

He spun the plane in an easy half turn, and Evelyn saw the whole world turn upside down. The sky was below them, and above their heads was Pearl Harbor. The polished edges of gentle waves caught the moonlight, making curved bands of white that, in Evelyn's imagination, looked like elongated stars, and the lunar illumination reached all the way to the harbor's shallow bottom, so that she felt she could see beyond the limits of her new topsy-turvy world, all the way to the limits of heaven.

The P-40 soared easily out of the sky and glided back to earth, its tires chirping as softly as a sparrow as they touched the runway. Danny guided the plane back to its exact spot outside the hangar without ever having to touch the throttle. Evelyn had forgotten her weight upon his lap and the cramped confines of the cockpit and even the pull of gravity. Now, as Danny shut down the engine, she heard the silence, saw the invisible, thought the unthinkable.

Danny carefully removed the harness around her. She looked overhead. The stars were still bright above them.

"I didn't realize until tonight that I had stopped wanting to live," she said.

She turned in his lap, and looked at him. And all he saw was her eyes.

Tentatively, almost reluctantly, they kissed. Their passion grew, neither of them prepared enough for that moment to find the strength to resist it.

15

Betty still lay asleep in her bunk, but Evelyn was already up and dressed; she sat silently on her bunk, staring at the pressed rose.

Still she could not throw it away.

So she placed it back into the diary. She closed the pages around the rose, put the book back into her foot-locker, and closed it too, quietly but firmly, like something final.

She walked quickly, practicing what she was going to say. *Danny, last night was wrong . . . Danny, last night was not wrong, but it was—it was too soon. You're a wonderful man, and so special to me, but I'm just not— I'm just not—*What was the right word? *Ready*, she thought. *I'm just not ready.*

She collided with Danny, coming from the opposite direction in an athletic, hurried jog. He laughed as he realized it was Evelyn, grabbing her shoulders, talking over her as she said, "Danny!"

"Evelyn! I was just coming to find you!"

"Danny, I—"

"Evelyn! Last night was so beautiful! I hope you feel that way too."

"I do, Danny, I just . . ."

He saw her struggle, and felt he understood. "I know, Evelyn, it was too soon. But I can't say I'm sorry." He smiled, his face all teeth and happiness. "I'm sorry I've gotta run, I'm going on duty—but I had to find you and tell you something." He paused, steadying himself by taking a breath. "I've always had this dream that maybe someday I'd write something, something worth reading. I never did. But when I woke up this morning, I had words in my head."

She noticed the piece of paper clutched in his hand. Now he unfolded it carefully, took another breath, and read from it. . . .

> *I soared above the song birds*
> *And never heard them sing*
> *I lived my life in winter . . .*

He lifted his eyes to hers . . .

> *. . . And then you brought the spring.*

He placed the poem into her hand, kissed her cheek and trotted away in the direction from which he'd come, calling back, "Can I see you tonight?"

"Okay . . ." she called back softly, and saw him grin as he turned and sped up his pace to a run.

Back in her quarters, with Betty still in the sweet guiltless slumber of the young, Evelyn placed Danny's poem within the same pages that sheltered Rafe's rose and closed the book with the silent prayer that her heart, like her diary, could contain two loves.

Book Two

INFAMY

16

Deep in the War Department's intelligence section, Captain Jesse Thurman had lost track of time, or more accurately, he had transcended its relevance. He did not know the hour or even the day; to him, the only time was Now. A perfectly Buddhist achievement—not a bad trick, for a Baptist.

The only indications of how long it had been since he had slept or showered were the sour sweat fragrance of his clothes and the heavy beard around his jaw. If any ranking officer had entered his basement lair, he would've told the captain to clean up and get some rest. Thurman would've told him to go to hell, and would've been forgiven for it. Not a bad trick, for a military officer.

In the last hours and days, he had pored over decoded messages, over reports marked TOP SECRET, over spy photographs of Japanese carriers in port being loaded with planes, bombs, torpedoes. Something was happening soon, and no one on earth could convince him otherwise.

Thurman became aware that he was thinking in circles; he forced himself to stand upright, and the screaming muscles in his back reminded him that he was in possession of a physical body. He took two steps away from the papers spread on the table in front of him, and it occurred to him that on the other side of the world, Admiral Yamamoto worked with much the same obsession, studying timetables, maps, potential developments both manmade and natural, along with strategies for dealing with them.

Thurman admired Yamamoto and wondered if the two of them might have been friends, had they known each other. In a real sense they were aware of each other, Thurman reflected, and were connected even more than if they drank together in the same bar, and shared dinner every Wednesday, as Thurman did with the woman he had married.

Wednesday! Thurman thought. *My wife! . . . My family! What the hell day is it, anyway?* He grabbed for a calendar and stared at it for as long as it took for him to realize it was useless to him in this state. His watch said 12:15—midday or dead of night? He rubbed his chin, felt the stubble and looked at his reflection in the polished brass base of a desk lamp. He looked awful. He grabbed his coat, he had to get out of there, kiss his wife, hug his children.

He was just reaching for the door handle when a security messenger, an ensign who had never needed to shave, entered from the hallway, carrying an envelope. The envelope was marked SPECIAL URGENT. It was a designation used so often that no one got excited about it. The ensign hadn't broken a sweat; no one had told him to hurry. "Where's this from?" Thurman asked.

"Diplomatic liaison office, Cap'n," the ensign answered, stifling a yawn.

"Find a bed or get out of the Navy, but don't ever yawn in front of me again, you understand?" Thurman snapped, as he grabbed the envelope and tore it open.

"Yes sir!" the ensign said.

"Get out of here."

Thurman read the message quickly, then read it again. He had already turned back to his desk and grabbed up the telephone, before the ensign had closed the door behind him.

"Mr. President," Roosevelt heard, from somewhere within his dream. "Mr. President." It was the voice of George, his valet, that he was hearing, but as Roosevelt groped for the spectacles on his bedtable and hung them over his ears, it was the face of one of his presidential aides who came into focus.

"What is it?" Roosevelt said, in a strong voice.

"Mr. President," said the aide, "we've just received a message from the Peruvian ambassador to Japan. His sources tell him the Japanese are assembling their fleet to attack us."

Roosevelt's voice was clearer than his thoughts. He took a moment to let the echoes of his dream drain away and said, "We've received warnings about every American base in the Pacific. Why does this one seem particularly alarming to you?"

The aide blinked, awed at Roosevelt's power. Pulled

from a tortured sleep, with two questions the president already had the aide on the defensive and looking to deflect responsibility. "I . . . it wasn't I who became alarmed, sir, I . . . General Marshall called and told me to wake you. He said he'd been called by the War Department's intelligence section, and would have a briefing assembled for you in two hours, if you were willing to cancel the Senate breakfast on the banking legislation."

Roosevelt used his powerful arms to push himself more upright on his pillows, and his valet helped position them behind him. "Did General Marshall say whether this Peruvian ambassador knew the target?"

"The general said the ambassador was not sure," the aide said. "But he thinks it's Pearl Harbor."

The admirals, generals and key civilian advisors sat behind Roosevelt and saw the silhouette of his large distinctive head just above the high back of his wheelchair as the reflective screen in front of him flickered. The film was black-and-white and without sound—it was even jerkier than the earliest silent movies—and showed a Japanese harbor, its piers almost completely empty.

An admiral spoke over the rattle of the projector. "Our naval intelligence officer in Tokyo secretly shot this, it confirms the Japanese fleet has set sail . . . somewhere. We can't find it anywhere, the fleet is under radio silence. They could be on simple maneuvers or lining up a major attack. It seems to me an attack is inevitable. The question is where? And how?"

As the film ran out and its loose end slapped in its spool, the admiral nodded for the overhead lights. As they came on, everyone in the room cringed; no one had slept much the night before.

The admiral moved to an easel display showing scout planes moving out in all directions from every American base in the Pacific; he was steeped in the craft of military briefings, and loved visual aids. "We keep sending scout planes in wider vectors but they get nothing." He paused for a moment to give the president time to absorb the chart, though the chart was perfectly simple, and began to uncover his next display, saying, "We have sent ships to the following areas—"

Roosevelt had had enough, and broke in: "Two whole Japanese carrier divisions have just disappeared, and we can't find them, correct?"

"Yes, Mr. President, and we—"

"I'm aware the Navy is doing its best, Admiral. Let's move on. Tell me where you think they are."

"Yes, Mr. President." The admiral tossed off the next three charts as if he'd suddenly become angry at the aides who had prepared them, and found a large flat map of the Pacific Ocean. "Between America and the Far East are the sea lanes where the winds and the currents make the best route for shipping." He sketched these out with a pointer. "Far above is the northern route, between Canada and Russia. Between these two routes is something we call the Vacant Sea. If I were the Japanese, I'd send a task force there. You could hide the entire land mass of Asia in the Vacant Sea and nobody would know."

"So they pop out and attack where?" demanded the president.

"That's the problem, Mr. President. This latest diplomatic intelligence suggests Hawaii, but as you know we've received warnings for every conceivable target, and the truth is that from the Vacant Sea the Japanese could hit anywhere they want. The Philippines, Borneo, Guam . . ." The admiral saw the president was losing his patience. "Captain Thurman of naval intelligence has been focusing solely on this problem, and he has something to tell us."

Everyone in the room looked at Thurman. The admiral sat down quickly. Thurman did not waste time. "Our cryptology team has recently broken Japan's Wind Codes, which are for high-level military traffic," Thurman said. "We've been developing a preponderance of evidence theory for some time, and this recent message from the Peruvian ambassador helps confirm our suspicions. I think the target is Pearl Harbor."

"You have hard evidence?" one of the generals asked.

"If I had hard evidence, we'd already be at war, sir," replied Thurman.

The general's eyes snapped, and the vice admiral who had stumped for Thurman's inclusion on this team winced and looked into a far corner of the room. There was no question that Thurman was brilliant; it was equally obvious that his intellect did not include political wisdom.

"Then what kind of evidence do you have, Captain?" demanded the general.

Thurman knew he was on shaky ground. How could he explain instincts to a fact-rooted man? He paused, looked the general cleanly in the eye and answered, "Our decoding machines miss words and have garbled

lines, so to explain the decrypts we have to interpret what we think they are trying to say."

"Interpret. You mean guess," said the general.

"They use their informed intuition—" began the admiral.

"Thank you, Admiral, but the general's right," Thurman interrupted. "We guess. Any goose bump, weird wart or spine tingle—we pay attention to, and read like a drunk gypsy, because somebody's gotta step outside to see inside. And what I see is a strike on Pearl Harbor. It's the worst thing that could happen. A blow to Pearl could devastate our Pacific Fleet's ability to make war."

"So you want us to mobilize the Pacific military force, at a cost of millions of dollars, on this weird little gut feeling of yours?" the general said.

"No sir," Captain Thurman replied. "I understand that my job is to gather and interpret information, and that making difficult decisions, based on incomplete information, from my shitty decoding machines, is yours."

They realized then—everyone in the room—that Roosevelt had said nothing but was listening to the exchange. They paused, and still the president did not speak.

Finally the admiral said, "Then bring us better information so we can make a better decision, Captain."

"Yes sir," Captain Thurman answered.

He would've sworn he saw President Roosevelt nod then, in approval or dismissal, he could not be sure. Afterward he was not even sure he had seen the nod. But he was sure Roosevelt had listened.

———

Yamamoto's two battle groups met in the open ocean, at precisely the coordinates he had planned. Under the strictest radio silence they assembled for the run to Hawaii.

Yamamoto stood on the bridge of his flagship as the signalmen flashed code to each ship to confirm all was well. Six aircraft carriers: *Akagi, Kaga, Soryu, Zuikaku, Hiryu, Shokaku*. Six carriers with a total of 441 warplanes. Along with them he positioned two battleships, nine destroyers, three cruisers. A whole flotilla of protection, though Yamamoto did not expect that they would encounter a single ship upon their route.

For they were in the Vacant Sea. The American War Department had been right about that.

At Pearl Harbor were ninety-six American ships. Eight battleships, all named after states: *Arizona, California, Maryland, Nevada, Oklahoma, Pennsylvania, Tennessee, West Virginia*. Eight cruisers, two light and six heavy, named after cities: *New Orleans, San Francisco, St. Louis, Helena, Raleigh, Detroit, Honolulu, Phoenix*. Thirty-five destroyers, named after distinguished navy men; four submarines, named after sea animals. And minelayers, seaplane-tenders, repair ships, target ships. On the airfields surrounding the harbor were fighter planes: P-40s, P-36s, P-26s, F4Fs. And bombers: SBD dive-bombers, B-17 heavy bombers, B-18 medium bombers, A-20 light bombers. And PBY patrol/recon seaplanes, and utility planes. And ammunition, and fuel, and spare parts, and warehouses sheltering the supplies that keep a massive military force in motion.

Only this force was not in motion. Most of it sat calm and still, in the Hawaiian sunshine.

It was the military machinery that Yamamoto was after. Most of all he wanted the American aircraft carriers: the *Lexington, Saratoga* and *Enterprise*. They were based at Pearl Harbor, but Yamamoto had no way of guaranteeing that they would be there when his planes struck.

There was no doubt, however, about the human beings. Thousands of sailors, soldiers, civilians. Men, women, and children. Yamamoto was targeting only military installations, but he knew the phrase from Shakespeare: *Cry havoc! and unleash the dogs of war.* Once the attack was under way, many people would die.

In the coming months and years, many Americans would think of Yamamoto as blood-thirsty and murderous. Many among the warlords who ruled Japan would consider him not ruthless enough. As a tactician, Yamamoto was trained to focus on eliminating an enemy's means of making war, and that is what he had set out to do. He knew that people would die. But how many, and how he would deal with the fact of their deaths, was a question that he, like any other human being in his situation, could offer only to his gods.

17

At a surveillance base on the island of Oahu, three tired soldiers assigned to Army intelligence sat at their telephone monitoring equipment. One, a Japanese American, had been given the job of listener, monitoring the telephone traffic between the Hawaiian Islands and Japan. He wore earphones and sat at a console from which he could monitor every trans-Pacific line. Next to him was the tracer, who handled the local side of the equation: if the listener picked up something suspicious leaving the Islands on its way to Japan, the tracer could track down the Hawaiian site of the conversation, right down to the address of the local phone being used. The third man on their team was an intelligence supervisor, whose job was to decide what suspicions were important enough to be passed up through the chain of command.

The listener, who always spoke quietly even though his equipment prevented any possibility of his presence being known upon the phone lines, pulled the headset cup off one ear and said, "I've got something on line three. Two men, who don't seem to know each other. The one in Japan is asking if the aircraft carriers are at their moorings."

The supervisor looked to the tracer, who was already at work and soon said, "It's a dentist. His office is . . ." He paused and looked at the supervisor. "It overlooks Pearl Harbor."

Admiral Kimmel was in a barber's chair having his weekly trim when his aide entered and asked the barber if he would give them a moment alone. The barber stepped out the back door into the shade of a palm tree, leaving the admiral and his aide alone in the shop.

The aide spoke crisply, having learned to give information quickly but without hurry. "Admiral, one of our listening stations picked up an exchange between a local dentist and someone in Japan. The dentist didn't know the caller; the caller talked like he was the friend of one of the dentist's relatives, interested in hearing about the local sights before he invests in a trip to Hawaii. But what he asked about specifically was the location of the aircraft carriers."

"Why would he ask a dentist?"

"His office looks out over Pearl."

"He a spy?"

"We don't think so. Intelligence is checking him out. They say he grew up here, but was born in Japan. Our listening section says this kind of conversation happens often; a friend of a friend, a relative by marriage, anybody with any claim on loyalty calls from the old country and asks for information, and the local feels it would be rude and insulting to refuse. It's the stuff about the carriers that made our guys suspicious; the caller from Japan kept coming back to questions about the carriers. Why couldn't the dentist see them? Had they moved? Could they be in another part of the harbor?"

Admiral Kimmel gave himself a moment to consider. "Let's assume the worst," he said. "The Japanese want to know about our carriers, so much that they make reckless phone calls. Their fleet is missing. They're out there planning it. But what's their target?"

Outside, the barber lit a cigarette. This was lasting longer than the admiral's usual interruptions.

When his aide had no answer, Kimmel asked, "And we've gotten no sniff at all of where their fleet might be?"

"No, Admiral. We've checked with Washington too, and they've got no updates."

"How many of our subs are out on patrol, nineteen?"

"Exactly, sir."

"Nineteen. Covering half the world." Kimmel shook his head. "You've turned this dentist thing over to the F.B.I.?"

"Yes sir."

"They'll investigate the dentist. But they won't find the Japanese fleet."

"No sir."

"Carry on," Kimmel said.

As the barber heard the front door closing, he snuffed out his cigarette and resumed cutting the admiral's hair. But the admiral was quiet, even quieter than usual.

———

It was the magic time of night on the islands, when the sun had been down just long enough for the temperature of the sea and the land to reach equilibrium and the winds to fall so quiet that there remained only enough breeze to stir the dry fronds in the tops of the palm trees and give them a soft and peaceful rattle, like the first toy of a newborn child.

The stars had come out as brilliant pinpoints in a night so clear that the ones that "shot"—the meteorites burning in the earth's invisible atmosphere—left sparkling white glory like that of fireworks as they flew to their deaths.

The figure walking toward the base hospital had paused and was looking up at the night sky at exactly the moment when one of these shooting stars died in that way. He wondered if it was an omen.

That very thought, the consciousness of it, kept him rooted in his place. For days it seemed he had not been thinking at all. In reality, thoughts had been flashing through his head at such a rate that none of them seemed a part of him, and he was moving forward like an animal, driven by pure instinct toward a secret lair where he would either recover from his wounds or die. Now here he was, stopping for the first time and experiencing the disturbing thought that forces beyond his own control determined his destiny. He wondered, *Why am I thinking this now?* He had never been noticeably superstitious. The God he believed in was just, fair and ultimately loving, though His ways were mysterious to the descendants of Adam and Eve. But this moment of glimpsing a shooting star falling to its death through the mechanics of a universe hurled into motion at the very beginning of time itself had a disturbing impact on him. The shooting star had its destiny. What was his? Did he have one at all?

This last thought was even more confusing. Whether random or divinely determined, he had some fate, didn't he? And he could shape it some way, like he'd always done, because he was alive and he had choices.

Ah, choices. Now he understood. He related to the rock flying and dying in space through no choice of its own because he felt himself utterly powerless now.

He argued with himself. *I'm alive! I've never been more alive than I am right now!* And yet he knew that to be arguing with himself in that way was a sign that he had become something less than alive, just an echo of something no longer living, a ghost.

Anyone seeing him might have felt the same thing. He stood with an eerie stillness, and when he moved again, forcing himself forward, he seemed to float in a drifting silence, like one who has seen worlds unknown to the mortals of earth.

He stopped again in the darkness outside the hospital.

The lights were on. Its white interior glowed. And moving within it, more luminous than the crisp white bedsheets, was Evelyn, alone and beautiful, like a ballerina in a giant's jewel box.

He stood dead still, transfixed in watching Evelyn through the windows.

The brightness of the hospital's interior would have made it hard if not impossible for her to see out; had she looked toward the windowpanes she would have seen her own starched image reflected back to her. If she had really stared through the glass and forced her focus outside, she might have caught the outline of his uniform cap, or the silhouette of his shoulder.

But Evelyn was not looking out. She was moving like a machine through her solitary work at the hospital—her busywork for escape—but she was finding no relief. Even as the man outside inched closer to the glass, Evelyn moved to the desk that faced the windows and sat down.

At her desk, the one reserved for the nursing supervisor, Evelyn turned the calendar back to October, where she had written on the square of October 22, "Order supplies." It was on that same date that Danny had taken her for the night flight over Pearl Harbor.

Slowly, deliberately, she counted the weeks from then to today, December 6.

Out in the darkness, Rafe—for Rafe it was—moved closer to the windows.

He could not see what was on her desk. He would not have looked even if he could have seen. He watched only her.

He stood there, separated from her now by only a few feet and the thickness of the glass window, almost close enough to touch. And though he felt like a ghost, without substance, without the power of movement, he was very much alive, and never felt life in all its longing and desperation more than he did now, even as seeing Evelyn and standing this close to her had taken his breath.

Life. She meant life to him. And love. Life and love: to him, at that moment, one and the same. The reason was not a dreamlike sentimentality, it was concrete and real. His love for Evelyn had kept him alive.

As the images of what he had been through since seeing her last flashed through his mind, he reflected on that literal fact. He remembered, remembered with all the immediacy of wounds still tender and not completely healed, tearing off the flying harness of his Spitfire, standing upright on his seat and throwing himself away from the plane as it raced its last few feet of flight through the fog floating on the sea. He remembered the crazy instant, so brief to the rest of the world but so eternal for him, when he seemed to have all the time in the world to consider whether he would hit the water at a sharp enough angle to skim the surface, or instead would slam into the water full on, with the same sudden result as hitting a stone fence. Then the blinding brain-flash from an impact that was something between the two, and the cold, the devastating cold, against his seared flesh.

It had been the cold that first told him he had lived through the impact, but would soon be dead. And that was when Evelyn's face had leapt to his mind. He heard her voice in the fragments of the letter she had written him.

Dear Rafe . . .

The cold shock was traveling up his body faster than his body sank. He was in his own netherworld, cloaked in the fog, a cocoon, a womb, a place where the surge of the icy sea seemed to be offering the same comfort as a rocking cradle, offering endless sleep. He realized then that the aftermath of the impact was still with him; his thoughts drifted free of reality because he was barely conscious. His flying clothes had lost all pockets of air, his heavy leather jacket was soaking with seawater, he was sliding under the surface.

. . . *Every sunset* . . . he heard Evelyn say.

Standing outside the hospital, staring at Evelyn within, his chest jerked as his lungs fought for air, as they had months before in the North Sea. In vivid flashes of memory he saw the bubbles from his mouth rising toward the surface as his body sank. If he heard anything then it was the voice of his own longing, yelling *Evelyn! Evelyn!* He fought his way back up to the surface, sucking air, kicking off his shoes, shedding the jacket, stripping off his pants.

The effort had exhausted him. He was trying to think clearly, slowly, wisely; but when his limbs refused to move he had no idea if it was fatigue or stiffness from the cold. He did not have the strength to swim, and where would he swim, even if he could have? Float. *Stay alive*, he thought. *Evelyn.*

His pants had already drifted below the surface but he grabbed at where they had been and his fingers managed to snag them. He tied knots at the cuff of each leg and gathered the waist together, blowing air into the legs. It was the crudest of flotation devices, but it would keep him alive a few more minutes.

How long he floated, he did not know. For a while he stayed alive by making a series of tiny private bargains: *Stay alive one more minute*, he would say to himself, *and then you can quit. . . . Just fight the pain for one more minute*. His body shook, his teeth clattered in his aching jaws; then nothing trembled, nothing moved, nothing hurt.

He had no strength, no will to live. His face settled into the water . . . his body slipped from his makeshift preserver, and what had been Rafe McCawley drifted beneath the surface.

. . . *gather its heat into my heart*, Evelyn's voice said within him, *and send it to you* . . .

He heard her so clearly that he opened his eyes to look for her. He found himself under the surface of the sea; how far under he did not know. He looked up and saw bright rays of light from a source above the surface; through the dancing rays reaching down into the water, he saw Evelyn's face, staring at him as he had imagined her staring toward the Hawaiian sunsets.

His limbs came to life and he fought toward the light, breaking the surface. The sea was dark and empty, but he grabbed the knotted trousers, re-inflated them, and held on—for life, and for Evelyn.

Now Rafe stared through the window at Evelyn, in flesh, in form, in reality, and he wondered, *Does she still love me? Did she ever, really?*

With those doubts another image flashed into Rafe's mind, his next memory after the jumbled and numb agony—there was nothing else to call it—of clinging to life in the water. He saw men in heavy coats, seamen's gear, standing over him. He was still so wet and cold he thought he was in the water, but he felt a throbbing below his back and realized he lay on the deck of a boat that he would later learn was a Norwegian trawler. The crewmen spoke to him in a language he did not understand; one of them called to him in German and then another argued with the first one and spoke in English that Rafe had a hard time realizing was English at all. Rafe's limbs were stiff, even his lips felt frozen, and he wondered himself if he were already dead. But there

was pain growing in his chest, spreading out from his
heart, beneath the blankets the seamen had covered him
with, and he tried to force a word through his rigid jaw.
The Norwegian seaman who had spoken to him in English leaned down to him and listened, and Rafe was able
to articulate the word again, but the seaman did not understand. The word Rafe spoke was *Evelyn*.

Inside the base hospital, Evelyn set the calendar back
into its place upon her desk and straightened out the
pencils and other insignificant clutter upon it with the
strange carefulness of someone who has felt a loss of
control over the greatest matters of life and so takes special care to control the smallest.

She stood, found her purse, switched off the lights to
her office and left for the night.

She had taken several steps along the path toward
her barracks when she saw someone ten feet away in
the shadows, standing frozen, like a wooden carving of
a man. It was a form she knew, a posture hauntingly
familiar.

It was Rafe.

Her body lost all its weight. She felt she was floating,
flying, as the world tilted on its axis and the stars spun
above her. She fainted.

Seeing her fall, Rafe regained his ability to move and
caught her before her face hit the pavement.

She felt the strength of his arms, the solid reality of
them as he gathered her limp form, held her. She lifted
shaky fingertips to his face. "Evelyn," he said.

She drew unsteady breath. He helped her to a seat on
the bench beside the path, and words began to spill

from him. "I couldn't tell you with a telegram, I had to see you, face to face. I watched you through the window, and . . . and couldn't . . . couldn't bring myself to look in your eyes and ask if it still mattered."

"How . . . ?" was all she could say at first. "How did you . . . ?"

". . . Survive?" He paused a long time, and it seemed to her that he was unsure of something—how to answer the question, how much to tell her. But then when he spoke again, the story came out with bare-bones economy, when it had clearly been such an adventure. She wanted every detail, but did not interrupt because what she wanted most of all was for her life, which had suddenly lost all the predictability that had once given her a sense of organization and control, to make sense again. "Jumped into a patch of fog," he said, "and the Germans couldn't see me. But the R.A.F. boys couldn't see me either. I got the nose up and made it out of the plane before it hit, and I was in the water and it was so cold . . ." He paused again, and now she was sure it wasn't lack of memory that made him hesitate; he was censoring something. "I don't know how long I was in the water. . . . They say in water that cold you can live a couple of hours, and it sure felt a lot longer than that. A Norwegian freighter picked me up, they were headed to Spain. They docked in La Rota, right beside a German ship, and told me to stay hidden below. I was afraid they'd turn me in, so I stole some clothes, jumped ship and found a church, where the priest contacted the Underground, and got me on a freighter to New York. I called my folks, then Colonel Doolittle. The Colonel sent a man to pick me up. They wanted to debrief me. I told the Colonel I needed to see somebody first, I had some personal business in Hawaii, and he had a supply flight heading out in an hour." He paused again, and looked at her. "I've done a lot of talking. You haven't said anything."

"I'm just . . . so amazed, so glad to know that you're okay. You are okay, aren't you?"

"Nothing that won't heal. I guess."

At these words she looked at him steadily, pain in her eyes. And Rafe, seeing that pain, and having craved at the parched fountain of his soul for a fertile reunion, felt a dreadful uneasiness creeping into his belly. She said nothing further, just looked away, and Rafe, unable to bear the silence, said, "That's what I was wondering, standing out here watching you. If . . . the wounds would heal, if . . . the distance could be made up. If it would matter that I had made it back."

She realized what he was asking. And the only answer she could give him was to say, "Rafe, I . . . It's been so different, being so sure you were dead."

"I'm sorry for what you must've gone through. But I'm back now. Alive. Like I promised." He hated himself for that last bit, reminding her he'd made a promise to survive and come back to her, as if she'd made a promise in return. But hadn't she? Not with words, but with her eyes, her touch, her kiss, those silent sounds from her heart. Had he made all that up? How could he? Was it possible to feel so connected to someone and have life and love united in what they are to you, without them feeling much of the same thing?

He couldn't miss the troubled look lingering on her face, and said, "I'm sorry, I . . . I guess I've assumed too much."

"It's not . . . It . . ."

"It's something."

"Rafe, I . . ."

"It's all right. I've always been like this, seeing things with my emotions instead of my eyes. Maybe making things up, real in my own mind but not in anyone else's. Overdramatic. It's not your fault."

"No, it is my fault. The letters I wrote you, I—"

"Don't worry about that. A guy's away from home and lonely—goodhearted girls like you try to cheer him up." He knew he was babbling. What was he trying to salvage—pride? No, something far beyond pride. Life and love, love and life, the belief that they are the same.

"Rafe," she said, "it's not that I didn't mean everything I wrote. It's just that . . . I thought you were dead."

"I don't see what—"

"I thought you were. And now . . . I've . . ." She couldn't say what she knew she must tell him.

"What?" He looked at her, seemed to hesitate and then blurted out the question he feared most. "Have you met someone else?"

She still couldn't tell him; she nodded instead, and saw his eyes go dead.

Then another voice called "Rafe!" It was Danny, hurrying through the darkness. "You're alive!" He held a telegram in his right hand, and gestured as he spoke. "Your parents sent me a telegram, it just arrived at the barracks. . . ." He hugged Rafe with true excitement, but as he did his eyes flickered in Evelyn's direction, a glance Rafe saw.

Rafe's face was clouded as he pulled back from

Danny, and that halted Danny's celebration. Danny glanced again at Evelyn, who could not bear at that moment to look at either of them. Then another expression came onto Danny's face, an unmistakable look of shame.

That was when Rafe knew.

"Aw, God," he said. "Oh my God."

Almost simultaneously, both Evelyn and Danny spoke his name: "Rafe—"

He put up a hand, silencing them, and walked away.

18

Rafe stood by the shore of Pearl Harbor and stared at the dark water. The stars were still bright above him, but he felt no connection to them, no link with anything in life or in love. Two things, the same thing, both of them as dead as the meteor he had seen earlier, falling to its death.

The water, it seemed to him, had accepted the soul of the shooting star, but had not preserved it, any more than it had treasured whatever meteoric ash had ultimately reached its surface. The sea just swallowed its essence into eternal darkness, as it had the soul of Rafe McCawley, once a pilot, a Tennessean, a friend . . . and once a lover of something that was not real.

The problem was, that love had never been an illusion to Rafe, it had never lacked the substance of life. As he stood feeling as alone and fragmented as the flaming chunks of meteor he had seen falling, the image of the Norwegian seamen leaning over his frozen and half-drowned body with the stars bright over their heads flashed again into Rafe's mind, and with that image came the whisper of that single word he had spoken, "Evelyn."

Rafe stared into the darkness of the uncaring sea, and struggled to bury that memory of his love so deep that he would never feel it again.

Neither one of them spoke on the walk back to the nurses' quarters, but when they reached the barracks door Danny said, "Don't worry, I'll find him." He hugged her, their embrace earnest yet tinged with guilt, and left quickly, his first few steps accelerating into a trot across the palmetto grass and out to the road that led back to his own base. *He's going back to his own barracks, to get his friends*, Evelyn thought. *He needs help*. She felt for Danny then, ached for his situation more now than she had on the walk home.

Turning to the door, Evelyn ran into Betty, on her way out to work the hospital's graveyard shift. "Evelyn!" Betty said, "You're so pale! What's wrong . . . ?"

"Not wrong, just . . . just news. Rafe's alive."

"Evelyn . . . !" After the first shock cleared from Betty's girlish face another look seeped over her, far more mature and thoughtful than most people had ever seen on Betty. With pain for Evelyn pinching the corners of her blue eyes she said, "Oh Evelyn. Oh my God."

The P-40s on Hickham Field sat in clusters, like chicks gathered for warmth beneath a henhouse light bulb on a winter night. The planes were easier to guard when they were bunched that way. But none of the guards patrolling the airfield would accost a uniformed American pilot, and none of them said anything to Danny as he moved out among the planes.

It was out in the cluster farthest from the main hangar that Danny found Rafe, sitting in the open cockpit of a P-40. Rafe did not react as Danny stepped up onto the wing, and Danny thought, *He knew I would find him. He knows me well enough to be sure that I would never quit until I did.* Danny said, "You'd always go sit in the plane whenever you were upset."

"Upset?" Rafe said. "Why should I be upset?"

"Let's go get a drink. We can talk about it. That is, unless you're scared to talk about it."

Rafe cut his eyes toward Danny.

The first of several Mai-Tai "volcanoes" hit the wooden table with a heavy thud. Rafe looked at the carved-out lava holding the pink liquid surrounded by tropical flowers, and frowned. "Looks like a sissy drink to me," he said.

"Drink up. Then we talk."

Rafe gave Danny a long stare, then accepted the challenge and took a long pull from one of the straws protruding from the pink liquid.

They drank for a long time without saying anything at all. There were moments when the silence between them was agonizing but each of them refused to be the first one to break it. Finally, Rafe tossed his straw into the potent Mai-Tai like a spear fisherman in a real lagoon, sat back in his chair and yelled at the bartender, "Four beers!" He looked at Danny and said, "I ain't drinking this slop anymore."

"Four beers?" Danny said. "You've become a big drinker."

"Not so big. One's for you."

A big Samoan waitress brought over the four beers, and as she chunked them onto the table the barroom door opened and the carnival atmosphere of downtown Oahu came spilling inside, along with Billy, Anthony and Red. Danny had been expecting them; when he sent them off to help him find Rafe, he had told them to come here if their search of the base clubs and other hangouts had netted them nothing. Now he tried to warn them off with a subtle shake of his head, but their excitement over seeing Rafe was too great; they rushed up to him, banging him on the back, mussing his hair, shouting, "You're alive, you son of a bitch! You're alive!"

Two hours later they were on their third Mai-Tai volcano and Rafe was using empty beer bottles as fighter planes to demonstrate dogfighting tactics over the Channel. "The Germans'll go under you because their planes are faster. Then they run so you can't catch 'em." He showed the movement in a beer bottle ballet, his hands graceful, his sense of space and position marvelous, even when drunk. "But then they'll come around and take you from behind—like some Americans will."

Rafe slowly put the empty bottles down and stared across the table at Danny. For a moment nobody spoke.

"Maybe we ought'a let you guys talk alone," Billy said.

"Naw, it's okay, it's okay!" Rafe said loudly. "Give Danny a shot'a Jack—straight up, Tennessee style."

But Billy stood and pulled Red and Anthony away to the bar, where they found stools among the sailors crowded there.

"You got something to say?" Danny challenged. "Then come on. Say it."

"We gotta face some facts here."

"Yeah? What facts are those?"

"I know why any guy would love her," said Rafe. "That's not hard for me to understand. I can't blame you that it happened. You thought I was dead, she was upset, you were trying to help her."

"Upset?" said Danny. "She was torn up, Rafe! We both were! What brought us together was that we cared about you—hard as that is for you to believe right now."

"Yeah, sure, you were both just caring about me, so that's why you two got cozy."

Danny's eyes met Rafe's; they glared at each other.

Rafe continued, "Anyway, you didn't know."

"What are you saying?" Danny demanded.

"I'm saying now you know. . . . So it's time for you to fuck off."

Billy, Red and Anthony, watching from the bar, could not hear what was passing between Rafe and Danny over the loud talk of the barroom and Hawaiian music oozing from the radio. But they saw Danny stiffen.

"Hey," Danny said at the table, "you asked me to take care of her."

"Take care. Not take advantage."

"Take advantage?" Danny's lips went white, pressed tight against his clenched teeth, but he struggled to hold back his anger. "You know, you're a lousy drinker," he said. "You always have been. Liquor makes you illogical."

"Illogical? Is that a high-falutin' way to call me stupid?"

Danny grabbed the edges of the table to keep from grabbing Rafe's throat, and barked, "You left her! You left her, to fight somebody else's war!"

Rafe looked back like a water moccasin, pleased to see the anger. Then he said quietly, "I didn't know how much I loved her until I was dying and her face was the last thing to go through my mind."

Those words touched Danny, and he knew they were true—but he couldn't change that. "Well I stayed," he said. "I stayed, and things changed. It's gonna take some getting used to."

Rafe stood, nodding as if in acceptance. Then he said, "Get used to this."

With a short straight punch he knocked Danny out of the chair, onto the sticky floor. Danny lay on his back, his feet tangled with the overturned chair; he wiped the blood from the corner of his mouth. "You want it," he said, "you got it."

Rafe was already over him, kicking the chair aside. Danny slammed a foot into the back of Rafe's knee, then mule-kicked him in the chest as he went down, and the fight was on.

The bar's bouncer was another Samoan, the boyfriend of the waitress, and he had fists as big and hard as coconuts. But he never got a chance to use them; as he moved from behind the bar, Anthony stepped in his way and said, "Let 'em fight, they need it."

The bouncer knocked Anthony aside with a single wave of his giant hand, but before he could take another step, Red had broken a lava volcano of Mai-Tai over the bouncer's skull.

The bartender grabbed the phone and called for the MPs.

Out in the middle of the barroom, Rafe and Danny exchanged punches, encircled by the other servicemen, who had cleared a space for them. The sailors sitting at the bar had swung around on their stools to watch the action, and rather than choose a favorite they cheered every punch thrown by either man. Billy, Red and Anthony winced with the punches their friends exchanged, and bobbed and weaved as if in the fight themselves. A sailor next to Billy tapped him on the arm and said, "Is this a private fight or can anybody jump in?"

Billy, revved beyond his redline on anxiety and adrenaline, hit him cleanly on the right cheekbone, and suddenly the whole bar erupted in fighting.

Rafe and Danny were really having at it, fueled by so much emotion that nothing hurt. Having stood up to trade punches, they now tumbled to the floor again and tore at each other's arms as if trying to rip each other apart. They again wrestled their way to their feet and Rafe managed to knee Danny in the groin. Danny doubled over in pain.

"That hurt?" Rafe said. "I didn't think you had any balls."

Without looking up, Danny lunged at Rafe, tackling him around the waist, driving him at the wall. But he was off target, and they tumbled through the back window—not covered in glass, but fronds and wood—and

out onto the sandy pavement of the alleyway. They lay
groggily in the debris, then they saw the MP Jeeps coming. They dragged each other to their feet and ran.

Inside the bar, the Hawaiian music still played from
the radio.

Most days of the year, Radio Station KGMB shut down
at 11 P.M. and did not resume its broadcast until the
hour of daybreak the next morning, but between the
sixth and seventh of December, 1941, it continued sending out its signal uninterrupted. The hidden intention of
this decision was to aid the United States military. On
that very night a flight of B-17 bombers on transfer orders from the mainland was making the journey across
the vast Pacific to the tiny speck of Hawaii, and the music playing from Oahu's radio station served as a secret
beacon to bring the big birds home. The American
bombers carried no explosives or ammunition and had
even been stripped of their guns to save weight for the
arduous trip, and inside their otherwise vacant fuselages
their navigators stayed tuned to the Hawaiian music and
listened to it with gratitude as it guided them to
safety.

At exactly the same time, 320 miles north of Hawaii,
the huge Japanese task force rumbled through the darkness of the Vacant Sea, the bows of the great ships blasting through the rough seas. And on the bridge of his
flagship, the aircraft carrier *Akagi*, Admiral Yamamoto
listened to the Hawaiian music that his navigators were
using to guide them right to the throat of American
power in the Pacific, Pearl Harbor.

Yamamoto, like any military commander worth his

brass buttons and gold braid, was ferociously alert, not only for every confirmation that his operation was unfolding as planned but also for any hint that it might not, and he knew, better than anyone else in the world at that moment, that the success of his plan was dependent on surprise. The American firepower at Pearl Harbor was greater than everything Yamamoto had been able to bring with him, and if they were waiting for him, their guns loaded and pointed into the sky, their fighter planes already scrambling into the air, their battleships making steam and their bombers out searching for the Japanese attack force so that the hunters became the hunted, then this operation could become an incomprehensible disaster for Yamamoto's nation. He stood on his command bridge, hearing the Hawaiian music, and thought, *If the Americans had any suspicion of our attack, the radio would let us know.*

The clock on the gray bulkhead over the radio reached midnight, and one of the Japanese charting officers promptly tore a page off the calendar and made an entry of their position in the *Agaki*'s log.

It was now December 7, 1941; the date that Franklin D. Roosevelt was destined to declare would live in infamy.

Yamamoto was too preoccupied with worries to spend much time thinking of the significance that date would assume. His main concern of the moment was the threat of early detection of their attack, and the greatest danger of that lay with the submarines that the Japanese High Command had agreed to include in the operation. Various members of the war council had competed for their share of what they were sure would be the inevitable glory and honor of the attack, and the naval leaders had objected to Yamamoto's plan because it used their ships only as a transportation system for aircraft but did not call for direct engagement; in fact the plan rigorously avoided it, and the Navy men, already used to grumbling about Yamamoto, said his strategy treated their warships as nothing more than ferry boats. No one could argue with its brilliance and simplicity, however, and the council reached a compromise, ordering that submarines be allowed to approach and seek to enter Pearl Harbor—*before* the planes arrived. Yamamoto opposed this, pointing out that discovery of the submarines, which he considered likely, would jeopardize the entire attack. He was overruled. There was no such thing as war without politics.

Yamamoto looked at his watch. The subs would be approaching Pearl Harbor right now.

Just outside the mouth of Pearl Harbor the American destroyer *Selfridge* was on patrol. Lookouts with binoculars stood on the destroyer's bridge, sweeping the dark water. One of them paused in his movements, and asked another lookout to train his binoculars on a spot he pointed to.

Inside the *Selfridge*'s control room, the watch officer listened to a report from the bridge on his headset and told the captain, "Sir, lookouts report a sighting, two points off the starboard beam."

The sonar operator, sitting close by, looked to them and nodded; his equipment had also indicated a large moving object in that direction.

"How big?" the captain asked the sonar operator.

He tried to get a better reading, and shook his head. "I've lost it now."

"Probably a blackfish," the captain said. "I've seen them look like subs."

Patrolling the same waters, just behind the *Selfridge*, was another American destroyer, the *Ralph Talbot*. Its lookouts spotted the same thing those on the *Selfridge* had. The captain of the *Ralph Talbot* was standing on the bridge of his ship when his duty officer approached him and said, "Sir, *Selfridge* reported a contact, then lost it. Now our sonar reports the contact."

The captain looked toward the *Selfridge*, then trained his binoculars on the water where the duty officer pointed. He saw something dark and black slipping along beneath the surface. He reacted instantly, grabbing his intercom and calling, "Radio room! Raise the *Selfridge*. Tell the squadron commander we have spotted a sub and request permission to depth charge." He looked again at the black shape passing a few hundred yards from them. America had its own submarines on patrol in the Pacific, but none of them would be trying to run submerged right into the mouth of Pearl Harbor, and there were standing orders for the destroyers to sink any ship violating these protected waters. The captain said to his duty officer, "We're five miles from Pearl Harbor and it's moving in from the open sea. Prepare to move to attack speed."

The intercom came alive with a call from the radio room: "Sir, the squadron commander on *Selfridge* denies permission."

The captain of the *Ralph Talbot* couldn't believe what he'd heard. "What?" he said.

"Denies, sir," confirmed the radio room. "He says it's a blackfish."

The captain choked back his frustration and shut down the intercom. But he said to the duty officer as they watched the shape disappear toward Pearl Harbor, "If it's a blackfish, it has a motorboat up its ass."

Danny drove along the back roads into the hills above Oahu, away from the people and the traffic, the convertible top of the Buick open to the fresh air. He had bought the car from an Air Corps captain who had already received his transfer orders and was going Stateside on the next plane out in the morning. The car was old but immaculate, and the captain had sold it to him on a handshake; send me the money when you have it, he'd said, and I'll send you the title.

It was the first car Danny had ever almost owned, and he had bought it in the first flush of hope that he and Evelyn could form something together that would last. It was the car of somebody who's going to be somebody, that's what Danny had thought. But now, with Rafe riding beside him, and the noses and knuckles, the chins and shins of both men battered from their recent scuffle, Danny despaired of ever again riding in the car and feeling a sense of celebration.

Rafe had not spoken since they left the bar. Now as they reached the top of the hill and turned down again, he said, "You got yourself a nice ride."

The anger swelled in Danny's throat. "That's all you can say?"

Rafe turned his head slowly; he looked toward the rear seat as if to admire the upholstery, turned forward again as if inspecting the dash, leaned his head outside the doorway as if appraising the fenders . . . and began to vomit. Danny slammed on the brakes and the car skidded to a stop.

Danny got him to the side of the road and stood there waiting for the retching to subside. He rubbed at his own face in frustration, and felt the bruises of his fight with Rafe; he was sober enough that they hurt, and he knew he'd have plenty of head pain in the morning.

Rafe tried to straighten up, but the waves of sickness came back over him and he bent again. He choked out, between heaves, "How come you're not pukin'?"

"Guess I'm used to it," Danny said.

"Mai-Tais?" Rafe gurgled, wondering through his misery how anybody would ever get used to this.

"Wanting to throw up. I've felt that way ever since you got home."

Rafe's nausea exhausted itself, but he remained bent at his waist, his hands on his knees. "Welcome home," he said bitterly.

"Hey," Danny spat, "knock that bullshit off. Rafe . . . you're the only family I've got. The only real family I've ever had. When you were gone, I was alone, the most alone I'd ever been. So was she." He paused. "You and I are a part of each other. And now Evelyn's a part of both of us."

"Shut up, would ya? You're just making me sicker."

"Don't blame her, Rafe. It's not like you're thinking. She loves you. I know that." Rafe didn't seem to be listening, but Danny knew he was. He added, "And I know she always will."

Rafe stood to face Danny; he knew this was hard for Danny to say.

Danny's eyes were wet with emotion. He needed Rafe's forgiveness, needed him to understand how far it was from him to want to betray a friend. He said, almost pleading, "Part of what she loves in me is how much of you she sees in me. I told her that, Rafe."

"How sweet," Rafe said. "Is that when you put the moves on her?"

Danny slammed his fist into Rafe's gut. Rafe doubled over, coughing, nothing left in his belly to come up. Danny just waited, satisfied now to see Rafe's pain, glad to have hit him.

Rafe stood slowly, nodding as if he knew the punch was what he deserved. Danny was about to apologize when, for the second time that night, Rafe kneed him in the groin. Danny folded, dropped to his knees, and started to retch himself.

"That's better," Rafe said.

Rafe crawled into the back seat of the car and passed out, Danny still collapsed at the side of the road.

Out in the stormy waters north of Hawaii, Admiral Yamamoto's battle fleet made the course correction that would position them for their launch, just before dawn.

Another American destroyer, the *Ward*, cut through the water, moving back into port after a night patrol. Its captain stood on the bridge, and its lookouts were still scanning the waters. One of them noticed something and pointed it out to the captain. "Sir, do you see that, in our wake?"

The captain raised his binoculars and looked across the waters in the trail behind the ship. He saw something small and black there. "That's a conning tower," he said.

"Could it be one of ours?" an officer said beside him.

"He's trying to follow us through the sub nets, into the harbor. Sink the son of a bitch."

The crew of the *Ward* responded to their orders with crisp efficiency, wheeling around their deck gun and firing a round at the exposed conning tower of the submerged vessel in their wake. It was America's first shot of World War Two.

It missed. The explosive round sailed directly over the conning tower and detonated harmlessly in the waters beyond.

Inside the Japanese submarine the sub commander was watching the *Ward* through his periscope, and when he saw a flash of flame erupt from the destroyer's deck he realized he was being fired upon and shouted the order to his crew, "Dive! Dive!"

But the second shell from the *Ward* did not miss. It slammed the sub squarely, ripping it like an axe striking a tin can. The submarine shuddered and rolled over.

The captain of the *Ward* stood on his bridge watching the sub sink, and snapped another order. "Radio Pearl. From Destroyer *Ward*. Have fired upon and sunk enemy submarine seeking to enter Pearl Harbor."

19

The stars had begun to fade and the sky had begun to lighten into gray. Through the night the Japanese crews had armed planes with bombs and torpedoes, and now they were rolling the final planes into position.

Below deck, the young pilots prepared themselves spiritually for what they were about to do. Some sat before personal shrines, saying private prayers. Some wrote death poems. Others wrote letters to wives, lovers, families.

One pilot, too young to have a family and too shy to have a girlfriend, sat down and wrote these words:

Revered father, I go now to fulfill my mission and my destiny. I hope it is a destiny that will bring honor to our family, and if it requires my life I will sacrifice it gladly to be a good servant of our nation and a worthy son.

On the command bridge of the *Akagi*, Yamamoto stood

staring through the windows out over the carrier deck. The deck crews had formed perfect ranks and stood at attention as the color guard raised the Japanese flag into the dawn sky. The banner of the Rising Sun snapped proudly and potently in the wind. The crews watched quietly and Yamamoto wondered if the power of the moment had silenced them with a sobering fear of the unpredictability of the chaos they were about to unleash. *Cry havoc! and unleash the dogs of war.* But the men were not sobered, just disciplined enough to restrain their excitement for a moment. As the flag of Imperial Japan cracked in the wind, and the battle pennants of the fleet flew up to dance beside it, the sailors roared.

Whistles sounded, orders rang out, the wind sang—calls to action. The deck was a rush of activity, and though Yamamoto had the authority to give any order he chose at any time, he had the feeling that the power to shape events was completely out of his hands now. He could not stop the momentum of the moment—and who would want to? The Zeros, their blunt wings scrubbed, their wheels oiled, their canopies polished clean, were stacked on the deck. Pilots wearing Rising Sun cloths wrapped around their foreheads ran to their planes and climbed into the cockpits. Propellers turned over, and engines raced to life. Deck crews pulled chock blocks from beneath the wheels of the planes. They were ready to go.

An officer on the deck stared up toward Yamamoto, waiting for his signal. When Yamamoto saluted, the deck signaled the first planes. The first of the Japanese planes started to taxi. And once again the seamen

saluted these men that they already took to be the heroes of their nation.

A person with a fondness for history could ponder the
events of that morning in a detached way and argue that
the next few hours were the most significant in the
twentieth century, and possibly in the twenty-first, for
they saw the launching of a war that would reshape the
world.

Such an argument is idle. How can any moment be
said to stand alone, without all the other moments that
brought it into being, or the infinite chain of responses
that followed? This much is certain: there was nothing
detached about the moments when they were not history but the present for those who experienced Pearl
Harbor and saw it from their own perspectives.

In a new radar installation on the island of Oahu, an officer and a private sat yawning over their equipment.
Their orders were to operate until 7 A.M., and it was
past the hour, but because the technology was new and
his men wanted further training with it, the officer had
allowed the private an extra few minutes over the
screen. So when the private said, "What's this? I've got
a haze," neither he nor the officer were much alarmed.
It was daylight now, they were no longer the first line of
defense, and the equipment was so unfamiliar to everyone that no one had the experience of relying on it.

The officer moved over, setting down the paperwork
he'd been filling out, and peered at the screen, thinking
at first that the private had fiddled with the controls and
clouded the picture. But he saw immediately that the

screen was not projecting an ambiguous blur. There were distinct blips on the radar, moving in from the northeast—so many of them that they looked like a cloud.

"I've never seen anything like this," the officer said. He picked up the telephone. The private tapped the radar screen, then slapped its side, but the blips did not go away.

Over at watch command, another Army officer answered the telephone, listened to the radar station report, and asked, "Coming from which direction?" He listened to the response, covered the receiver—there were standing orders for all intelligence-gathering units to keep information compartmentalized, to thwart suspected spying activity by the Japanese—and reported to the watch commander, "Radar station has picked up a cloud of blips, coming in from the northeast."

The watch commander switched on the radio on his desk and tuned it to KGMB. Hearing the station broadcasting Hawaiian music reassured him. He nodded at the radio and said, "They're on early. That means we've got a flight of B-17s coming in from the mainland, they use the radio music for a homing beacon. Don't say that over the wire, just tell the radar guys not to worry about it."

Back at the radar station, the officer there listened in dismay, and said, "All right, sir." He hung up the phone and told the private, "They say don't worry about it."

The radar station did not know about the peaceful flight of bombers coming from the mainland. And the watch command did not realize there were far too many blips on the radar screen for the approaching force of planes to be the Americans.

One of the blips showing up on the American radar was a Japanese light bomber with a three-man crew. The planes were sturdy and compact, painted a sandy brown that made them harder to see in the skies above the Pacific. One of the crew functioned as navigator, and his job was made simple by the Hawaiian music coming from his radio, tuned to Oahu's commercial station, leading them in like a homing beacon. The pilot of the Japanese bomber looked to his left and saw the sun rising over the eastern horizon, shooting out rays in all directions, resembling the Japanese flag. He considered it a wonderful omen, and said so to his friends.

The first aircraft off the Japanese decks in the predawn light had been a scout plane; now, undetected by any radar, unnoticed among the peaceful civilian air traffic in the Sunday-morning skies, the Japanese plane flew high over Pearl Harbor and radioed back to the battle fleet, "Harbor quiet. Ships in place." To this excellent news the scout added two words that were not comforting. "Carriers gone."

When Yamamoto was handed this decoded message, he read it in silence and then told his staff, "We have achieved surprise, but their carriers are not in port. I don't like this." This was an understatement; the absence of the three American aircraft carriers stationed at Pearl Harbor troubled Yamamoto to his core. The other American ships were there, heaped together and waiting

before the ravenous tiger of his battle group like raw
meat . . . or bait. Yamamoto had no idea where the
American carriers were; could they be scouting for him
and waiting to attack? Once he sent his planes toward
Pearl Harbor, if the Americans found him they might
sink his carriers; then all his planes would be lost
too. . . .

In fact the American carriers were hundreds of miles
away. One was on training maneuvers. The other two
had steamed toward Midway, under the suspicion that a
Japanese attack might be coming, and would, if it came,
be far from Pearl Harbor.

The possibility of calling his planes back loomed in
Yamamoto's mind. But the submarines had begun their
incursions hours ago, and even if the Americans hadn't
been alarmed by any of them yet, their discovery was inevitable, and all opportunity for surprise would be
gone. It was now or never.

Air Commander Genda knew what Yamamoto must
be thinking, and reassured him, "We have a fighter
screen up, in case we are attacked."

Yamamoto said, "We must go ahead. This is our
moment."

There were already 190 Japanese warplanes swarm-
ing through the skies of paradise, within sight of Pearl
Harbor.

Admiral Kimmel was leaving his home early that morning, anticipating a round of golf with his friends and fellow officers. He was just about to step out into the
beautiful sunshine when his phone rang and a member
of his staff reported to him, "Admiral, one of our de-

stroyers reports having fired upon and sunk an enemy submarine seeking to enter Pearl Harbor."

"Relay that to Washington," Kimmel said immediately, "and—"

But before he could ask, there was a Jeep already pulling up in front of his house, ready to rush him to headquarters.

In Washington, D.C., deep in the lower levels of the Naval Intelligence Center, an 18-year-old typist was struggling with a decoding device. Thurman stood at his shoulder, with the waistband of his trousers hiked up to his ribs. When Thurman was tense, he always pulled his pants up high. "Son, you new at this machine?" he demanded.

"Yes, sir, very new and very nervous, sir," the typist said.

Thurman took a deep hot breath to try to bolster his patience and watched the decoded words coming out of the machine: FURTHER PEACE TALKS USELESS . . .

It was too much for Thurman. He grabbed the telephone, a direct line upstairs, and said without formality, "We've picked off a Japanese message that looks like a declaration of war! I'm down here trying to save the free world and you guys have sent me a decoder with pimples older than his typing skills. I need some help— NOW. Thank you!"

In his bones, Thurman knew it was already too late. But he tried to reassure himself with a mental reminder that his instincts had been wrong before. He just couldn't remember, for the life of him, when that had ever been.

When he reached his office Admiral Kimmel was handed the latest dispatches by an aide who had already read them, and who reported: "Naval Intel has intercepted a transmission from Tokyo to the Japanese embassy in Washington, instructing them to burn all secret documents and break up their decoder machines."

"Has the War Department issued alerts?" Kimmel asked his aide.

"No, sir."

It was not a declaration of war, of course, but no professional officer could hear such news without concluding that the Japanese expected a war. And whether Admiral Kimmel or his brethren in Washington should have expected the same thing can be debated. But the messages sent from Washington could not be considered an advance warning; by the time Kimmel read them, the bombs had already begun to fall.

As the first squadron of Japanese planes came within direct sight of Pearl Harbor, they increased throttle and nosed down, diving toward the surface, hurtling into attack mode.

The harbor lay quiet below them. It was a sleepy Sunday morning, and most sailors, soldiers and civilians in and around Oahu were still drowsing in their beds. Christmas was coming, decorations of red and green hung on trees fragrant with tropical plumeria. Children dressed as shepherds, wise men and angels were piling into family cars to arrive early at church to prepare for the Christmas play. In the military housing communities, officers in T-shirts and lounging shorts stepped out onto their front porches to retrieve the morning paper.

————

On the lower decks of the battleship *Arizona*, the ship's brass band, having won a musical competition the night before, were indulging in their prize: the right to sleep late this morning.

Out on the main pier, a young bugler nervously rehearsed in preparation to play for the first time in the morning flag-raising ceremony.

On the *West Virginia*, Dorie Miller mopped the floor of the kitchen. Out in the dining area, a young sailor sat down to open a packet he had received from his girlfriend back home, and had savored unopened until a quiet moment when he could best salve his loneliness and stoke his hopes; he unwrapped the paper cut from a brown sack and discovered she had sent him a picture of herself, along with a rabbit's foot on a chain. He warmed to the sentiment, and hung the good luck charm around his neck.

Back in Washington, Thurman's eyes grew wide as the teletype punched block letters of the message intercepted from the Japanese and decoded: BROKEN RELATIONSHIP . . . HOSTILITIES IMMINENT . . .

In the mountains overlooking Pearl Harbor, day hikers and overnight campers had been stirring since before dawn in a windless silence that was broken by a rising rumble that some of them thought must be the ancient gods of Hawaii, shaking the ground. But the sound did not come from Madam Pele, goddess of the earthquake and volcano; the air was suddenly full of Japanese planes skimming overhead—dozens and dozens of them, headed toward Pearl Harbor.

In the waters of the harbor the American ships were silent, their engines cold, their anchors steady in the sand of the harbor bottom.

A half mile away, the Japanese torpedo planes dropped down to level flight just a few feet above the waves, and their engines, revved to their limits, screamed.

High overhead, formations of Japanese bombers settled into the steady flight of a bombing run.

On the airfields around Pearl Harbor, American planes sat in bunches, like the ships at anchor, unarmed, unready, unprotected.

In his flagship, Admiral Yamamoto and his staff huddled over their battle maps, awaiting news. Even before news of the first explosions reached them the Japanese seamen below the carrier decks were arming and bringing the second wave of planes up to the flight deck.

At a few minutes past 8 A.M., two sailors stood on the deck of the U.S.S. *Oklahoma*, a proud battleship as fine as any in the fleet. They were sharing a smoke and looking out over the quiet harbor. One of them saw planes—his mind registered only the first few—streaking directly at them, low over the water, and he pointed the planes out to his friend, saying, "Look at that."

"It's the Army again," his buddy answered, "practicing on us." Something dropped from the lead plane and splashed easily into the water; the plane banked away. "Practice torpedoes," he said. They watched the torpedo's path, a white streak coming through the water at them. "Now listen, you'll hear a little thud when it hits the side of the ship."

They watched calmly and with an amused curiosity as the torpedo rushed to the *Oklahoma*, below her waterline. Then a massive explosion threw a fifty-foot wall of water over the deck, hurling the sailors and everything else not lashed down into the sea on the other side of the ship.

As stupendous as the explosions in and around Pearl Harbor would be that day, there were residents of central Oahu, just a few miles away, who would hear and see nothing and remain unaware of the attack until it was long over.

20

Danny felt the sun, warm on his face, and realized its red brightness outside his eyes before he opened them, but it was not the light that woke him. A strange rumble was filling the air around him. It was unusual and out of place enough to reach the subconscious levels of his pilot's mind and draw him from his stupor. He rubbed at his stinging eyes, opened them—not without some wincing—and found himself in the front seat of the Buick. He groped around to make sense of it all, and found his shirt ripped and crusted with dried blood. He remembered the fight now, remembered everything.

He looked into the back seat and saw Rafe there, just waking, in the same condition. Except that Rafe was looking up into the sky, his face fixed. Then Danny remembered the rumble that woke him, and looked up too.

The sound had grown louder, rising into a thudding vibration, and the light on Danny's face began to flicker as objects passed between him and the sun. It was a formation of planes, a massive formation, larger than any

Danny had ever seen in the skies above Hawaii or anywhere else.

He looked at Rafe, just as Rafe looked at him, wanting answers. How could there be such a flight of Hawaii-based planes, without Danny knowing about it?

Then they both understood, in a moment that wiped away their headaches and the soreness of their split lips and torn knuckles, what it had to be. Rafe scrambled into the front seat as Danny slid behind the wheel, and gunned the Buick toward the base.

In Washington, Thurman read the first part of another secret message intercepted in its journey between Tokyo and the Japanese embassy, and he knew, even before the rest was decoded, that he was too late.

The first instruction of the message read: TO BE DELIVERED AT 1:00 PM, EASTERN TIME. Thurman looked helplessly at the clock; in Washington it was already past 1:00.

It was meant to be a declaration of war, precisely timed. That clearly meant to Thurman that the acts of war were also precisely timed, and already in motion.

He reached for a phone and called the highest-ranking admiral he knew, and though he did it in a rush of near panic, a voice inside him spoke with quiet resignation and told Thurman, *Too late. Too late. Too late . . .*

That day heroism wore many faces.

The Marine color guard on the battleship *Arizona* was conducting the ceremony of raising the flag of the United States at the stern of the ship when the first Zero fighter planes, flying 250 miles per hour twenty feet off the water, began strafing Battleship Row, raking the decks with machine-gun fire. The Marines completed their ceremony, a task sacred to them, before running for their weapons to return the fire.

An unknown pilot of one of the Zeros, while skimming low over a strip of land surrounding the harbor on his way to the attack, saw children playing and waved them away, in a silent but unmistakable gesture that told them to flee from the coming danger.

Belowdecks on the battleship *West Virginia*, Dorie Miller was at work cleaning up the breakfast trays of the white sailors who had just eaten when he felt the ship shudder, the force of an explosion transmitted through the entire steel skeleton of the vessel. The intercom came alive: "Battle stations! Battle stations! This is not a drill!"

Men ran to the ladders, and the shaking of the ship from a second bomb blast tossed them off. Dorie was at the foot of the ladder when men fell back on top of him and knocked him to the floor.

Several stories above him, the captain of the *West Virginia*, Mervyn Bennion, raced up into the command bridge, where he found most of his staff lying wounded from the blast of a 500-pound bomb. "Stay calm," was his first order of the war. "Alert the crew, prepare to sail. Corpsmen, get the wounded to sick bay! Load and—"

The bridge ripped apart. A chunk of shrapnel tore into Captain Bennion's stomach and ripped his guts open. He fell but did not lose consciousness. He saw that the corpsman he was just giving the orders to had been blown apart. Captain Bennion, gripping his hands to his stomach to keep the organs inside his body, struggled to stand, all the while asking himself what he must do next to save his men and his ship.

On the main deck below him, Dorie Miller emerged into the sunlight and saw carnage and confusion in every direction. A bloody officer grabbed him by the shoulder and shouted, "We need stretcher bearers on the bridge!"

Dorie ran into the fire and smoke, toward the bridge. His hands found a railing leading upward, and he leapt up the stairs.

He arrived at the command bridge to see the corpsmen crouched over the disemboweled captain, who was still giving orders. "Radio for air cover and initiate fire control," Dorie heard Bennion say. Japanese Zeros were still streaking past the ruptured walls of the ship, wing guns spitting machine-gun fire that tore into the steel all around the Americans huddled in the command bridge. Dorie helped a corpsman lift the captain to take him below.

They carried him together, Dorie gripping Bennion's legs just behind the knees, and the corpsman holding him with his hands passed under the captain's shoulders and joined above his chest. The tilting and movement was agony to Bennion, who still clutched at his stomach. Dorie wanted to be gentle but there was nothing he could do but grit his own teeth against the captain's stifled torture and hurry on, as more bombs exploded both on the *West Virginia* and on the neighboring ships, and shards of iron whistled through the smoky air around them. When they reached the ladder to the lower decks and could no longer carry the captain as a team, Dorie took his full weight, using one arm to steady himself as he climbed down and one to hold the captain like a child's teddy bear. The corpsman waited on deck for Dorie to clear the ladder, and even before Dorie's head was below the level of the deck the corpsman's chest exploded as machine-gun bullets from another strafing Zero caught him in the back and tore through his body.

Moving down the ladder, Dorie could not feel the captain's weight; but the pain he knew he was inflicting seeped through Dorie Miller's skin.

When they reached the bottom the pain had grown too much for the captain; he knew he was dying. "Put me down here," Bennion told Dorie simply.

Dorie put him down. He cradled Captain Bennion as he trembled in death throes. Through the shaking the captain said, "Find my executive officer and tell him he's in command. Tell him to fire the boilers and make sure the gunners have enough ammuni—"

He did not finish the last order. Dorie could not at that moment think of feeling for a pulse; he didn't have to. He laid the captain's head as gently as he could upon the deck, then ran back to the ladder, and climbed out into hell.

Fire and smoke were everywhere; even the water between ships was burning from the oil that floated on the surface. The decks were slick—but not from oil; blood was everywhere too, along with screaming and confusion. Everyone seemed to be moving as fast as he could, and yet time had slowed; men ran as if through mud, and the Zeros screaming through the smoke with their guns flashing had a terrible grace. Their bullets caught the running men and ripped them down. Somehow

Dorie found the executive officer and yelled to him, "Captain said you're in charge!" The Ex-O nodded and continued giving orders; he had witnessed the captain's wounds.

Then Dorie saw it: an unmanned anti-aircraft gun— empty because the gunners assigned to man it were lying beside it with their chests shot open. Dorie ran to the gun, through the strafing. He saw the belt of ammo had already been loaded by the dead gunners. Dorie Miller swung the business end of the gun toward the Zeros coming in out of the black smoke, and he began to fire.

The avalanche of events created all the wild experiences of some men caught off guard by others who had planned extensively. One gunner, belowdecks in the battleship *Pennsylvania*, had just finished an early-morning shower when the bomb blasts began to shake the ship. The *Pennsylvania* was sitting in dry dock, perched on massive blocks beneath its open hull, and he wondered if its entire mass was about to be knocked off its supports. He knew torpedoes could not reach them; it had to be bombs—Japanese bombs—and his warrior's instinct to fight back overwhelmed every other thought. He ran to the ladders and climbed out onto the deck, wearing nothing but a towel wrapped around his waist.

He had begun a routine service of his gun, a flak cannon, the day before, and so had left it with its cover unsecured. He ran to the gun, tore its cover away, and slammed a shell into the breach. Other men in the crew were racing onto the deck, looking for any way to fight back, and they joined in to help him. He knew that all he had to fire was training ammunition, rounds that would explode as aerial markers for target indicators, but would release no shrapnel; still he thought if he could hit one of the Zeros head on he could bring the son of a bitch down. He fired the first round and the blast of the gun blew his towel off. He cussed and grabbed it and recovered himself as his shipmates re-loaded the gun. They kept firing, and with every blast his towel blew off, until a sailor behind him stripped down to his underwear and gave the gunner his pants, saying, "I'm tired'a lookin' at your ass!" Then they went back to firing the gun.

On the decks of other ships the same kind of mad-ness was going on. Gunners found their ammo boxes locked, so they found hammers and stood in the hail of strafing fire pounding on the locks until they broke open; they then discovered their locked ammo boxes were empty. Officers responsible for bringing order to the chaos were being shot down in every direction; with characteristic American spontaneity the enlisted men organized relays to bring ammunition up to the guns from the ships' magazines.

The air was alive not just with bullets and shrapnel but also with flying chunks of iron from the ships being torn apart by bomb and torpedo blasts. One seaman saw a buddy go down with one of his butt cheeks torn away; they never saw the missing body part, but a base-ball-sized chunk of iron that had un-assed him landed at the seaman's feet. He kept it in a shoebox, and brought it out to show his buddy every time they met again for the rest of their lives.

The survivors would keep strange mementoes like

that. They would also keep the memory of their friends blown apart, burned to ash before their eyes, screaming of agonies unimaginable; they would see these images not only in their sleep but at random and unpredictable times in their waking hours too, for the rest of their lives. And they were the lucky ones.

Evelyn had been awake all night. The shock of Rafe's return had knocked time out of its orbit, and she felt no sense that she would ever sleep again. She spent many hours of the long night waiting outside her barracks for Rafe or Danny or both of them together to return and tell her the miracle they'd worked out—how happiness and peace could somehow arise from the situation the three of them now found themselves in. It was a miracle she could not imagine, could not even pray for; it seemed to her wrong to ask God for the impossible, especially when she felt herself responsible for the hopelessness.

A couple of hours before dawn she had moved inside the barracks and had lain down on her bunk, still wearing her clothes from the evening before, and still as far from sleep as ever. Every moment of her life—a life that began the moment she met Rafe and ended when he and Danny left her in the darkness of this endless night— played out again and again on the ceiling over her bunk while she kept her eyes open, or on the backs of her eyelids if she squeezed them shut.

When the sun rose she was sitting on the edge of her bunk with the diary open, Rafe's rose beside Danny's letter. She wasn't worried about Betty returning from her shift and finding her this way; she was anxious to talk with her and maybe find some kind of release by crying on her shoulder. She looked at her watch and saw that it was just after 8 A.M. Betty would be on her way back soon.

Then Evelyn heard a distant rumble. At first she thought it was naval gunfire; she'd once heard a battle cruiser fire off its deck guns during a 4th of July celebration at the naval base where she had trained. But these sounds were fuller, deeper. The sound elongated. And they continued. *Why would anyone fire off naval guns on a Sunday morning?* she wondered. She looked out the window and saw clouds of smoke rising in the sky, and then she knew without a doubt, without ever having heard them before, that the explosions she was hearing were bombs.

"Oh my God . . . EVERYBODY TO THE HOSPITAL!" she shouted, and ran from room to room, banging on the doors of her fellow nurses.

As Barbara and Sandra rolled out of bed and grabbed for their clothes, Evelyn ran outside, toward the hospital. Planes unfamiliar to her—Japanese Zeros—zoomed low over her head, barely missing the tops of the palm trees growing beside the nurses' quarters.

She heard the cracking of wing guns and the whiz of bullets through the air; she did not know if they were shooting at her, but she could not have been more terrified. She reached the hospital and fell inside, gasping; she found three nurses, newly arrived for the morning shift, staring at her, wild-eyed, waiting for her to tell them what to do.

Evelyn scrambled to her feet and darted to the cabinet, pulling out boxes full of supplies; Barbara and Sandra appeared at the far door, both terrified.

"Get everything out!" Evelyn yelled to them, and the other nurses. "Bandages, sutures—"

A bomb exploded outside, so close it shook the hospital's wooden walls. "They're getting closer!" Sandra screamed in near panic.

Evelyn paused and listened; there was another bomb blast outside, nearer still. A terrible thought struck her. "Come with me!" she shouted, and Barbara and Sandra followed her as she sprinted down the hospital hallway and into the traction ward, where four men from a Jeep accident lay with their casted limbs roped in the air. Trapped and helpless, they had heard the bombs too and were crying out for help. Evelyn raced to the medical cabinet and grabbed razor blades for Barbara, Sandra and herself. "Cut them down! Get them away from the windows!"

Evelyn jumped to the nearest bed and sliced the traction ropes of a man with both legs broken. He moaned as his limbs fell free of their support, and yet through his pain he kept saying, "Thank you, thank you . . ." as she rolled him out of the bed and dragged him to the wall farthest from the windows.

Barbara and Sandra were following her lead, and a doctor with the same thought as Evelyn appeared at the door with orderlies he'd grabbed on his way down the hallway. With all of them scrambling they hauled all four traction patients to the wall, then shoved mattresses against the windows as the bombs outside seemed to be walking their way toward the hospital like an invisible giant with explosive footsteps. Evelyn, the other nurses, the doctor and the orderlies snatched up the free mattress and were just covering the patients and themselves as a bomb struck just outside the hospital, punching huge holes through the walls and blowing the windows into shards that shredded the mattresses jammed against the windows.

They waited for the next bomb to fall, right on their heads. But it did not come.

"Everybody all right?" the doctor asked, raising his head.

No one was cut more than slightly, everybody was alive. "Holy Mother," Evelyn heard the sailor she'd dragged to safety whisper, and she saw him looking at the bedframe where he had rested moments before. Caught in the bare springs that had supported his mattress was a five-pound chunk of shrapnel, still smoking from its explosive journey from the bomb and through the wall.

One large formation of Japanese bombers approached Pearl Harbor at a level of twelve thousand feet. Yamamoto had ordered them equipped for high altitude so that he could put the maximum amount of planes over the target in the least amount of time, with minimal interference from each other, and his bombers flew in exactly as designated.

So meticulous was Yamamoto's planning that the Japanese bombardiers had each been given a specific American ship as their target, and they had trained with hours of practice drills, both with aerial photographs and with miniature ships floating in their mockup harbor, to identify their personal target. The bombardier in one of the planes flying toward the *Arizona* was good, very good; but in his wildest hopes he had not imagined the accuracy and the fortune of the first bomb that he would drop.

Through his bombsight as they approached the moorings, the ships looked like toys far below. The bombardier ticked off the other ships passing through his sights, "*West Virginia . . .*" he muttered, "*Oklahoma . . .*" He was able to identify them though some were already burning, and he worried that smoke would obscure the *Arizona*. But then he saw her, distinct in his bombsight as the crosshairs reached the battleship amidships. He pulled his bomb lever, and a huge steel bomb fell away.

He watched the ship as the bomb dropped toward it. He knew the small propeller on the bomb's tail was spinning in the air, running the arming mechanism into the bomb's explosive core. He counted the seconds and almost felt the speed of it as it fell faster and faster, its fuse set to delay after the initial impact, allowing the momentum of the drop to carry the high explosives down through the upper decks so that the rupturing would occur deep in the ship's guts.

He did not see the moment when the bomb first connected with the teakwood deck and smashed through it; the optics of the bombsight were not that good. It took but a fraction of a second for the bomb's weight and speed to carry it through layer after layer of decking, right into the ship's magazine, where 200,000 pounds of black powder rested next to stacks of cannon shells.

The explosion was almost beyond comprehension. Over twelve hundred men died instantly.

The Japanese bombardier had wondered for the briefest moment if his bomb had actually missed and been swallowed by the water itself, without detonation. Then, even from a height of twelve thousand feet, he saw the *Arizona* leap into the air, the ship's spine broken, its innards ripped out in one explosive instant. Men on the deck were thrown into the burning oil already floating on the water from the other ruptured ships. The concussion sent tons of debris up into the air and down again with devastating impact for the *Arizona* and her neighbors. The *West Virginia*, moored alongside her and already a mangled mess of blood and flame, took even more damage as sixteen-inch guns flew like iron telephone poles and chunks of the *Arizona* as big as house trailers rained down.

21

After a night of drinking and brawling, Red stirred and staggered toward the toilets. He bumped into the wall, backed up like a windup toy and lurched blindly forward again, into the urinals, where he unleashed a marathon piss stream. He stood there, still more asleep than awake, enjoying the relief of his bladder, when a rumble penetrated his brain and his eyes came open a fraction. Through the window slits above the urinals, he saw a cloud of Japanese planes rushing past.

He squeezed his eyes shut, and looked again; the planes were bombing the distant hangars. Red pissed along the wall as he raced out of the head, trying to get his pecker back into his drawers. He shouted to the sleeping guys.

"Th-th-th-th-th-" He slapped his face with both hands, and stomped his feet. "Th-th-th-th-Dammit! Th-th-th-" He still couldn't get it out, couldn't wake them. Bursting with frustration he blasted out singing, "The Ja-a-a-ps!! The Ja-a-a-ps!!"

He stood there belting it out like a baritone in a

bizarre opera. His friends stirred. Anthony winced as his hangover shot its ice-pick stab through his temples, and groaned, "What the hell . . . ?"

Red pointed outside and tried to talk, but now he couldn't mutter a syllable. Then the waking pilots heard the explosions, and tore themselves from their beds.

Over at the Hickham Field mess hall, soldiers had been sitting down to breakfast when machine-gun bullets began chewing up the outer walls. Men ran for the doors so fast that they clogged there like panicked people at a theater fire; the soldiers would've sorted themselves out if they'd had the time, but they did not; a bomb that came through the wooden roof killed everyone in the structure.

Three hundred yards away, the Japanese low-altitude bombers, with Zero escorts, zoomed in over the airfield, blasting the clusters of American warplanes—whole squadrons taken out with one bomb. The mechanics and pilots who were running for their planes, desperately hoping to get something in the air to fight back with, found themselves caught in the strafing. The men ran in every direction, and the Zeros raked them down with machine-gun fire. It was carnage.

The men of Danny's squadron staggered out into the sunshine, half drunk and half dressed. Japanese planes were racing over their heads; the ground seemed to be erupting in all directions. The pilots raced toward their own flight line. They had reached the tarmac when the clustered American planes began blowing up like a line of falling dominos. The concussion of one bomb knocked all the pilots to the ground.

"Goddamn Japs!" Billy screamed. He looked around and saw several anti-aircraft guns around the field, most of them unmanned because the men meant to be their crews had been strafed to death on the way to their action stations. "Come on!" Billy yelled, and jumped to his feet, running toward a sandbag bunker protecting a fifty-millimeter gun.

"Billy!" Anthony shouted, but Billy kept running, and a stream of bullets from a strafing Zero slid by him, pitting the tarmac but never touching him.

He had almost reached the bunker when a steel bomb came skipping across the tarmac. It clanked and bounced past the fallen pilots, then collided with the side of the sandbag bunker just as Billy reached it. The bomb stopped without detonating. Billy was bug-eyed. His heart stopped. His friends, watching from fifty yards away, couldn't breathe. "It's a dud," Anthony said at last.

But Billy heard a sound within the bomb, a metallic *flit-flit-flit*. Then the sound stopped, and the bomb detonated, blowing Billy to bloody dust.

Red, Anthony, and the others looked on as their friend was vaporized, and their innocence, like America's, was gone in that moment.

Danny drove the Buick right through the main gate; the guards had taken cover in their shack and were firing their rifles into the air at the planes passing above them. Danny never slowed, and blasted the Buick onto the tarmac, where some of the planes were still undamaged. Rafe was out the door before the car stopped rolling, and Danny was right behind him.

They were running toward a cluster of fighters near the hangar when both hangar and planes went up with bomb blasts. Rafe and Danny dove to the ground and watched as machine-gun bullets thudded into other planes on the flight line and ripped along the walls of the main buildings, shredding the flight tower.

"Get me into a damn plane!" Rafe said through clenched teeth.

"My thoughts exactly," Danny shot back, above the noise. He stood and sprinted toward another cluster of planes, Rafe running with him. As they drew near the planes, parked wingtip to wingtip, a bomb exploded among the aircraft, tearing them apart. Blown to the ground once more, Danny and Rafe looked around to see what seemed to be the entire American Air Force being destroyed.

"Dammit!" Rafe spat furiously.

The size of the Japanese attack was obvious to them now; the enemy bombers were filling the sky overhead, and Zeros skimmed helter-skelter over the treetops, strafing individual soldiers who fled from the buildings, shooting them down like dogs. Danny was thinking furiously. "Come on!" he said suddenly, jumped up and sprinted toward a phone booth.

Again Rafe followed. Danny reached the phone booth, grabbed the receiver and dug a coin from his pants pocket. "You're making a phone call?!" Rafe shouted.

Danny stood in the booth dialing, and Rafe stood outside, dancing as waves of bullets swept the area around them. Rafe thought Danny had lost his mind until he heard him shout into the receiver, "This is

Walker! We're under attack at Wheeler! Get those planes fueled and armed RIGHT NOW!"

Danny slammed down the receiver and turned toward the car. Rafe, in the nonsense of battle, reached in to hang up the receiver before Danny grabbed him and led him on a sprint to the Buick. Behind them, the phone booth shattered in a flood of machine-gun bullets fired from a passing Zero.

They reached the convertible and dove in. "Where are we going?" Rafe shouted.

"Auxiliary field at Haleiwa, ten miles north of here!"

"What's there?"

"Two P-40s."

"Damn right."

As the Zero pilots saw the Buick moving, they swarmed in to strafe it.

Danny drove like a madman through the hail of bullets, zigzagging and gunning the Buick's big V-8 engine.

Out in Pearl Harbor, the battleship *Nevada* had gotten under way, plowing through the harbor as the water erupted with bombs. Sailors on the surrounding ships, engulfed in flame, fear and defeat, saw the *Nevada* moving and cheered her on with shouts of "Go, *Nevada*, go!"

On the *Nevada*'s bridge her captain was struggling to save his ship, knowing they had a fighting chance if they could make the open sea.

But above him the lead pilot in the next group of Japanese planes spotted the moving battleship and led his squadron down after it.

They came whipping in over the waves, dropping

torpedoes and bombs. On the *Nevada*, the captain felt
his ship shudder as she took a torpedo blast below her
waterline. "We're not gonna make it," he said to his officers, "and if we go down here we block the channel."
He scanned the shore. "Beach her there!" He pointed to
a spot where he could ground his ship outside the harbor's main lane. His officers relayed the order to the
helm, and the ship's rudder turned as more blasts ripped
her hull.

The *Nevada* swung off its course toward the sea and
ran aground, its bow plowing into the volcanic rock of
the shoreline.

Inside her dynamo room, the impact jolted the boilers, already bursting with the pressure of the steam that
powered the huge ship. Jets of steam from rupturing
pipes scalded and blinded the engine room crew. The
leader of the crew was a man named Dan Ross; his men
remember him shouting, "Everybody out! I'll keep it
running!" They also remember that they obeyed his order, and they regret that they did it so quickly. The
smoke and steam were blinding to Ross too, but he
stayed behind and kept the boilers going, struggling to
read the gauges and regulate the valves to feed power to
weapons and pumps, to give the *Nevada* a few more
minutes of life.

Above decks, the *Nevada* was like a beast cut from
its herd; predators swarmed her with torpedoes and
bombs. The attack was frenzied and chaotic; one torpedo launched toward the ship missed her hull and
skimmed up the beach itself, striking a house on the
shore and blasting it to fragments—but none of the
bombs seemed to miss; they detonated along the ship's

length, engulfing the entire upper deck in flame. Sailors
with their flesh on fire leapt into the water and struggled out onto the shoreline as charred wrecks of hu-
manity. Their doctors, their medical corpsmen,
everyone who could have helped, were burned too. But
men on the shore were screaming and pointing the way
to the hospital.

It was the one where Evelyn worked.

Back out on Battleship Row, the black smoke had
turned day into night. The number of attacking planes
seemed endless—and their strategy flawless. Even luck
was with the Japanese. Torpedoes hitting one ship
would lift its hull with a blast, enabling the next wave of
torpedoes to rush under and hit the next ship anchored
behind. The American battleships were bobbing like
seesaws.

The *Oklahoma* was already listing, its deck splintered, hundreds of sailors already in the oily seawater,
thrashing to keep their heads above the surface, when
another barrage of torpedoes blew thirty-foot holes
along its hull.

Inside the ship, the thundering detonations deformed
the hull and water came racing in; some of the doors,
designed to shut watertight, could not be closed in the
twisted structure; others wedged shut and could not be
opened for routes of escape. As the listing grew ever
more severe, ladders that had been vertical were becoming horizontal; men fought their way toward any
opening they could imagine, only to find sailors blown
apart ahead of them by more detonations of bombs and
torpedoes.

On the ruptured and now almost vertical deck, sailors slid into the water. Still the Marines on deck were firing back at the Japanese planes; some of the Marines were even using handguns.

But courage could not save them or their ship. The *Oklahoma* rolled over.

The capsizing of a ship of that magnitude, equal in mass to that of the *Titanic*, sucked everything around it to the bottom of the harbor. One survivor, already in the water when the ship turned turtle, would remember being pulled down so fast that the hair on his head streamed out behind him until he was pressed into the sand of the harbor bottom. Some men—many—were crushed there, below the ship. For others, however, the contact of the *Oklahoma*'s superstructure with the harbor floor was their salvation; the fluid forces reversed themselves and men who had been snatched to the depths were then propelled toward the surface, launched almost completely out of the water before splashing back into the burning oil on its surface. A few of the survivors began to swim toward a motor launch they saw carrying men away from the wreckage. The launch itself was then struck by a Japanese bomb and became a geyser of debris and body parts. The men in the hell-like water decided to swim the other way.

At least they had some choice. Most of their shipmates—the ones not already dead—were trapped alive inside the submerged hull of the *Oklahoma*.

The tiny auxiliary airfield at Haleiwa sat tucked among the green volcanic hills of Oahu. Its runway was barely paved, and its only permanent building was a Quonset hut—if a semicircle of corrugated metal bolted to a concrete base could be called permanent. Earl Smith was the only man at the facility that morning. He thought of this small field, nothing more than a military maintenance facility, as his personal property; but he was even more attached to the two P-40 fighter planes parked on it. To these he was as emotionally bonded as he would be to his own offspring. He had given them loving care—which in Earl's case meant lots of attentive cursing.

He was wrestling to load an ammunition belt into the wing guns of one of the fighters when the Buick slid to a stop on the grass beside the runway and Danny and Rafe jumped out. There were bullet holes punched in the trunk of the Buick, and Earl glanced at them, cursing through clenched teeth.

"They ready, Earl?" Danny said, running up.

"They stay ready," Earl said, insulted. Then he looked up and said, "Oh shit." He saw, for the first time, the cloud of Zeros and dive-bombers in the distance. Remote from the main facilities in and around Pearl Harbor, Earl had been oblivious to the action going on. What he saw now was the second wave of Japanese planes, moving in on new angles.

Earl slapped the ammo covers into place. "Get 'em up!" he said. "Just don't hurt my planes."

" 'Preciate your concern, Earl," Danny said. He and Rafe climbed into their separate cockpits, and above their heads they saw Zeros breaking off from the main group and heading down in their direction.

Rafe was used to scrambling takeoffs in hot-engine

Spitfires; now it frustrated him to find the P-40's engine cold. "You're flooding it!" Earl yelled, as the engine sputtered.

"The hell I am!" Rafe shouted back. "The plugs are dirty!"

Earl glared at Danny and shouted, "Who is this asshole?" Whatever else he said was drowned out as Danny's engine and then Rafe's roared to life. Inside the cockpits they switched on their radios, and taxied to the end of the runway side by side. They could see the Zeros racing closer, coming at them for sure. There was no time for revving the engines or warming them to operating speed; Rafe pushed the throttle forward and Danny followed, rolling with what felt like agonizing slowness as the wing guns of the Zeros began to flash and the P-40s surged right through the strafing fire and lifted into the sky.

"Stay low!" Rafe barked into his radio, and broke to his left, away from Danny. Danny broke hard right, and the Zeros divided to follow them.

There was a moment—it could not have been more than a few seconds, but it was plenty—when Rafe and Danny felt themselves connected once again, joined without discussion or decision. They were in planes, they were aware of each other's position, of everything going on inside and outside their own cockpits. They were together.

And they felt the Japanese planes coming on.

It was Danny's first time in combat. But Rafe had been there before. He analyzed what was happening, not on the conscious levels of his brain but deep in his gut, where he always lived, and radioed, "Bet they don't dust crops in Japan."

Danny understood immediately, following Rafe's tactic as he broke into another sharp turn and used the hut, palm trees and low hills to shake the Zeros. The Japanese pilots were skilled and disciplined, and their light powerful planes well suited to dogfighting; but the crop-dusting technique of the P-40 pilots was a surprise, the American planes skimming less than a meter from the ground, then bobbing up, banking left and right. The Zeros, dividing into two groups to chase the pair, stayed close and sprayed the air around the P-40s with machine-gun fire, but when the Japanese plane on Rafe's tail caught the top of a palm tree with a wingtip and spun into the ground in an instant fireball, the others backed off enough for Rafe to catch his breath and radio to Danny, "How many on you?!"

"Four, I think!" Danny answered, out of breath. "You?"

"I don't know. . . ." Flying 200 miles per hour, twenty feet above the ground, he threw his plane into a sweeping turn so he could look over his shoulder and count the planes behind him. At three he stopped counting. "Danny!" he snapped. "Let's play some chicken."

Danny banked hard, away from Rafe, knowing exactly what he meant him to do.

The four Zeros behind Danny followed him confidently. Their Mitsubishi engines were more powerful than his, and their planes were lighter and more maneuverable. They could gain altitude more quickly than anything the Americans had ever made. The P-40's only mechanical edge was that it could dive faster, and what kind of advantage was that when you were skimming the grass on the hilltops? Danny's turn was tight and hard but the Zeros could turn even tighter if they had to; by the time he straightened his course they had lost contact with the other Zeros, but since the American planes had broken off in different directions it was clear they were just frantically scattering to get away any way they could. But they would not get away; the Japanese pilots spread out to broaden their field of fire and pushed up their throttles to close the gap between themselves and their enemies, and rip them from the sky.

Earl saw it from the ground, even before the Japanese pilots did: the two P-40s rushing headlong at each other, like two bullets aimed at each other's noses. "Oh shit . . ." Earl muttered. "Oh shit, oh shit . . ."

The P-40s seemed to be flying right into each other's propellers; the Japanese pilots realized too late that they were flying directly into their comrades.

At the last instant Rafe and Danny did what they had done back in the States, each snapping a quarter spin to the right so that the P-40s flashed by each other, belly to belly.

The Japanese were lucky; only two of them collided in mid-air, exploding into a double fireball.

The others scattered, and when the shock of one collision and the closeness of several others passed they realized they had lost both P-40s behind the hills, and they banked away from the tiny airfield to reunite with the main Japanese attack.

Danny and Rafe rejoined each other in the open sky and watched the squadron of Zeros from behind as they headed away. The P-40s were flying smoothly and so far had expended no ammunition. So far.

Danny and Rafe looked across at each other. Neither man smiled, neither frowned; they showed no emotion at all, but they felt a strange peace. For now, at this moment, there was nothing more than this, going into battle together.

"You hear me okay?" Rafe said into his radio.

"Yeah. So you can call me if you need help."

Now Rafe did smile. "I got half a tank," he said. "You?"

"Little less."

Danny fired a short burst to see if his guns worked. They did. Rafe did the same. Up ahead they saw another formation of Japanese planes, headed toward Pearl.

"No trouble finding targets," Danny said. "How you wanna go at 'em?"

"They're in strafing formation. We'll just blow right through their line.

Once more they looked across at each other. "Land of the free," Rafe said.

"Home of the brave," Danny answered.

22

There weren't nearly enough ambulances in Oahu to handle the wounded.

Military trucks brought piles of bodies to the hospital, those in screaming agony, those in unconscious suffering, those with a pulse, and those without. In all the chaos it was often impossible for the overwhelmed Army medics and Navy corpsmen on the airfields and in the ships to judge who might be saved and who had no hope, so they did their best with tourniquets and compresses and left it to the doctors and nurses to sort them out. Wounded men rode in lying next to corpses; it could not have been a comforting journey.

Evelyn worked among the frenzy in the main ward like a frantic traffic cop, shouting, "Put criticals in ward one, stables in two! Barbara! Fill every syringe you can find with stimulant and antibiotic!"

There were moments when no one seemed to hear her; the sight of something like the blood-spattered rabbit's foot that Sandra had just seen around the neck of a young sailor with half his face blown away would make a nurse lapse into stillness like a clock with a broken mainspring. Others of the nurses, none of them ever having seen a battlefield casualty, stood trembling and helpless over the crowds of horribly wounded men, not knowing which to try to help first. Some, like Barbara right now, ran around frantically, grabbing at syringes, spilling them.

It was in moments like these, when Evelyn saw herself losing control of the nurses she was responsible for leading, that she felt most overwhelmed herself. With the screaming chaos all around her, she needed to do something, shout some order that would organize everything—but what? She saw two corpsmen bringing in an officer on a stretcher. The blood was a bright red blossom on the white front of the officer's uniform, but he was conscious, holding a compress to his own neck; the corpsmen, finding no place to put him, looked to Evelyn, and she said, "Just set him down right here." They lowered him to the floor at Evelyn's feet. She knelt and said, "Let me see."

His eyes were fixed on her but clear; he was conscious, but he would not let her pull his hand away from the wound on his neck. His name was printed above the pocket of his uniform shirt, and she read it through the bloodstain. "Jackson . . . Major Jackson. Let me see." He pulled back the compress to show Evelyn the wound and blood spurted over her starched white apron; it was arterial blood, bright red. She gawked down at it and felt as if it were hers, from a widening gash torn into her soul. Without thinking, reacting only to her instinct and her training, she shoved her hand right into the wound of Jackson's slick hot neck, found the spurting artery, and plugged the hole with her finger. Her eyes locked on the face of the dying man, as his eyes begged her for help.

Evelyn began to hyperventilate. She could not move, could not think what to do. In the reflection on the chrome medical cabinet she saw other nurses crying, frozen, shocked by the shattered bodies all around them. Something about the warm slickness of the blood on her bare hand, the pulse of life she could still feel through her fingertip in the wound, brought her back to life. "Doctor!" she shouted. "Doctor!"

The doctor who appeared at her shoulder was young himself, and like everyone else in the hospital had never seen battle injuries until this moment. Evelyn, from some reserve she never knew she had, found the strength to speak simply and clearly. "It's an artery—responds to pressure—edges are clean," she said.

The doctor drew focus from her clarity; he leaned down over the wounded man and went to work, Evelyn still keeping her finger in the wound.

"Barbara!" Evelyn called. "Two bags of plasma! Barbara!"

Barbara was kneeling on the floor beside the supply cabinet, picking up the syringes she had dropped. Hearing Evelyn, she turned back to the cabinet, grabbed for more plasma, and dropped that too.

"Listen to me!" Evelyn shouted. "LISTEN TO ME!" For a moment, the noise in the hospital diminished; even the wounded men seemed quieter. "We can do this!" Evelyn said, loudly, but low enough to sound calm. "Just focus on one thing at a time!" Everyone went back to work, but things did not seem so frantic now. "Barbara," Evelyn said firmly, "get two bags of plasma, let's go."

Barbara snapped into action. Evelyn worked in the center of the hurricane that had hit them all in a storm of horror and dying; and something about the way she worked—about the way the wounded man she was saving looked up at her—made her feel, for one shining moment, that she had to be, and could be, a beacon of life.

Everywhere, it was madness.

The B-17s approaching Oahu after a fourteen-hour flight from the mainland found themselves attacked by Zeros and had no way to fight back because their guns were unmounted, packed in grease. And the enemy fighter planes were not their only danger: as they flew over the island anti-aircraft fire burst around them, the frantic American gunners on the ground now believing that everything they saw in the air was Japanese.

At the radio station whose signal had guided both the American and the Japanese planes to Pearl, a disc jockey received instructions to stop playing the soothing Hawaiian music and make the announcement: "All Army, Navy, and Marine personnel are to report to duty."

General Walter C. Short was commander of U.S. Army forces in Hawaii. Surrounded by his aides, working frantically to mobilize all the forces, he sent a terse message to Washington: "Hostilities with Japan commenced with an air raid on Pearl Harbor."

President Roosevelt received the news in the White House, where he was having lunch with his friend and advisor, Harry Hopkins, who answered the ringing phone, then quickly handed the receiver to the president, who listened for a moment and then hung up, shaken. "The Japanese have attacked Pearl Harbor," he told Hopkins.

"My God. Do we have damage estimates?"

Roosevelt glanced up at him, anger in his eyes. Hopkins had seen Roosevelt show his temper, and it was not pretty; one of his other advisors would later say of him, *When angry, he could say things that would end a relationship forever*. Hopkins knew the outrage he saw in Roosevelt's face was not directed at him, but still it was chilling. "Our Pacific Fleet, at anchor, unprepared?" Roosevelt responded. "It's terrible. It has to be. And it's not over."

In the skies of the mid-Pacific, Lieutenant Commander Shimazaki, leader of the second attack wave, spoke calmly into his radio. "Second wave, we will deploy over the military bases. High-level bombers to the air stations, dive-bombers attack ships in harbor. Fighters strafe and cover."

He nosed his plane down for the attack run.

Below, the harbor was a mass of destruction and panic. Everywhere there was screaming; men tried to fight fires and move the wounded. As the next wave of Japanese planes struck, the smaller American ships that had been spared in the first attack now found themselves targets. A tremendous explosion rocked the destroyer *Shaw*, blasting it apart, and as other secondary vessels began to light up around the harbor it seemed clear that no one would be spared.

The American resistance was sporadic and mostly in-
effective; far more bothersome to the Japanese pilots
was the thick black smoke coming out of the damaged
ships and off the oil fires along the water. One torpedo
plane, its pilot flying blind, clipped the superstructure of
a burning battleship and spun to a crash.

The sailors in the maelstrom of terror and calamity
struggled inventively to survive. Men trapped on one
flaming ship used the severed barrel of a five-inch naval
gun as a bridge to cross to the less damaged ship anchored beside them. Others jumped into water and
swam through the burning oil, using the sweeping mo-
tions of the breaststroke to brush the flames away from
their faces as they towed buddies too wounded to swim
themselves.

The once-pristine hospital, that place that Evelyn had
first seen as a snowy white, perfectly ordered arrange-
ment of luminous empty beds, was now a nightmare of
crimson horror. Blood was everywhere; it soaked the
mattresses and dripped through them onto the floor, the
puddles connecting with the rivulets running there already, fed by the tributaries of weeping wounds of men
lying upon the bare wood. Burned and broken soldiers,
sailors and civilians all mixed together, dying everywhere, screaming in pain, begging for help—and Evelyn, her uniform covered in blood, working in the
middle of the chaos. Seeing Sandra's hands shaking as
she tried to give an intravenous injection to a charred
sailor, she said, "Don't look for a vein, just poke. And
mark them somehow! We've got to keep track of who's
already gotten morphine!"

Sandra obeyed, gritting her teeth and stabbing the needle into the blackened flesh. She carried a grease pencil in her uniform pocket, intended for use on medical charts; she withdrew it and called back, "Mark them . . . where?"

"On the forehead!" Evelyn answered, wondering how many of the wounded had already received doses of morphine amid all the madness.

Sandra tried to make a mark on the sailor's smoke-darkened face; the grease pencil slipped across the soft dirty skin and its line did not show. Evelyn ran to her purse, dumped it out, grabbed her lipstick and marked an "M" on the patient's head. The other nurses followed suit.

Out in the hallway the doctors amputated limbs; a veteran Navy doctor, setting his saw against a sailor's shinbone, called out, "Evelyn! Get me a tourniquet." She raced to the cabinet and found their supply of tourniquets already exhausted. "I need a tourniquet!" he said again. She squirmed out of her nylons and gave them to the doctor.

His eyes met hers for just a moment. "You have to do the triage," he said. "They're bringing them in truckloads!"

At the doorway, she became the gatekeeper of who should be given medical help and who should be passed over. Outside the hospital was a surreal world of white smoke, with black-charred sailors emerging out of it like walking dead coming for help. Trucks kept pulling up—military trucks and even civilian pickup trucks—loaded with wounded. Young naval corpsmen with wild eyes lifted the bodies as carefully as they could and car-

ried them to the hospital door. Once more Evelyn had to
steel herself. These were life-and-death decisions,
shouldn't doctors be making them? What if she were
wrong, what if she couldn't . . .

She pushed all this from her mind and looked at the
first wounded sailor carried to the door; his stomach was
a mass of blood-soaked bandages. She felt his neck and
found a weak pulse, but his skin was cool—he was already going into shock. "Critical—front ward . . . !" she
said to the corpsmen, and they carried the sailor inside.

Next was another wounded sailor—a boy really—
clearly dying, his chest a mess of sucking wounds, but
his eyes were open, imploring her for help. She touched
his shoulder, and all she could think to say was, "It's going to be all right." His eyes fluttered shut and she wondered if he had already died, but she could not bring
herself to feel for his pulse, and more wounded men
were coming faster than she could look at them. She
straightened and whispered to the corpsman at the front
end of the litter, "Just give him morphine, he's too far
gone." The young corpsmen had heard such words
more than once that day. They carried the sailor to a
shady area along the outer wall of the hospital and laid
him gently upon the grass among other young men who
had already slipped into death. The shady side of the
hospital was already looking like an outdoor morgue.
Evelyn watched them go and thought, *So this is what
war looks like.*

The first thing she saw as she turned to the next body
coming to the door was the flyer's uniform, the wings
on the chest—and that chest riddled with bullets. The
pilot's face had been shot off. Evelyn's legs went numb.

Her eyes darted to the patches on the uniform sleeve, and they were just like those Rafe and Danny wore. For a moment she lost her equilibrium and found herself on her knees beside the stretcher; whether she had fallen or knelt, she could not remember. She stretched her hand out to the flyer's dog tags, read them . . . and saw a stranger's name.

Evelyn sagged in guilty relief. Then she told the stretcher bearers—Army medics, these—"Take him into the shade and cover him; he's dead."

She steadied herself as the next body came through, a woman on a stretcher, in a white uniform, her stomach shot open, pale hands clutching at the open wound. Evelyn felt for a pulse and found none. "She's gone too, take her to—"

It was Betty.

23

Evelyn sagged against the doorjamb of the hospital entrance. Voices around her spoke but she did not hear. Some called her name and she did not answer. The enlisted men bringing their fallen friends in search of medical help no longer waited for her triage but moved on wherever momentum carried them.

Evelyn tried to focus, to find anything that would force out the image of Betty's face and the shock of her death. Looking away from the hospital she saw more horribly burned sailors staggering out of the smoke; behind them the beached hulk of the *Nevada* burned at the harbor shoreline.

Evelyn turned and grabbed an orderly. "Go to the base exchange," she told him, "and get some of those canister spray things they use for killing bugs."

"Insecticide . . . ?" He frowned at her.

"No, just the sprayers. We'll fill them with tannic acid. It'll sterilize them and cool the burns! GO!"

The orderly raced away. As Evelyn hurried to assist

the burned sailors, she shouted back through the hospital door to the orderlies, "We're gonna need every bed! If they can breathe, make them get up and move someplace else!"

The Americans on the ground were not the only ones experiencing chaotic conditions, and perhaps the natural confusion of such an event explains some of what happened that day. Japanese pilots, in the high temper of battle, revved up by months of training and under orders to find targets, dove out of the skies and strafed trucks trying to carry civilian dependents to safety, away from the housing areas of the bases the Japanese were attacking. The trucks were military, and surely that is all the attackers saw. Miraculously, none of the women and children carried by those trucks were killed.

There were many opportunities for the Japanese to kill civilians, opportunities not taken, and violence against the civilian population was clearly not their intention. Downtown Oahu did experience considerable damage—attributable to the shells fired from American anti-aircraft guns, falling back to earth after missing their targets.

On the other hand, it cannot be argued that the Japanese intended to soften their blows against the people who wore uniforms. Men struggling for survival in the burning waters of the harbor were strafed by passing Zeros, and there was no merciful intent in the killings.

At Hickham Field a bright red engine from the Honolulu Fire Department raced up to an Army building already engulfed in flame from the air attack, and as the pump engine stopped and the firemen jumped off and ran to fight the fire, they were cut down by machine-gun bullets from the Zeros.

Two of the planes involved in that strafing pass were chased down by P-40s they never saw coming, and the wing guns of the American planes ripped them into flaming debris.

Not many American planes got into the air that day, but there were some, and Rafe McCawley and Danny Walker were two of them. Between them, they shot down six Japanese planes.

At some point during the fighting of that morning, Danny changed from a frightened pilot who had never seen combat into an avenging warrior. He was not aware of the moment of his passage. But he realized, as he watched the last Zero he would shoot down that day spiral out of the air, that he had fulfilled part of a destiny that he had been born to—or at least had found at an early age, sitting on a nail keg inside the fuselage of a plane that would fly only in his imagination, on a farm in Tennessee.

And he was conscious of the fact that it was Rafe who had led him to those flights of imagination, and Rafe who had bequeathed him that destiny.

As the two planes wheeled and turned back to their base, Danny settled his fighter alongside Rafe's wing and reflected that he no longer felt any guilt for loving Evelyn, and no self-reproach. What Danny felt for Evelyn had been as inevitable for him as this day of combat had been. Whether it had been the Lord God Jehovah or the Fates of Mount Olympus, a force greater than Danny had determined his destiny. There was no denying he had been led to that destiny by Rafe.

Yamamoto's staff, working in the command center of his flagship, were steeped in good news. The Japanese battle group was performing with magnificent efficiency, and the maps and models they used to track the progress of the attack recorded one American ship after another struck with bombs and torpedoes. Out on the flight decks the planes that had struck the first blows were returning with grinning pilots, exulting with the support crewmen who greeted them as conquering heroes.

On the bridge of the *Akagi*, Air Commander Genda summed it all up for the admiral he so deeply admired. "We have achieved complete surprise. The first wave is returning, the second is attacking right now, and out of three hundred fifty planes we have lost only twenty-nine." He paused to see how much the scope of this result, so much better than they had anticipated, would affect Yamamoto; when the admiral remained silent, Genda added, "We are prepared to launch the third wave."

Still Yamamoto said nothing.

"What is troubling you, Admiral?" Genda asked.

"We have no idea where their carriers are. They are surely looking for us right now. If they should find us and attack us while our second wave is still out—or worse, landing with no fuel and empty guns . . ."

Yamamoto did not have to finish the sentence. Genda understood what a disaster it would be to have the Americans catch them at a moment when they could not defend themselves, and if the Japanese lost their carriers this entire day would flip from victory to total disaster. Genda was aggressive; he understood that it was his duty to be so, just as it was the duty of the admiral to weigh the risks. But Genda was certain they should attack for a third time.

"We need a damage report," Yamamoto said quietly.

Almost as if the war gods were listening to him, the communications officer said, "We have Commander Fuchida on the radio now, Admiral."

Yamamoto nodded and Fuchida's voice came over the intercom. "I am over the harbor right now," he reported. "We have a tremendous victory." *Victory*. The first time that word had been uttered among the excited souls of the Japanese command group. Yamamoto's staff wanted to cheer, but their admiral was straining at every word coming to him from his scout in a Zero high above Pearl Harbor. "Many ships damaged, some totally destroyed," Fuchida went on. "But the second wave's attack is being hindered by the smoke."

That was enough for Yamamoto. He gestured for the communications officer to keep him informed of any new reports to come from Fuchida, and turned to face the open sea, where the American carriers and the unknown future lay. Genda moved up beside him. "The more we attack," Yamamoto said, "the harder it is to find targets. And we no longer have surprise."

"If we launch the third wave and annihilate their fuel depots, we destroy their ability to operate in the Pacific for at least a year!" Genda said.

"And if we fail, if we lose our carriers, we destroy our ability to fight them at all."

Each man knew he was stating the obvious. Sometimes that was the only way to arrive at a decision.

And Yamamoto arrived at his. "As soon as the second wave returns," he said, "we will withdraw."

A short time later, the Japanese battle group turned for home.

Are facts the truth?

The facts are that the American carriers were nowhere near the Japanese when Yamamoto called off the attack; Genda had been quite correct that a third wave of planes launched against the American oil storage tanks would have encountered virtually no opposition, and the devastating effects of the surprise attack on Pearl Harbor would have been multiplied many times over.

It is also true that Yamamoto would soon become aware of his missed opportunity, and it would haunt him so much that when he faced an almost identical dilemma months later during the Battle of Midway, he would make the opposite choice, launching a follow-up attack in spite of the danger of discovery. This time the American carriers were close, and would find him and sink his carriers.

Those are the facts. Would different decisions have changed the outcome of history? No one knows—and that is the truth.

24

The planes had stopped coming.

Pearl Harbor was a place of shattered bodies and shattered ships; blood, body parts and debris covered every surface above the once pristine waters, now hellish from the oil fires on its surface sending sickening black smoke into the choking air.

While he struggled to organize defenses in case of further attacks, save the men trapped within his sunken ships and pull together the remnants of his shattered fleet, Admiral Kimmel received a telegram from Washington. It told him: "Be on alert. Attack by Japan considered imminent."

General Short, at his headquarters, told his staff, "I want lookouts and sentries everywhere, with orders to shoot first and ask questions later. We have to anticipate a landing of enemy troops."

One of his colonels asked him, "Do you think a follow-up invasion by enemy ground troops is possible, General?"

"After this morning, we'd better not consider anything impossible."

An aide handed him a telegram that had come from Washington by way of Western Union and been delivered to Army Headquarters by a messenger boy—who happened to be a Japanese American—on a bicycle. The telegram read ULTIMATUM FROM JAPAN TO BE GIVEN PRECISELY AT 1.00 P.M. WASHINGTON TIME. JUST WHAT SIGNIFICANCE THE HOUR SET MAY HAVE DO NOT KNOW, BUT BE ON ALERT ACCORDINGLY.

Outside the Japanese embassy in Oahu, cars from the Honolulu Police Department squealed to a stop and disgorged officers who burst through the embassy doors and stormed through the hallways. They found the Japanese staffers there burning documents. The police officers stopped the fires and took the Japanese staffers into custody. The officers would comment later that they felt the members of the consulate looked terribly ashamed.

All the shooting was not done for the day. American planes trying to return to their bases in the aftermath of the attack were fired upon by skittish air defense crews, but none of the pilots were hurt. One more Japanese pilot would die, however. During the onslaught against the anchored ships his plane had been damaged so badly that he could not crash it like a flying bomb against any available military target, as pilots of other damaged Japanese planes had done; instead he had gone down on the shallow shoals of the harbor waters, and had climbed out onto the wing of his Zero. When the skies had cleared of the other attacking Zeros a crew of American seamen armed with rifles took a motorized dinghy over to take him prisoner; as they approached, the pilot drew out a pistol, and they shot him dead.

None of the downed Japanese planes were approached without caution, but no other Japanese pilots were found alive. Orders were given that all their bodies be treated with respect. One, however, was placed inside a new garbage can until a proper container could be found for his body; when asked why they had put him there, the men who did it explained that they had meant no disrespect; in the aftermath of the fighting, they said, it was the only thing they could find that would hold the body.

All the wounded bled, even those who were burned. The blood that came from those men charred by the fires looked all the more red, so cruel were the openings torn into their blackened bodies by the bullets and the shrapnel. Outside, the sounds of the planes roaring overhead and the bombs exploding had died away, replaced by the howls of sirens—sirens everywhere, their cries of warning seeming ridiculous now, like the telegrams that had come too late.

Inside the hospital there was a different kind of wailing. Men shrieked in pain, called for their mothers, shed tears down torn faces, screamed out until their voices were shredded, as the nurses moved amid the sound and the blood, grateful for the noise, for the men who could still cry out were the ones who were not dead.

Those who had died were carried out the way they had been carried in, and the steps of the hospital were tracked with gore, the doors themselves propped open, ready to swallow the living and spit out the dead—the mouth of hell.

Along that trail of spattered blood and into that open mouth walked lieutenants Daniel Walker and Rafe McCawley. They had not spoken since agreeing to come. They had not even mentioned Evelyn's name when deciding on this destination, had said only that the hospital seemed the first place they should go, on their way back to the air base that they already knew was shattered.

They walked in and stood with their backs to the wall, and just as the sight of men being shot had made them terrified and furious, what they saw now made them sick. Neither vomited; both wanted to.

Out among grisly and stinking wounded, Evelyn was showing two other nurses how to use the fly sprayers to spritz cooling antiseptic on the charred bodies. Danny and Rafe watched her until she glanced up and her eyes caught on them and hung. Her eyes registered relief, but they were the only part of her that could show emotion now; the rest of her was taut with stress and covered in blood. She moved to them and stopped several feet away, touching neither.

"How can we help?" Rafe asked her.

Three minutes later they sat in folding chairs at the end of a corridor, clear plastic tubes conducting blood from their arms into the green glass of sterilized Coca-Cola bottles, all other transfusion containers having been put into service long before. Evelyn made sure the shunts in their arms were not leaking and moved quietly back to work, as Danny and Rafe sat side by side, their blood flowing into identical bottles; and once again they felt their bond, as if their blood went not only to the same destination, but came from the same source.

As night began to fall on Pearl Harbor, the fires had all been put out but the smell of oily smoke still lingered everywhere, added to now by the acrid odor of welding torches, their sparks cutting through the darkness of the blackout the military had now imposed. There was no shooting, except for the sporadic bursts from the still jumpy sentries; the war now was to save trapped men.

Teams working frantically followed the sounds of tapping transmitted through the ship hulls, and cut through the layers of the *Oklahoma*'s capsized hull; as the night wore on, half-naked men began to emerge, men who had believed they would never draw a fresh breath again. As they stepped out into the open air and saw the devastation around them, they were perhaps the only ones who could look upon that scene with a sense of gratitude.

Most of the unaccounted for had been aboard the *Arizona*, and while the overwhelming size of the explosion that ripped her, and the scale of her destruction made clear the extent of her casualties, the men of the Navy were tortured by the knowledge that even as she lay on the bottom of the harbor she must still hold some survivors, trapped in air pockets within the hull. The agonies of the rescuers increased when the divers who first reached the hull swore they heard tapping coming from within. The Navy rushed in all the equipment they could muster, and more divers hurried down to the wreck. No one had any idea how they could extract any still left alive; if they were there, their brothers were going to find them, or die trying.

And that is what happened: they died trying. Divers moving among the shattered ruins of the ship were killed as debris collapsed upon them, and it became clear that the lives sure to be lost in trying to save anyone left inside the *Arizona*, much less recover the bodies of the dead, were greater than the number of those with any hope of being rescued.

The admirals made the agonizing decision to call off the efforts to penetrate the *Arizona,* and she became a monument of what happened there, and a silent whisperer of the deaths that were to come because of it.

Book Three

INVINCIBILITY

25

Every journalist and press photographer in Washington was waiting for him, fresh flashbulbs in their cameras. Yet as the president was wheeled out to meet them, not a single photographer took a picture. Not yet.

Aides helped Roosevelt from the chair, the president struggling on legs that had no strength, to the podium. His aides locked the steel clasps at the knees of his braces into place, and now President Franklin Delano Roosevelt, standing at the microphone, looked powerful, even majestic.

Now all the camera bulbs popped and flashed. Roosevelt looked at his audience, an audience that he knew was all of America, all of the world, all of history. His eyes were icy, his voice pinched with anger.

"Yesterday, December 7, 1941—a date which will live in infamy—the United States of America was suddenly and deliberately attacked by the naval and air forces of the Empire of Japan.

"The United States was at peace with that Nation and, at the solicitations of Japan, was still in conversation with its Government and its Emperor looking toward the maintenance of peace in the Pacific. Indeed, one hour after Japanese air squadrons had commenced bombing in Oahu, the Japanese Ambassador to the United States and his colleague delivered to the Secretary of State a formal reply to a recent American message. While this reply stated that it seemed useless to continue the existing diplomatic negotiations, it contained no threat or hint of war or armed attack.

"It will be recorded that the distance of Hawaii from Japan makes it obvious that the attack was deliberately planned many days or even weeks ago. During the intervening time the Japanese Government has deliberately sought to deceive the United States by false statements and expressions of hope for continued peace.

"The attack yesterday on the Hawaiian Islands has caused severe damage to American naval and military forces. Very many American lives have been lost. In addition, American ships have been reported torpedoed on the high seas between San Francisco and Honolulu.

"Yesterday the Japanese Government also launched an attack against Malaya.

"Last night Japanese forces attacked Hong Kong.

"Last night Japanese forces attacked Guam.

"Last night Japanese forces attacked Wake Island.

"*This morning Japanese forces attacked Midway Island.*

"*Japan has, therefore, undertaken a surprise offensive extending throughout the Pacific area. The facts of yesterday speak for themselves. The people of the United States have already formed their opinions and well understand the implications to the very life and safety of our Nation.*

"*As Commander-in-Chief of the Army and Navy I have directed that all measures be taken for our defense.*

"*Always will we remember the character of the onslaught against us. No matter how long it may take us to overcome this premeditated invasion, the American people in their righteous might will win through to absolute victory.*

"*I believe I interpret the will of the Congress and of the people when I assert that we will not only defend ourselves to the uttermost but will make very certain that this form of treachery shall never endanger us again.*

"*Hostilities exist. There is no blinking at the fact that our people, our territory, and our interests are in grave danger.*

"*With confidence in our armed forces—with the unbounded determination of our people—we will gain the inevitable triumph, so help us God.*

"*I ask that Congress declare that since the unprovoked and dastardly attack by Japan on Sunday, December seventh, a state of war has existed between the United States and the Japanese Empire.*"

WAR! The word echoed out across America, and young men all across the country, on country farms and in city pool halls, put down their plows or their cue sticks and headed to military recruitment centers, where lines stretched out the doors and down the streets. WAR! The years of German aggression on the other side of the Atlantic had not done it; the conquest of Europe, the air war against Britain, the incursions into Africa and Asia—none of this had shaken the United States from its choice to remain aloof and unconcerned, but with the news of Pearl Harbor the dam had broken and the floods of anger flowed. It mattered not at all that Japan was about as far away as it was possible to be on the face of the planet Earth; this had been an attack on America, an attack on home, a sudden, deliberate *sneak* attack, and somebody, by God, was going to pay.

Congress had answered with a declaration of war, not only against Japan but against her European allies, Germany and Italy, as well. Roosevelt promised the American people that he would lead them to take their vengeance. But the news from the War Department and the discussions within the White House were neither positive nor powerful; all it seemed America could do was to try to slow the rate of its defeat.

To fight back, the country not only had to train soldiers, sailors and airmen, but it had to mobilize its industries to manufacture the weapons to arm them, and all of that took time. Time was the one thing America could not manufacture. Her enemies had prepared for years, and had already piled up victories—the Germans

and Italians in Europe and the Japanese in Southeast
Asia, Korea and on the Chinese mainland.

And while it had been the Germans who had most
occupied Roosevelt's mind as being the greatest threat
to Western civilization, he now found Japan looming as
the most immediate danger to the United States. The
Japanese offensive was in high gear, and America was in
retreat everywhere in the Pacific. Yes, repair work had
begun right away on the ships of Pearl Harbor; even
some of those that had been sunk were being raised and
repaired. And the American aircraft carriers had escaped. But still it was not an adequate force for defense,
much less for fighting back to victory. The risk of a
Japanese invasion of the American mainland was considered more than possible; some military planners—the
public never knew how many—thought it likely. Roosevelt received reports from the War Department that its
best tacticians had studied the scenarios and believed
that if the Japanese did mount a full-scale assault
against America, landing on the West Coast and driving
inland, the United States would not be able to stop the
invaders and turn them back until they had reached as
far as Chicago.

Roosevelt gathered his advisors in a meeting room of
the White House and told them, "We are facing a crisis
greater than any of us could have imagined. We've been
trained to think that we're invincible, and now our
proudest ships—the heart of our fleet—have been destroyed by an enemy we considered inferior." He did
not give this point long to settle; the president was not

in the mood to listen to expressions of forced optimism. "We are on the ropes, gentlemen. That is exactly why we have to strike back now. Hit the heart of Japan, the way they have hit us."

There was silence around the table, the president's advisors, both civilian and military, wondering whether he was stating broad and indefinite goals, as politicians were given to do, or actually had some specific military action in mind. The latter made no sense to them; every military professional around that table considered an American offensive operation to be impossible in the foreseeable future.

One of the admirals seated at the table leaned forward, the brass and ribbons of his uniform reflecting in the polished mahogany surface, and said, "Strike back, sir? With all respect, Mr. President, we're still pulling corpses and wreckage off the bottom of Pearl Harbor."

Roosevelt's distinctive chin, already jutted forward, remained fixed; only the muscles of his jaw flexed.

The others left it to General Marshall, who had always been able to disagree with Roosevelt and still retain his respect, to speak up now. "Mr. President," Marshall said, "Pearl Harbor caught us because we didn't face facts. This isn't a time for ignoring them again. The Army Air Corps has long-range bombers, but no place to launch them from. Midway's too far, China is overrun by Japanese forces, and Russia refuses to go to war with Japan and won't allow us to launch a raid from there."

Roosevelt glared. "If the Army is incapable of doing what must be done, let it be the Navy then."

The admiral who had been leaning forward now sat

back and said, "The navy's planes are small, carry light loads, and have short range. We would have to get them within a few hundred miles of Japan, and therefore risk our carriers. And if we lose our carriers, we have no shield against invasion."

Roosevelt erupted. "Does anyone in this room think victory is possible without facing danger?! WE ARE AT WAR! Of course there is a risk!"

"But consider the risk, Mr. President!" General Marshall said, his voice steady but strong. He knew he was speaking to the man who had told America in the depths of the Great Depression, *The only thing we have to fear is fear itself.* But then they were facing lost jobs and idle factories, not bombs and bayonets. "Sir, there is not a man at this table who rose to his position by being overly cautious. We know the military value of going on the offensive, and we have all been trained to be aggressive. But we don't serve you or the American people if we tell you we can accomplish something that we simply can't do."

Roosevelt said, "Gentlemen . . . most of you did not know me when I had the use of my legs. I was strong and proud and arrogant. Now I wonder, every hour of my life, why God put me into this chair. But when I see defeat in the eyes of my countrymen—in your eyes, right now!—I start to think that maybe he brought me down for times like these, when we all need to be reminded who we truly are. That we will not give up—or give in!"

"But Mr. President," the admiral pleaded, "I must agree with General Marshall. With all respect . . . what you are asking can't be done."

Roosevelt placed his hands on the arms of his wheel-chair, and struggled to lift himself. Aides jumped to help him, but he waved them off. With a physical effort that had his neck veins bulging and sweat popping on his face, Roosevelt stood on his withered legs and looked at the men around him. "Do not tell me . . ." he said, "that it cannot be done."

Francis Stuart Low, nicknamed "Frog" among his friends, was a submarine captain in the U.S. Navy. He, like the rest of America, had felt outraged by the attack on Pearl Harbor, but he had been less surprised than most at the coming of war, for he was part of that network of officers within the Navy's overall chain of command who were informed and consulted as to problems concerning strategy and planning. He was used to hypotheticals and war game scenarios and always tried to view them with professional detachment. The outbreak of hostilities had put a new edge on such intellectual endeavors, and in the question of how to mount a raid against the Japanese—spread throughout Naval Intelligence channels on a secret basis—he caught a whiff of something far beyond the speculative. He smelled something dead serious, and the challenge of inventing a way to do what seemed impossible, something the Navy clearly had been unable to come up with a plan for, captivated him.

He found himself thinking about it day and night—not always at the front of his thoughts, but constantly turning the issue over in the lower levels of his brain.

He felt he had given up on the question—like everyone else clearly had—when he happened to visit the

Norfolk Air Station. While he was there, carrier pilots were practicing their landings out on the runways; painted on the tarmac was the outline of a carrier's flight deck, and the naval pilots were using it to hone their skills of approaching such a limited surface. Captain Low paid little attention to the Navy pilots; such practice was necessary and routine.

What did get his attention was the flying of the Army Air Corps pilots, who were returning from a training mission of their own just as the Navy planes were breaking off their practice. The Army pilots decided to make a few runs at touch-and-go landings, aiming at the carrier deck outline on the tarmac.

Low stopped and stared at them the entire time they practiced the maneuver.

Not long afterward, he called his commanding officer, who then called someone else, who called someone else . . . until the calls reached the White House.

26

So many caskets, so many flags draped upon them.

They lay in ranks, arranged on the tarmac of Hickham Field, an army of the dead.

It had taken many days to gather them this way. In the aftermath of the attack there had been so much to do. Reorganize crews and squadrons, repair or replace equipment, clear away what could not be salvaged. And among all that could not be salvaged were the bodies of the dead. They deserved respect, and those still living deserved their time of grief, but that was a luxury when every second was devoted to keeping the army of the dead from growing.

Now here they were, stretching everywhere in long rows, ready to be sent home or buried locally if that had been their wish.

Rafe stood among the mourners, the military people in their finest uniforms, the civilians in their Sunday best, and as he looked out at the sea of flag-draped coffins he thought about their destination—home—and wondered where home was for him now. Danny stood to his right, Evelyn on the other side of Danny. That was the way it was now. Rafe could be this close to her, and no closer. Evelyn was Danny's now. She was no longer home.

So where would home lie now, if not with Evelyn? Not back in Tennessee, where Danny was a part of everything he remembered. And the other places he had seen—among them the great cities of New York and London—were only places to him, not a union of body and spirit and self and others that altogether made up that place we recognize as home. Where was it now, for Rafe McCawley?

No, it was not among the dead. Love and hope had kept him alive, and though the hope was gone the love still lingered. Painful though it was, it was enough to remind him that he might love again. But he could not find hope in that now, could not imagine it, or home.

Yet as he stood there, he knew of a place where he felt he belonged. That was inside the cockpit of an airplane, in a place called War.

Evelyn could feel Rafe's thoughts, even in their very remoteness. He would not look at her; he had not let his eyes linger on her since he had walked away from her on that first night at the hospital, before the attack began, and at the hospital later, when she was setting up the transfusions, he had tried to make his arm limp and lifeless and had glanced through her as if she had become invisible to him.

There was so much she wanted to say to Rafe, though she had no words for any of it.

And Danny . . . what could she give him, how could

she comfort him, in the pain and helplessness that she knew he was feeling?

Evelyn was empty, fresh out of solace. One of those flag-draped coffins—the one directly in front of her—held Betty's body.

Danny Walker stood between the friend he could never replace and the woman he could not possibly love more than he did at this moment, nor could he ever love her less than totally, and felt himself without options. He could not retreat from Evelyn, he could never go back to being her admirer, protector, and friend. He was as stuck where he was as were his friends in the coffins.

But Danny being Danny, his mind took flight on its own, and he found himself thinking of the coffin that held the distorted dog tags that had belonged to Billy—dog tags because the metal relic was all they had located of Billy's bomb-vaporized body. The poet in Danny could not help reflect on this strange state of death and memorial, as if Billy had in a single instant crossed the boundary between body and spirit, and so—it seemed in Danny's lyrical hopes—had become freer to fly and shimmer in that unbounded world of love and reverence that gives life its only real meaning.

To Danny, this was not sentiment. He believed in survival, and knew that a body without a soul was dead, and a soul without a body was as alive, maybe more alive, than it had ever been.

That belief gave Danny his own kind of faith. And from that faith he could hope for a miracle—for only a miracle could make things right now between himself and Evelyn and Rafe.

". . . Where is God in this?" the minister was saying. "Though we cannot understand why our friends should die while we live, we can believe that with our lives comes the opportunity, the duty, to make our lives matter, as theirs did. To affirm our truest selves in our belief that any God worth divinity would choose justice, and mercy, and would take these fallen brothers and sisters into eternal peace. Amen."

Evelyn stepped forward and placed a lei of plumeria flowers on Betty's casket. She felt someone else move up beside her; it was Red, and as she glanced up to his face and their eyes met, Red burst into tears, as if something in Evelyn had made it impossible for him to hold them back any longer. Evelyn reached out to him and he fell into her arms, sobbing. Maybe she had some comfort left after all.

As Evelyn stood at Betty's coffin with Red crying on her shoulder, an Army Air Corps major stepped up to Rafe. "You Lieutenant Rafe McCawley?" he said, emphasizing the first name, since the last name was clearly printed on the nameplate of Rafe's uniform.

"Yes sir?" Rafe answered.

"And Lieutenant Daniel Walker, is he around?"

"Right there," Rafe said, as Danny, hearing his name, turned to the major.

"I have orders for you," the major said. "You're both going Stateside. We fly out in two hours." He handed them both envelopes, containing printed orders.

"What's this for, sir?" Rafe asked.

"Ask Colonel Doolittle," the major said, and walked away.

Rafe and Danny were left staring at each other. Then they both looked at Evelyn, grieving at the casket of her friend.

"Let's go pack," Danny said. "I'll tell her later."

When Rafe first arrived in Oahu he had checked into a small hotel. Officially he had been on leave; finding a place to sleep had been his own responsibility—and at that time all he could think about was his reunion with Evelyn. Now here he was, packing to leave, having had a reunion so different from any he had imagined, and still all he could think about was her.

He tried to force all that from his mind and retreat into the routine of a soldier's ordered life: he dried his shaving gear, wiped his toothbrush on the towel to remove the dampness and packed his personal gear carefully in his travel duffel. He buttoned his spare shirt, folded it and tucked it in with the last of his clothes, then tied it all tight as they'd taught him in basic training camp to do. Then he made the hotel bed as his mother had taught him to do. Always leave everything tidy, she had told him, no matter what you expect will happen after you've left.

That advice had worked for his mother's life, he reflected now, brushing the last wrinkles out of the white bedspread, but how could he heed it now?

Before he could come to any good answer, there was a knock at his door. He thought it was the cab driver, calling for him early, but when he moved to the door and opened it, Evelyn was the one standing on the other side.

He stood there looking at her. "May I come in?" she

asked. He stepped back and she walked inside. She
moved into the center of the room and looked around at
everything, the woven mat carpeting the wood floor, the
broad plantation shutter on the window, filtering the
sun into narrow slits, the ceiling fan turning slowly
overhead and his duffel bag at the foot of the bed.
"Packing?" she said, though his bag was all ready to go.

"Orders," Rafe answered.

"What kind of orders?"

"The secret kind."

"The dangerous kind," she said.

Involuntarily, her hand touched her belly. "I can't
find Danny," she said. "Did he get the orders too?"

Rafe nodded. "He's probably saying good-bye to his
squadron." . . . *Before he finds you and takes you in his
arms and kisses you good-bye like a lover should,* Rafe
wanted to add. *Like I would, if I were your lover.*

Evelyn just stood there in the center of the room, not
moving, watching Rafe flush red and look away from
her. She said, "I couldn't have you go away without you
understanding something." She moved closer to him,
and for a moment he thought—and desired with all his
being—that she would kiss him. The longing for her
touch was an agony so real it hurt him physically. His
hands wanted to reach for her; he fought to keep them
at his sides, and forced himself to turn away.

Evelyn stopped as he turned away from her. She stared
at his back as he said, "You don't need to explain."

"Yes I do," she said. "Because you're acting like I
didn't love you. You've got to get over that."

He spun around, his face reddening again. "Get over

that? Loving you kept me alive—don't you understand?"

"Don't say that . . ." Evelyn said, her voice weak, barely above a whisper.

His voice was hot and angry. "That's what you don't want to hear! You and Danny want to forget that you and me ever happened, but it's not so easy for me to do! I believed your letters, I believed you loved me, and that gave me a reason to go on, to come back."

His voice had risen far louder than he had meant for it to; he forced himself to pause, and as he did he saw the pain on her face. In that crazy moment he wanted so badly to snatch her into his arms, to kiss her. Quietly he said, "Now I feel dead already. And I just don't understand. Why, Evelyn? Why?"

"Rafe . . ." She paused. She was very pale. "I don't know any other way to say this . . . but just to say it. I'm pregnant."

The blood drained from Rafe's heart—yet he found the strength to move to her. She turned away, moved to the window and leaned toward the open slats of the shutters, as if the air could revive her.

"I wasn't really sure until the day you turned up alive . . ." she said, "and then everything happened. And now I can't tell Danny—and neither can you. All he needs to think about right now is how to do this mission and get back alive."

A pressure squeezed Rafe's head as if unseen hands meant to crush it, and the inside of his brain ached as if pierced by a screeching sound pitched higher than his ears could hear. Yet he felt painfully sober, finally understanding the truth.

She spoke to him again, her face lowered, her back to him still. "Rafe . . . all my life I've wanted one home, one place to call mine. But life has never asked me what I wanted. Now I'm going to give Danny my whole heart. But I'll never write a letter, or look at a sunset, without thinking of you. I'll love you my whole life."

She lifted her head and turned to him, the sun through the window slats catching the edges of her hair, making them strands of luminous gold. He knew he would never get the picture of this moment from his mind. Her eyes were bright with tears, but still she refused to cry.

She hurried past him, to the door and out of the room. He stood there, unable to move.

As the transport plane that would carry them back across the ocean to the mainland of America was being fueled, Rafe and Danny waited in the shade of a shelter. Their duffel bags rested beside the steel post that held up the tin roof above them; the post was scarred with shrapnel, but the crater of the bomb that had exploded on the runway had already been repaired. Rafe and Danny stood looking out over the runway until Danny said, "I told her not to come."

When the ground signaled that the plane was ready, they picked up their duffel bags and slung them over their shoulders; and just before they stepped from the shelter Evelyn came around the corner of the hangar behind them. Rafe saw her first, and Danny, seeing the look in Rafe's eyes, followed his gaze to her.

Evelyn stopped, still standing in the sunshine. Rafe's eyes held hers for a moment, and then he turned and walked to the plane, leaving Danny to move to her alone.

He reached her, set his bag down, and hugged her. "Take care," she said. "Don't be scared." She kissed him softly on the cheek, then looked at him with a smile. *Keep it light, Evelyn, she told herself. You can get through this if you just keep it light.*

Danny was not keeping it light. His eyes, soft and brown, fixed on hers as he said, "The only thing I'm scared of . . . is that you might love him more than me."

She found herself staring away from his eyes and down at the gray tarmac, baking in the sun. *Look at him, Evelyn. Look at him!* When she finally did lift her face, she gave him the best she could give him. "I do love you, Danny. And I'll be here waiting for you, when you come back."

He smiled, kissed her on the lips quick and hard, relieved and buoyed by her reassurance. He grabbed his bag, slinging it over his shoulder as he turned and hurried to the plane. As he ran up the steps she saw Rafe in the shadow of the plane's doorway—waiting for Danny, or looking at her? Danny turned and waved to her a last time before he stepped into the fuselage. He smiled and shouted something to her, but it was blown away in the wind and the revving of the plane's giant propellers. Danny ducked his head inside and the plane lurched forward.

She could not be sure, but she thought she saw Rafe, standing there in the shadows and still facing her as the plane's door closed and it began to roll away.

27

Eglin Airfield was a training facility of the U.S. Army Air Corps. It sat on the broad sandy plains of the Florida panhandle at the very edge of the Gulf of Mexico. Rafe and Danny were not told they were going to Eglin, not on the flight across the Pacific, not during their stop for refueling in Los Angeles, and not during the final leg of their journey across the United States. It was not until they stepped off the transport for the final time, and smelled the sea again, and were shown to a barracks and told to clean up, that they dared ask where they had been brought, and they were then informed of their location by a sergeant, who told them as if he found them surprisingly stupid.

The sergeant left them before either of them thought to ask what time it was; they had dozed off and on through the many hours of mind-numbing travel, but were still too tired to work out the difference in time zones. All they knew was that it was the middle of the night at Eglin Airfield, and they had twenty minutes to shower and shave.

In exactly twenty minutes a major showed up and led them across the flat sandy grounds of the airbase to a bunkerlike building built low into the ground. There were no windows; air conditioners to provide ventilation were mounted in holes cut in the bunker walls, and they hummed and dripped humidity in puddles.

The major led them inside the bunker and down a Spartan corridor. As they walked Danny and Rafe glanced at each other; the whole place reeked of secrecy. At the end of the corridor the major opened a door without knocking, stood aside for Rafe and Danny to walk in ahead of him, then closed the door behind them without entering himself.

The room was empty except for a filing cabinet, a lamp, two hardback wooden guest chairs, and Colonel Jimmy Doolittle sitting alone behind a desk.

Rafe and Danny snapped to attention and saluted. Doolittle casually returned the salute and motioned to the two chairs in front of the desk without looking up from the papers he was studying. "I heard what you did," Doolittle said.

"We can explain, Colonel," Rafe said.

"Explain what?" Doolittle said.

"Whatever it was you heard about us," Danny said.

"You mean the hula shirts you were flying in? Or the six planes you shot down? You're both being awarded the Silver Star, and promoted to captain." Doolittle sat back in his chair and looked at them.

Rafe coughed, and asked, "Is that the good news, sir, or—"

"You're just about the only pilots in the Army with combat experience, and I need you for a mission I've been ordered to put together. Do you know what 'top secret' is?"

Rafe and Danny looked at each other. How do you answer a question like that, coming from Colonel Doolittle? Danny wasn't about to try, so Rafe said, "Yes, sir. You mean the kind of mission where you win medals—and they send 'em to your relatives."

Doolittle allowed himself a smile. " 'Top secret' means you train for something never done before in aviation history, and go without knowing where you're going. And you have to accept on that basis, or not at all."

"I'll go, sir," Rafe said.

"So will I," Danny said.

"Go get some sleep," Doolittle said. "You both look awful. We'll start tomorrow, I want you to join me for breakfast. I've picked some other pilots—" he glanced down at the files he had been studying on his desk— "and I'll want you to get to know all of them in such a way that they're comfortable talking with you. The fact that you've been in combat and have come through it successfully will be important for their attitude."

Doolittle went back to his paperwork. Rafe and Danny sat there, waiting to be dismissed, hesitating as if they thought the spooky major might magically appear again and tell them what to do. "Is . . . that all, sir?" Rafe asked.

Doolittle's eyes snapped up at them. They were pale in the lamplight, rimmed with red; they realized he had been awake longer than they had, and whatever it was he was planning, it had him edgy.

"I just . . . wondered if that was all you had to tell us, sir," Rafe said.

"There's only one other thing I can tell you," Doolittle said. "You won't need any hula shirts." Rafe and Danny winced, stood, and moved to the door. "By the way, McCawley," Doolittle said, "the Brits sent me that box, it's your personal effects, from the barracks in England."

There was a cardboard shipping packet the size of a shoebox on top of the filing cabinet beside the door. Rafe tucked it under his arm, and his eyes met Doolittle's for only an instant, before Doolittle went back to his paperwork and Rafe and Danny stepped back out into the corridor.

The night was cool, even this far south, even on a Gulf Coast beach. It was winter, after all, and even the few stragglers who walked the beach thought nothing of Rafe's lone figure building the tiny fire of driftwood. The wood burned well—he had found it back among the dunes, soft and dry—and he soon had a small but vigorous little blaze.

He knelt beside it, and opened the box containing his letters from Evelyn, the ones the Brits had sent back to Doolittle among Rafe's personal effects, after he had been shot down. While in Spain with the Resistance, he had wondered what would become of these letters; he had thought his parents would end up with them, then maybe pass them back to Evelyn. But now they were in Rafe's hands again, and there was no one to whom he could pass them on.

He could not keep them himself. He knew that now. Back in the new barracks after meeting Doolittle he had been tempted, once in his room—here at Eglin each pi-

lot had his own cubicle—to open the letters and read
them again, but he could not put himself through that
torture.

So now he watched the flames dancing up from the
driftwood, and upon those flames he laid the letters
from Evelyn, laid them as tenderly as a warrior would
lay the body of his children upon a funeral pyre, placing
them there tenderly but feeding them to the fire
nonetheless.

He did not watch them burn, but stared instead out
toward the water, where the waves were low and dull
and the night fog blotted out the stars. He heard a voice
behind him say, "You can't sleep either?" and turned to
see Danny stepping out of the darkness.

Rafe glanced down at the fire; the letters were already weightless black flakes. As Rafe continued to
stare into the flames Danny sat down beside him.

They sat there a good while, until Rafe spoke, still
looking into his little fire. "This ain't no time to leave
things unsaid."

"You got that right," Danny answered.

"Gotta face facts," Rafe said. "And the fact is, we
both love the same woman."

"Not gonna hit me again, are ya?" Danny asked,
smiling.

"Even before you came to live with me and my folks,
we were brothers—"

"I know that, Rafe, but I couldn't have stopped what
happened with me and Evelyn, any more than you
could'a quit loving her."

"That's what I'm trying to tell you. You and I are
family, and I figured Evelyn and I would be family too.

But if I blame you for what happened—for what's a fact now—I lose you both."

"What are you saying?" Danny said.

"You're a good man already, Danny," Rafe said. "You'll be a good husband. And a great father . . . someday. And maybe all of us can still be a family."

Danny understood exactly what Rafe was giving him: better than forgiveness. Danny nodded.

"But I don't want you to go on this mission," Rafe added.

"What do you mean? How could I not go on this mission?" Danny felt himself growing angry again.

"She loves you," Rafe said insistently, as if that explained it all.

"You're not leaving me behind this time." There was no argument Rafe could make that would change Danny's choice, and that was clear to both of them.

"Then you listen," Rafe said. "You go, you gotta come back alive. You and me, we look out for each other. But if it comes down to a choice between one of us or both of us not making it—then you make the choice to come back. Okay?"

Danny looked at him, dead serious . . . and then smiled. "Ain't no Jap ever born, can kill us."

"You got that right, country boy," Rafe said. He smiled too.

And Danny hoped they would both laugh and joke, maybe even go drink some beer together. But Rafe just kept sitting there, looking out at the featureless sea and the starless sky.

28

Doolittle had ordered them all assembled inside a hangar at Eglin. The sun had only just cracked the horizon and the air still wore the morning chill, but the young flyers in that hangar were excited. Red and Anthony had come in late the previous night, and there were other airmen along with them who carried themselves like what they were, the best the Army Air Corps had to offer.

In the hangar was a bomber, a B-25, one of the Army's new medium range aircraft, quicker and smaller than a B-17. The plane was a rich green, with stiff wings and a distinctive tail punctuated by vertical stabilizers on either side; there was something bulldog tough about its stocky appearance and blunt nose. Its presence was nothing remarkable, here at a major airbase, but Rafe and Danny were already acquainted with some of the men assembled there, and knew at least two of them to be bombardiers. The B-25 carried a four-man crew and there were seventy or eighty men in the room. What was Doolittle putting together here?

"Attention!" a sergeant announced, and Doolittle strode into the room.

"At ease," Doolittle said. "Be seated." The young fly- ers settled into the folding chairs placed in a square fac- ing Doolittle, and the B-25 behind him. Doolittle stood before them, straight as an oak, chin high, eyes clear. At forty-five he was two decades older than most of the air- men there, but none of them would have readily tangled with him in a bar. He was steely, as colonels tended to be, but he was relaxed too; in the presence of airplanes, Doolittle exuded confidence.

"You've all been handpicked," he said. "The mission I've chosen you for is top secret. It is daring and it is dangerous. Look at the man beside you. It's a good bet that six weeks from now, either you or he will be dead."

Danny leaned close to Rafe and whispered, loudly enough for the other pilots to hear his bravado, "What color flowers do you want me to bring to your funeral?" The men around him snickered, and Doolittle himself was not displeased; cockiness was good among pilots.

Rafe said in return, "You choose—since I'll be the one bringing 'em for you."

"Okay," Doolittle said, serious again, "Anyone who'd like to drop out can do so now, no questions asked."

No one even thought of leaving.

Doolittle nodded; that was that. "In flight school," he said, "you all qualified both in single and in multi- engine planes. You'll be flying multi-engines here."

Rafe and Danny looked at each other. *Bombers.*

"I want to introduce a couple of people," Doolittle went on, and nodded toward an officer standing to his left. "Doc White here is a flight surgeon. He has volunteered for gunnery training so that he can go on the mission, because we can't spare the weight of an extra man."

Again Rafe and Danny exchanged a glance. A *long-range* bombing mission.

". . . And Ross Greening," Doolittle said, "our gunnery and bombing officer, who will oversee your equipment and your training in low-altitude work."

Low level? What the hell kind of mission is this?

Doolittle gestured to Greening, on his right, Greening nodded to the assembly, and Doolittle was essentially done with his briefing. "I emphasize for a last time that this is top secret," he said. "You tell no one, you do exactly as I tell you. Any questions?"

Rafe spoke up, "Who'll be the first one in, Colonel? I'd like to volunteer."

Danny elbowed him in the ribs so hard it took Rafe's breath away.

"I thought I'd made it clear," Doolittle said. "I'm not just putting this mission together, I'm leading it myself."

Danny leaned closer to Rafe and whispered again, this time so no one else could hear. "I take it back, about the flowers. We're *all* gonna die."

Evelyn worked at the hospital in rolling shifts, eight hours on, four hours off, around the clock.

Out in the harbor they were putting things back together again, repairing, restoring, renewing wherever they could.

Inside the hospital they did the same thing, and gradually the red of the place began to recede, and its whiteness was restored again.

She tried to think only of her duty—her immediate

duty, the bandages she had to change at that moment, the medications she had to keep track of, the letter she had to write for the sailor who now had no hands, or read for the one who had no eyes.

In two months, Evelyn herself received one letter from Danny. He wrote—

> *My dearest Evelyn,*
>
> *They censor our letters—an intelligence officer actually sits down and reads them before they get sent along—to be sure that nothing we are doing gets mentioned.*
>
> *This is all right with me. I don't have any wish to talk about what we're doing. I do want to talk about you and me and the future, and the fact that someone else besides you will be reading this first doesn't trouble me either, because I know that what is between you and me is—and always will be—just between you and me. No one else will know completely or understand fully just what it is that exists between us, and only God knows the future.*
>
> *But no, wait, that isn't quite true either. I know the future, at least this much of it: I love you, and always will.*
>
> *Danny*

Rafe of course did not write her at all, and she knew that he would not. She had no doubt that he would never write her another letter, ever again.

But he was the only person on earth besides herself

who knew of the baby growing inside her, and in that way they shared the deepest secret of her life.

No ... perhaps not the deepest secret. That secret was so deep that Danny could never know it, Rafe could only suspect it and even Evelyn could only half realize it herself. The deepest secret of Evelyn's life revealed itself to her one evening, when she was lying down in her bunk to get a few hours of rest before she had to rise again and work all night. Usually, in her exhaustion, she would fall asleep as soon as her head touched the pillow, but this night she thought of Betty, dying so young, and reflected for a moment that Betty had escaped growing old. The thought caused Evelyn to realize that since she had survived the greatest catastrophe of the century then perhaps she just might grow old herself.

The notion did not trouble her; it seemed nothing more than an idle thought. But as she settled down into bed and placed her cheek against the soft cotton of the pillowcase, she realized with sudden and disturbing clarity that, if and when she did become an old, old woman, then the letters that she would read again, if only in her mind, would be the ones that she had once received from Rafe.

Back at Eglin, they trained. Doolittle devised their preparation for the mission and personally supervised every detail. The objectives and methods of the mission remained secret to the young pilots, but whatever it was involved takeoffs from an extremely short runway followed by an extended period of low-level flying.

They spent hour upon hour struggling to get their bombers airborne in an impossibly short acceleration run, and Doolittle himself was right there with them, developing and honing the necessary techniques and skills. Once they had been taught to treat their planes like sensitive animals, giving them loving care and handling them carefully to insure their performance; now they pushed their equipment as hard as they drove themselves, revving engines to the redline before starting their full-throttle runs along the airbase tarmac, then tugging the control stick back so that the planes shuddered into the sky.

Ross Greening stripped the bombers of extra weight and dispensed with the Norden bombsights they had been designed to carry. The Norden, a watermelon-sized amalgam of gears, gyroscopes and timing equipment encased in black steel, was an amazing and highly secret weapon that enabled remarkably accurate bombing from high altitudes, but from what the pilots could tell from their training, the mission did not promise to involve anything above treetop level. Greening removed the heavy Norden sights from every plane and replaced them with a makeshift device he had made from a strip of aluminum on a swivel, used more like a gun sight than a tool for aiming bombs.

They practiced with this simple device, skimming the Florida terrain at high speed and dropping sacks of flour onto targets staked into the sandy ground. It was a challenge for the bombardiers, and the young pilots found the process fun.

In all that time they never practiced landing. The possible implications of this were not lost on the men. But none of them mentioned any fear. They revered Doolittle for his accomplishments, they respected him for training alongside them, they admired the skill he displayed. Most of all they trusted him. He would, they knew, lead them on a dangerous mission, if such a mission were necessary; but he would not do so without a plan for getting them back alive. If they knew anything about Jimmy Doolittle, they knew that for sure.

The days crawled by for Danny. Every hour he was away from Evelyn was an hour in which he felt separated from all that gave him identity and meaning. He loved flying as he always had, but the previous affections of his life had grown empty without her. His writing, however, had taken on new meaning, for though he could not compose or send letters to her, he could write her poems. Some of these he scribbled down on paper during the few private moments he could find, but mostly he kept them only in his heart, where he lived in the new knowledge that he loved someone on earth more than he loved himself.

Rafe, for his part, lost track of time—the mark of great happiness, or of intense misery. He accomplished the feat by plunging fully into the task at hand. Because that task involved flying, abandoning his private grief was easier. The bombers were not fast, nor were they nimble like the fighters he had been flying; piloting them on short takeoffs or tree-skimming runs required instinct and anticipation. The demands were a blessing. He did not think of living or dying, not while he was training. He was flying a plane, and for now that was all he wanted to think about.

But at dawn, when the sun first cracked the horizon, or at sunset, when the sky went deeper blue and the edges of every shred of cloud glowed pink and orange, he could not help but think of Evelyn—and not even so much now where she was or what she was doing, for he knew the physical reality of her life was now lost to him, but rather he remembered how full he had felt when he had been able to hope that one day their bodies would be as united as their spirits were, and he could not help but ache with the emptiness of an absence he no longer had any hope of filling, ever again.

29

They took off from Florida, sixteen B-25s, on a day when spring had already come to the Gulf Coast. Even now, leaving Eglin Field for the last time, they practiced their skills, flying low along the contours of the earth as they made their way across the continent, passing state after state, flying over the farms and small towns, the fields and the families of America.

They landed in San Francisco, near the harbor, and were told to report in a matter of hours to the docks where the U.S.S. *Hornet*, one of the aircraft carriers that had escaped the Japanese attack on Pearl Harbor, lay at anchor.

When they reached the *Hornet* they found their planes being loaded aboard the giant vessel, and the pilots were each assigned a sleeping berth aboard the carrier. Still they had no idea of their ultimate destination; even the sailors aboard ship did not know. The seamen were all aware of the uniqueness of the situation; they had never seen or heard of U.S. Army bombers being loaded onto an aircraft carrier, and rumors began to circulate. Some of the sailors thought they would be taking these planes all the way to Europe; others whispered that America must have a secret base from which these planes could be launched against Japanese targets in the Pacific.

The pilots kept their mouths shut. Doolittle would tell them when he was good and ready.

The moment came when the *Hornet*, accompanied by her escorts and support vessels, steamed from San Francisco Harbor. The battle group was just passing beneath the Golden Gate Bridge when the pilots received orders to assemble in the carrier's main briefing room.

They gathered there, pilots and their flight crews, and Colonel Doolittle got right to the point. "Well gentlemen. I can now tell you that our target is Tokyo. We are going to bomb it."

The men in the room, full of training, nerves, youth, and pent-up energy, broke into exultation. They yelled, laughed, slapped each other's backs and knees. Rafe, Danny, Anthony and Red, who had lived through Pearl Harbor and knew friends who had not, were quieter in their celebration, savoring the prospect of revenge.

Doolittle let the men have their moment of release from the suspense, but he did not let the exuberance get out of hand. "The Navy will get us to within four hundred miles of the Japanese coast," he told them. "We'll launch off the carriers from there."

This news was received with a protracted silence. The pilots were not prepared for the thought of a carrier launch. Doolittle knew they would be surprised, so he gave them time to let this sink in.

Anthony raised his hand and spoke up. "Sir, we all

thought you were just transporting these to some small airfield."

Doolittle just stared at him, and Anthony, wishing he had kept quiet, compounded his mistake. "I mean, sir . . . has this ever been done, launching army bombers off navy carriers?"

"No," Doolittle replied. "Any other questions?"

Red lifted a hand and said, "C-Colonel, we've been practicing t-takeoffs, but—" Not wanting to embarrass himself by stuttering in front of Doolittle, Red looked to Rafe for help.

"Colonel," Rafe said, "I think Red's just a little nervous because he doesn't know if any of us can land on this carrier deck."

"We won't have the fuel to get back to the carriers," Doolittle answered, "so they'll run back to Hawaii the minute we're airborne."

"B-but if the carriers head home," Red blurted out, "where do we land?"

Doolittle scanned the room full of young flyers, with not a trace of irony in his eyes or his voice as he answered, "I have a phrase I want you all to memorize: *Lushu hoo megwa fugi.* It means 'I am an American.' In Chinese."

———

Thirty minutes after Doolittle concluded his briefing, the *Hornet* was plowing her way westward, and Danny and Rafe stood alone at the end of the flight deck, far over the surging sea. They had just paced the entire length of the deck—repeating their measurement walking in the opposite direction, to be sure of the count.

"It's shorter than our practice runway," Rafe said. "And we'll be loaded with two thousand pounds of bombs and fifteen hundred pounds of fuel."

"I got another Chinese phrase for Doolittle," Danny said, "*Mug wump rickshaw mushu pork*. It means 'Who thought up this shit?' "

Anthony, Red and the other pilots were out pacing the deck too, everyone acting as if the measurement was simply a matter of professional curiosity. As Colonel Doolittle emerged from the main door and moved out onto the flight deck the pilots stopped their careful pacing and shifted into a casual stroll, as if all of them had happened to want a breath of fresh air out on the flight deck, all at the same time.

Doolittle pretended not to notice this; he moved up to Rafe and Danny and stood there with them, looking off the end of the flight deck. When neither of them spoke, he prodded, "Got a problem? Say it."

"Well, sir," Rafe said, "we've only got sixteen planes . . ."

"So . . . ?"

"So how much difference are we really gonna make?"

"We're not backing down, sir," Danny added quickly. "It's just something we'd like to know since we might die doing it."

Doolittle nodded. He took a moment, looking at them, at the other young pilots walking the decks behind them, at the endless sea before them, before answering. "At Pearl they hit us with a sledgehammer. On this raid, even if we get through, we only hit them with a needle—but it'll be right to their little sneak-attacking brains. You understand?"

Rafe and Danny both nodded, but Doolittle knew he hadn't made himself completely clear. "Victory," he said, "belongs to those who believe in it the most, and believe in it the longest. We're gonna believe—and we're gonna make America believe too."

Doolittle turned and walked casually among his men, strolling the deck as they did, letting them know by his very presence that he was confident they could do what no one had ever done before, showing them through his own calm determination that they could not only accomplish their mission, but survive it too.

Oahu, home of Pearl Harbor and all the other islands in the Hawaiian chain, now stood in a state of constant military alert. The damage had been repaired around the military bases, and the presence of war in the air had given the whole environment a new edge. Even around the base housing, where officers' families lived in individual bungalows, a squared-away military attitude now prevailed, with children's toys cleaned up from the lawns, and tricycles and bicycles returned to the front porches every evening. The officers came and went on exacting schedules; after the events of a few months before, none of them would be late to his post for the rest of his career.

It was from one of these bungalows that Major Jackson stepped and walked toward the Jeep that he drove every morning to his job on the base. But this morning as he reached his Jeep, a tired-looking nurse stepped from the shade of the palm trees where she had been waiting, and said, "Excuse me, Major Jackson. Do you remember me?"

Jackson would never forget her face, even if he had seen it from a different angle, lying on his back with his eyes rolled up toward her as she kept her fingers plugging the torn artery that was leaking his life away. "I do," Jackson said simply. He studied her face now. He remembered her as extraordinarily beautiful, literally having seen her as a guardian angel; she still looked beautiful, but she was exhausted, her face pale and underfed, her eyes red from too little sleep. Jackson had heard how hard the nurses were working; he had seen it himself, during his four weeks in the hospital. "Are you getting any rest at all over there?" he asked.

"Not much." She tried a smile; there was no joy in it. She seemed nervous to him. She obviously had come for something.

He touched the scars on his neck and said, "I meant to thank you—"

"I know a way," she said abruptly. "You can let me listen."

"Excuse me?" he said.

"When the news starts coming in, about the mission those pilots are on."

He hesitated, frowned. "I don't know what . . ."

"There's a mission. Something's going to happen. You're in Intelligence and—"

He turned toward his Jeep, trying to move away from her.

"I'm sorry, I don't know what you're talking about," he said.

"You're in Intelligence, you do know what I'm talking about."

"I can have you arrested."

"For what, proving that the guys in Intelligence aren't the only ones who have any?" she said. She gripped his hand upon the steering wheel. "Major! I don't want to know any more than I already do—that two men I care about very deeply are going into great danger, and I'm useless as a nurse and as a human being, worrying about what's going to become of them."

He took a moment to compose his thoughts. "Look," he said, "I can't discuss anything with you. You know that. We shouldn't even be talking."

"You're in Intelligence. That's no secret."

"Technically, it is."

"Technically . . . Listen to me, Major. I fell in love with a pilot. I lived for months wondering every minute where he was, how he was, if he was alive. Every twinge I had, every little fear, wanted to explode inside me, into panic, like maybe I'd just sensed his death or—" She knew she wasn't making sense; how was he going to understand? "Now two men I . . . Two men that matter to me are on a mission that's so secret they're not even allowed to write me."

"I understand it's difficult," Jackson said, and he hated his tone of voice. He knew he was sounding like he thought she was just a hysterical woman; the truth was, he envied any man who had a woman who cared about him that way. "But there is a war going on, there are missions everywhere, and I'm not free to discuss any of them—that do or don't exist," he added, unconvincingly.

Without wanting to, Evelyn touched her belly, where

the baby grew secretly. "Pearl will be the listening point, in that windowless building you go to, with the twenty-foot antennas on the roof."

He was surprised at how much she realized. He wondered for a crazy moment if this wasn't some test of his loyalty, worked out by the government's spooks.

"I worked in the War Department infirmary," Evelyn said firmly, "and I have security clearance. All I want is to be there, when the news comes in, to tell if they've lived or died."

"Most officers would have you thrown in the brig," Jackson said.

"Most nurses would've gone on to somebody else instead of keeping their fingers plugged in your artery."

Jackson stared at her. She stared back. Then she let go of his hand on the steering wheel and stepped back from the Jeep. He looked at her for a moment, then started the Jeep and drove away.

On Sunday the 12th of April, the *Hornet* rendezvoused with the U.S.S. *Enterprise* and its support ships, and the battle group made its way west through heavy weather. They traveled as Yamamoto had done, through the Vacant Sea.

The weather was against the American fleet, and their headway was slower than Admiral Halsey had hoped. Still, the timetable was less crucial than stealth, for discovery of his ships by the Japanese military would jeopardize not just the mission but the United States' entire military capability in the Pacific, and the closer they drew to the Japanese mainland the greater the danger grew. Once they were within range of

Japan's land-based bombers, a sighting of the battle group meant that Halsey could lose his carriers, and if he did that, the war was all but lost.

So while the heavy weather slowed them down, it made them harder to find; visibility was reduced, and scout planes were hampered. Halsey, in charge of the operation until the planes had left the deck of his carrier, did not curse his luck, and stared as objectively as he could at the cold hard facts.

Late that night the storm they had been fighting all the way across the Pacific began to weaken a bit, and though they were still many hours and hundreds of nautical miles away from their planned launch point, Halsey gave orders to begin the initial preparations. Deck crews began removing the lashings that had tethered the B-25s during their voyage. Ordinancemen hoisted four bombs into each aircraft, and the army gunners loaded ammunition for the machine guns.

Doolittle and Ross Greening oversaw the preparations from the shelter of the observation deck. Doolittle marveled at the way the Navy boys scurried around, fearless in doing their jobs, ignoring the heaving of the slick planks beneath their feet, the rain lashing their faces, the wind blowing their bodies off balance. As a boy he had read Robert Louis Stevenson's adventure novel *Kidnapped*, a story involving a soldier who finds himself surrounded by hostile sailors on a ship; the soldier in his arrogance thinks of the sailors as cowards, as they are uneasy with hand-to-hand battle, but when a tempest strikes, the terrified soldier stands in awe of the sailors scrambling high above the waves, among the spars and sails. Doolittle felt like that soldier now.

Next to him Greening continually fidgeted over a battered sheet of calculations, and Doolittle finally turned to him and said, "Ross, you keep messing with that slide rule, you're just going to wear it out."

"Colonel," Greening answered, "I've just about done that, and I have to tell you . . . even if everything goes right, I can't promise you they'll make it."

Doolittle looked away again, out over the rainswept decks. "I know," he said. "We might lose this battle. But we're gonna win this war. Know how I know?" Greening waited; he felt a reverence for Doolittle, and would not interrupt him. "Them," Doolittle went on, nodding to where Rafe and Danny were checking the mechanical and hydraulic systems of their bombers. "They seem rare, because they don't stand out in times when people are looking for the next hairstyle or the newest dance. But in times like these, you see young men like them stepping forward."

Doolittle looked directly at Greening with that distinctive stare of his and said, "There's just nothing stronger than the heart of a volunteer."

Together they looked again, out at the bombers and the men who would fly them.

And in that moment, Doolittle made a decision.

Once again he assembled the flyers in the carrier *Hornet*'s briefing room. "We'll take off late this afternoon," Doolittle said. "We'll drop our fire and then it's on to China. Simple as that."

A young flyer raised his hand. "Colonel, you've given us the homing beacons, but you've also told us that China is overrun with Japanese troops. What do we do if the beacons aren't switched on?"

"If that happens you get down any way you can, and do your best to avoid capture. The Chinese will help any way they can."

Doolittle paused and waited for more questions; he wanted to give his men a chance to feel that everything was settled, every loose piece of the plan had been found and tightened down. A pilot near the back of the room, behind Rafe and Danny, raised his hand and asked, "Colonel? What do we do if our planes are damaged over Japan and have to be abandoned there?"

Doolittle nodded, acknowledging the fairness of the question. "I wasn't built to be a prisoner," he said. "If my plane gets crippled, I'm gonna have my crew bail out, and then I'm gonna drive it into any military target I can find. That's just me. But hell, I'm an old man, I'm forty-five. You boys are just starting out in life, so what you do is up to you."

But the young faces in that room were committed to doing exactly what Doolittle intended; he was the man they wished to be.

For the last three months, Evelyn had watched wounds heal. Raw screaming mouths of ripped flesh had closed, had ceased to weep blood, had faded from angry red to tender pink beneath her clean and careful hands. Every day as she changed bandages, fought pain and infection and brought broken men solace from despair, she had seen the miracle of healing. She saw the men under her care make the trip from agony to health, from misery to hope, and wondered if the great and mysterious power that made this transformation natural would carry her heart on the same journey.

But every day the life grew within her belly, and every day she hid it, she knew she moved one day closer to the time when she could hide it no longer.

So she washed the wounds, changed the bandages, cut away the casts to expose the stale flesh beneath to the fresh and purifying air, and she prayed that the God who had turned His face from her would look down, not on her but on the men she loved, and spare her just enough to make her a fit vessel for the innocent life she carried.

It was late one morning, and she was removing the sutures from a sailor's arm when she looked up and saw Jackson standing at the door. He held a security pass in his hand, and she understood in that moment that somewhere in the vast unknown called War the dangers to the men she loved were about to begin, and all her questions about hope and the future were soon to find their answers.

30

They were fishermen, not warriors of the Japanese military. But when they were commanded to become part of the machinery of Imperial Japan they accepted their orders dutifully and took up their position in the picket line of vessels spread around the islands as an early warning system. They were even allowed to continue their fishing, whenever it did not conflict with their responsibility to keep watch for any intrusion of American vessels.

The men on the *Nitto Maru* were used to sailing the vast waters of the Pacific for days on end without seeing another boat, and so they could not have been prepared for the sight that greeted them in the early morning hours of April 18, 1942, when they sighted not one but an entire flotilla of huge ships steaming directly toward Japan. It was a confusing and disturbing sight for the fishermen; they had not been trained in the art of identifying enemy vessels or even of recognizing whether the ships coming toward them were enemy or friendly, but this was something they were sure they must report.

One of them, Nakamura Suekichi, ran to the boat's skipper, Gisaku Maeda, who had already begun radioing the *Kiso*, flagship of the Japanese Fifth Fleet, when they saw a flash from one of the ships steaming toward them—it was the U.S.S. *Nashville*—and shells began to explode near them in the water.

Rafe and Danny, like the other pilots, were in their bunks trying to rest for the long trip ahead of them when they heard alarms going off all over the ship and the intercom began to blare: "Battle stations, battle stations! All hands man your battle stations!" They poked their heads out into the hallway and saw sailors running everywhere.

"We're too far from Japan, is this some kinda drill?" Danny wondered.

"I don't know," Rafe said. "Something's got 'em stirred up."

Colonel Doolittle ran to the command bridge of the *Hornet* and found Admiral Halsey gathered there with his staff. "We've got a problem," Halsey said, and Doolittle had no doubt what that was; he could see the cruisers out in front of them firing their deck guns.

"How far are we from Tokyo?" Doolittle asked.

"Seven hundred miles," came the reply.

A few minutes later, the carrier's loudspeakers announced the order, "Pilots, man your planes!"

The building Major Jackson led Evelyn into did not look unusual at its entrance, except that there was no sign near the doorway to tell any visitor what it was. If anyone had asked, they would have been told it was a relay station, to explain the array of long-range antennae on its roof. Evelyn followed Jackson through two long hallways guarded by armed sentries and into a bunkerlike room where a dozen stenographers and code breakers worked at desks. Beyond this area she glimpsed, through heavy glass, a separate listening room where tense men manned radio receivers and Teletype relays. Jackson walked Evelyn through the double doors of this room and to an empty desk, where he whispered, "Don't talk to them, and they won't talk to you. Just pretend to type the information we pass you." The room stank of cigarette smoke and tension sweat, and Evelyn, wanting to vomit, felt her stomach twist and knot, but maybe that was her own nerves, more than just the smell.

Jackson had just taken a seat among the men wearing headphones when one of them, a Japanese American, turned to him and said, "We're picking up Japanese transmissions. . . . They've spotted our carriers."

Already Evelyn had begun to wish she hadn't come.

More than two thousand miles away, the men on the bridge of the carrier *Hornet* were turning their great ship into the wind and urging maximum speed out of her powerful engines. The Army pilots were running out onto the deck; the naval deck crew was already there, fighting the wind, checking signals, scrambling to deal with the sudden change in the launch plans. The cruiser next to the *Hornet* was still firing away at the Japanese patrol boat.

Doolittle ran onto the deck, and found Ross Greening already at work. "We're too far out to make it!" Greening shouted above the noise of the wind and rain. "The planes need more gas, but they've gotta be lighter to get off!"

Doolittle's plane was already set at the head of the line; directly behind it were the two bombers Rafe and Danny would fly, and he saw them both standing between their aircraft, waiting for his orders. He ran to them and said, "Strip everything you don't need out of the planes. I mean everything! Pass the word for everybody else to do the same!"

As they scrambled to follow his orders, Doolittle moved back to Greening and said, "Ross, you better figure something out fast."

The additional three hundred miles made every ounce of weight and every drop of fuel loom critical. The flyers in the line of planes behind them began tossing out the extra gear that they had planned to carry on their flight over Japan and into China. One navigator threw out a phonograph and records; another flyer threw out a large supply of toilet paper rolls, having heard there would be no such thing in China. Still, they weren't being ruthless enough for Greening; he jumped into a plane, unbolted the steel seat at the copilot's position and tossed it onto the deck in front of a shocked Red.

Red moved underneath the plane and poked his head up through the belly hatch. "Where am I gonna sit?" Greening's answer was to slap a light wooden crate into the seat's place. "I'm supposed to fly eight hours sittin' on that?" Red blurted out.

"You and your whole crew better take a piss before you take off, or you'll never clear the deck," Greening said as he climbed down past Red and moved on to the next plane.

Greening then forced himself to stop and think for a moment. He turned and grabbed a sailor. "Go get me brooms, mops, anything with a long wooden handle. And tar, black tar! And brushes!" The sailor didn't hesitate, but hurried away. When he ran back onto the flight deck he found Greening pulling the machine guns from the rear position of the planes. "Saw off the handles," Greening told the deck crews. "Paint them black and mount them in place of the guns. Then go to the kitchen and get those big soup kettles and fill them with fuel like spare tanks. Go!" Off in the distance the Japanese patrol boat took a hit and exploded.

Rafe and Danny met again between their bombers. Their rear gunners were tossing ammo belts out onto the deck and mounting the blackened sticks.

"Broomsticks instead of tail guns," Danny said quietly.

"At least maybe it'll scare the Japs," Rafe said.

They exchanged a glance, and climbed into their bombers.

In the Mission Monitoring Room all the technicians sat slumped, tired and tense like frozen mud, straining for every sound and hearing only static through their headsets. Evelyn had quickly given up on trying to look busy; no one was watching her anyway. Then one of the men on the headsets—he was the Washington relay operator—perked up, listening. He muttered, "Roger," into a mouthpiece, covered it with his hand, and announced to the room, "The War Department thinks they should scratch."

Jackson just shook his head. "Then they shouldn't have picked Doolittle," he said. No one in Washington had the power to order the mission called off now; of course a number of men had the *authority,* but that was different from having the *power.* The power would be the ability to tell Admiral Halsey, in the middle of the world's largest ocean, not to rely on his better judgment; or to tell Colonel Jimmy Doolittle, once the planes left the carrier, that you knew better than he did, and there was nobody in America who could do that.

So they waited, and they listened.

On the bridge of the *Hornet* they ordered the engines to *all ahead flank* and watched the wind-speed gauges, willing them toward the level that would assure the planes a safe launch.

Doolittle sat at the controls of the lead bomber and felt the steady pounding of the engines as he pushed them to their redline. Out on the deck, the flight master showed him the WAIT sign. Ross Greening was out on the deck too, holding a chalkboard and facing Doolittle. Doolittle glanced up at the battle pennants strung along the carrier's superstructure; they whipped in the wind but were not catching much rain now. Out on his wings—Doolittle felt the plane as an extension of his own body now—the props blurred, and he could feel the wheels straining against the brakes. Out ahead of him the flight deck looked impossibly short, and if it looked that small to him he could imagine how it looked to the other pilots in his command, most of whom had never made a takeoff into combat, even from a long paved airfield, much less from the deck of an aircraft carrier pitching on the high seas. Hell, they hadn't even done this in practice. Now they were loaded with bombs, overloaded with fuel. What was he asking of these men?

His eyes found the American flag cracking in the wind.

Outside, Ross Greening took a deep breath and showed Doolittle the chalked letters: GO!

Doolittle looked up to the flight deck and saluted Admiral Halsey. Halsey returned the salute. Then Doolittle looked back one more time at Ross Greening and released the brakes.

Rafe and Danny watched through the cockpit glass of their own B-25s as the tail of Doolittle's plane began to drift away from them. The forward movement of the plane seemed impossibly slow, the props clawing through the air rushing across the deck. The inner voices saying *He'll never make it* sang in dissonance against the other voice within them saying *Jimmy Doolittle can do anything he chooses to do with an airplane, and he chooses to do this*. Halfway down the short deck the plane still seemed barely in motion—and so it was, relative to the ship; but the carrier's momentum driving into the wind gave the planes airspeed, and the added lift from that headwind was their only hope.

The moment unfolded with almost unbearable slowness for the watching pilots, and they could only imagine how it felt to Doolittle himself. Each turn of the B-25's wheels brought the plane closer to the edge of the deck, and the pace felt so ponderous that there seemed to be no possibility that the craft would become airborne; he would drop like a stone into the sea in front of the ship, and the plane would either disappear without a trace or the bombs would explode and blow Doolittle and his crew to fragments.

Doolittle reached the end of the deck and pulled straight back on the control stick; the bomber stood on its props, as the flyers liked to say, hanging almost vertical yet not stalling, rising smoothly into the air, and as easily as that, Doolittle was flying, making a long sweeping turn around the carrier. The seamen on the carrier deck cheered. The admiral and his staff on the carrier's command deck nodded in approval.

The other young pilots did what Doolittle had done, and drove their planes into the air.

On his command bridge, Admiral Halsey watched until the last plane had cleared his deck and set its course for Japan. "You know," he said quietly, to no one in particular, "that's the first time I've ever launched birds into the air without planning to be around when they came home." He paused for only the briefest moment before adding, "Okay, let's get out of here." His battle group turned as quickly as it could, and began its race back toward Pearl Harbor.

In the Mission Monitoring Room they strained to hear, but nothing was coming over their monitors. Everyone sweated; the sharp smell of their tension overpowered even the stale stink of the cigarettes. Evelyn forced herself to breathe, feeling that somehow her lungs had forgotten how to do it on their own. Her heart, however, did not have that problem; it thumped within her chest, making her body shake with every beat.

———

Out over the Pacific, sixteen planes skimmed twenty feet above the waves. Rafe and Danny could see each other, flying fifty feet apart off each other's wingtip. Doolittle's plane flew in the lead, and the rest of the bombers trailed in a narrow line behind them. All of them seemed to have made it off the decks, but no one knew for sure; the American planes maintained strict radio silence.

President Franklin Delano Roosevelt, at almost the same moment, had gathered America for what he called a Fireside Chat, a time when he sat in a room of the White House and addressed the nation over the radio; more than half the population of the United States was listening as he told them

> *"From Berlin, Rome and Tokyo, we have been described as a nation of weaklings and playboys who hire British or Russian or Chinese soldiers to do our fighting for us. Let them repeat that now! Let them tell that to General MacArthur and his men. Let them tell that to the soldiers who today are hitting hard in the far waters of the Pacific. Let them tell that to the boys in the flying fortresses. Let them tell that to the Marines."*

Roosevelt, like every man, lived with his own particular fears; he faced down those he could, and those he could not he learned to live with and take responsibility for. He did what he could do and lived with what he could not change. He did not pray to walk again; he did not pray for any victory he felt he did not deserve. But as he said these words the silent recesses of his heart, from which all true prayers come, cried out to God that Jimmy Doolittle and the young men who flew with him would be borne upon the wings of righteousness, and would deliver a just wrath upon America's enemies.

31

They flew for hours on a low straight course, the steadier the better, to conserve fuel. Along the way the gunners in the rear of the B-25 added the extra fuel to the tanks. They kept the spare cans inside the planes for one single dumping once they'd reached the mainland, as a precaution against any possibility that the Japanese might follow the trail of empty fuel cans back to the aircraft carriers, so great was the American planners' fear of losing the carriers, and therefore the entire war.

For the pilots, there was plenty of time to think but not much mental room for it. The tension of conserving fuel as they fought against the unexpectedly high headwinds, and the anticipation of the action they were about to face in an air raid on Japan's holy and most heavily defended city crowded out almost everything else.

But Rafe was able to let his instincts fly the plane, while that part of his mind that was never tethered behind the same fences that everyone else's seemed to be was free to float on its own, to look out over the waves

in the flat morning light and see in their place the green
fields of Tennessee; he could smell the oil of his father's
overalls and the fuel of his father's plane; he could feel
that he had become the man he had expected to be, not
just doing what he had always meant to do but also
standing where he had always meant to stand, for something greater and more important than his own life. He
had not, however, expected to find himself feeling so
alone when he reached this moment of attainment; he
had believed that this sense of his, of having reached a
kind of destination of his life, no matter what fate lay
ahead of him in the skies over Tokyo, would include a
woman, and the completeness of love.

Then he realized, with absolute clarity, that his life
did include love, and that was why he felt complete. He
could never have Evelyn in his life, not in the way he
had hoped, but he would always love her, and he could
not imagine that she would not love him. And as Rafe's
father used to say to his family in the depths of the Depression, *It's not enough—but it'll do.*

Danny's reflections on the seven-hundred-mile flight
to Japan were different. He thought in words, in
phrases and sentences that he wanted to say to Evelyn,
to convey to her the depth of his feeling for her. Ever
since leaving Pearl Harbor he had felt a haunting sense
of separation from her, a sense that seemed more than
physical distance. There was some kind of gulf between
their souls, a distance that he had to close. He did not
know what this gulf was; he had never loved anyone as
he loved Evelyn, and so had not known her equal or the
person he became in relationship to her. He wondered if
this strange combination of unity and division was sim-

ply part of the great mystery of love itself; whatever it was, he reached out to her in the only way he knew how, with the poetry that ran through his mind whenever he thought of her, which was always. In that flight across the western Pacific, Danny heard himself saying to Evelyn, *I will be grateful for every drop I drink from that great river of spirit that you are.*

To someone else, that might not have been poetry. Someone else might hear those words as sentimental. To Danny, they were absolutely true, an expression of exactly who he was and how he felt. And in that, Danny felt complete.

The coastline of Japan came up slightly later than they had expected it to, and the navigators in each plane adjusted their calculations accordingly. Not all the planes were targeted for Tokyo; those few planned for other cities now sheared off from the main group, and all the planes continued to fly as low as possible, skimming now over the treetops.

In Doolittle's plane they calculated their expected arrival time over Tokyo itself. His original plan had been to fly over Tokyo at dusk, when he would have the protection of low light conditions but enough illumination for targeting. He would drop incendiary bombs, and the fires they created would guide his boys in behind him as they followed under the cover of night. Now, his navigator told him, they would be hitting Tokyo at noon.

High Noon, Doolittle thought. *So be it.*

The islands of Japan, like those of Hawaii, were ringed with watchers and coastal defenses, and in the spring of 1942, unlike the seventh day of December of

1941, the United States and Japan were officially at war. Still, when ground observers, both military and civilian, noticed and reported unidentified aircraft flying in from the direction of the open ocean, their warnings were ignored in Japan as they had been several months before in Hawaii. The alarms simply did not make sense to people who thought attack to be impossible.

In Tokyo it was a pleasant day, the city brimming with optimism. War was as distant as the moon; the warriors of Japan had not only humbled China but had humiliated America, and any reminders of the armed conflict seemed to reassure more than disturb. The air-raid drills the city experienced were comforting reminders that Japan's military leaders were protecting their emperor and his city. The sirens had gone off just before noon, and the young men manned their guns, but it was only practice. In the marketplace mothers strolled with their children, and when they saw the sleek green planes flashing by, so low over the tops of the buildings, they distinctly thought, *How beautiful.*

The emperor himself saw one of the four-engine bombers fly overhead as he sat in the garden of the Royal Palace preparing to enjoy his lunch. He did not recognize the aircraft and wondered if his generals might inform him about the new planes they were developing.

At the outskirts of the city the individual planes had diverged toward their separate targets. Rafe and Danny had exchanged a wave and banked away from each other, Rafe toward an engine factory and Danny to the oil tanks near the harbor. They had studied the aerial maps together, had memorized each other's targets and flight lines, and though they could no longer see each other, Rafe carried a sense of exactly where Danny would be at any given moment, and Danny did the same in return.

The planes were on their own now, without visual or radio contact, each crew in its own world, each pilot the captain of his ship's individual fate.

The final run to the targets was an experience of constant expectation. The pilots climbed to two hundred feet, and after so long a time of skimming the waves and the rooftops, even that altitude seemed high. But the ground still rushed past, the ground structures coming into view quickly, making it crucial to stay focused on the landmarks and the rapidly closing space between the plane and the optimum release point for its bombs—all the while waiting for the burst of flak, the sudden slash of machine gun and cannon fire that would let them know the Japanese had seen them coming and would not let them leave alive.

Even in the frenzy of their preparations, the bombardiers had found time to inscribe messages on their bombs, hasty but sincere phrases chalked on the noses of the five-hundred-pounders. FOR AMERICA, some had written. FOR THE ARIZONA. FOR PEARL HARBOR. On the nose of one of the bombs in Danny's plane, Anthony had scratched the words FOR BILLY.

Rafe's bombardier worked the aluminum pivot bombsight Ross Greening had rigged up at a total cost of twenty cents per plane, and Rafe held the plane steady, scanning the skies for fighters or anti-aircraft fire. There wasn't any. He opened the bomb bay doors, set the plane on a level course, and left the moment in the hands of the bombardier. He heard the report in his headset, "Bombs away," and they all held their breath, wondering for a crazy few seconds if they could have trained all this time and flown all this way to have the bombs be duds. Then a black mass of smoke and dust leapt from the factory that was their primary target and in the next instant debris from the explosion flew up around them, some of it rising even higher than the plane itself.

Suddenly bombs were going off all over Tokyo, and at first no one had any idea where they were coming from. The Japanese military soon realized that the unusual planes people reported seeing were the ones conducting the attack, and Radio Tokyo interrupted its relaxed broadcast to tell citizens to take cover because an enemy air raid was in progress.

The Japanese tried to organize themselves to fight back, but the bombers were gone almost before anyone knew they were there. The damage was hardly massive, but it was widespread: a factory here, a refinery there, a depot at one end of the city, a field of oil tanks on the other. The military had no clear sense of how many planes had participated in the attack, and more maddening still, they had no idea whatsoever where they had come from; therefore they did not know what steps to take to keep them from coming again.

The same men who had driven Yamamoto to commit to attacking Pearl Harbor and who had sold themselves and their nation on the concept of Japanese invincibility now had to call upon their emperor and explain to him that somehow, some way, through some method they did not understand and from some launch point that they could not yet locate, America had been able to bomb Tokyo—as if the emperor had not deduced this already.

In the Mission Monitoring Room at the Intelligence Center in Pearl Harbor they picked up the broadcast of Radio Tokyo, and the Japanese American listener who monitored and translated the transmission announced to those assembled in the tight smelly room that Radio Tokyo was reporting a raid in progress and telling the citizens to take cover.

For the next fifteen days and four hours, Evelyn would not hear another shred of news concerning the fate of the men she loved.

32

"Last bomb away," Rafe's navigator said, and suddenly holes ripped through the floor of the plane, hot lead flying through the interior of the plane and ripping through the gunner. The navigator, who had just turned to watch the bomb bays close, shouted, "Gunner's hit!"

Red slid off the crate in the copilot's position and hurried back to the rear of the plane, where he found the gunner slumped and lifeless. Red plugged his headset into the intercom and said simply, "Dead."

Rafe was scanning the sky in every direction. "If that's Zeros, you gotta get 'em off me!" he called back to Red.

"Whatta ya want me to do?" Red said, "sweep 'em out of the sky?"

"It's not Zeros, it's flak!" Rafe shouted, as anti-aircraft shells crashed in the sky in front of them. He banked the bomber left and right, but everywhere he turned the black bursts of flak tossed the plane and sent shrapnel tearing through the fuselage. Rafe pushed the engine to top speed, and threw the plane into maneuvers that sent Red and the navigator bouncing off the walls, but still the flak chopped at them.

President Roosevelt sat in his wheelchair beside the fireplace in his White House office. There was no fire in the grate—the blanket over his legs helped the White House furnace keep him warm enough—but he stared at the dark hearth as if it were alive with light and flame. The weight of the world was etched upon his brow; he was a lonely man, in the loneliest job in the world.

Lingering nearby was George, his valet. Unable to endure the silence any longer, he drifted silently to Roosevelt's side. "Is there anything I can get you, Mr. President?"

"No, George." Roosevelt did not lift his eyes from the black hearth. "I'm just thinking about my sons. I'm not the first president to have sons in a war. I just wonder where the others found their strength. Every time a general comes to me with a message, I think they're about to tell me that one of my boys is dead."

George nodded, and lingered for a moment. Then, uncharacteristically, he spoke up. "I don't have sons in this war, sir," George said, and the surprise of hearing George volunteer a comment caused Roosevelt to look up at him. "But I believe if I did, I'd thank God this country has a president who feels like you do."

Roosevelt and George were still looking at each other when they heard the door open. They turned to see General Marshall enter. His appearance at the very moment of this conversation was chilling for both Roosevelt and George, and it didn't help that Marshall's face looked so grave. George's mouth went dry and he looked to Roosevelt, but saw that the president did not flinch. If anything he seemed stronger than ever—ready.

"What is it, General?" Roosevelt said firmly.

"The Chinese didn't receive our request for homing beacons until it was too late to get them set. And the planes had to take off so early they may lack the fuel to make the mainland anyway."

"So our boys are flying blind and running out of fuel."

"The Chinese are sending out search parties to try to find the crews before the Japanese patrols do, if any of the planes make it."

"God help them," Roosevelt said. He turned and stared back into the lifeless hearth.

33

The anti-aircraft attack did not last long; they were almost past Tokyo's defenses before the gunners began to fire, and in a short time Rafe's bomber was out of range of the ground-based guns. He kept climbing now and scanned the skies for any signs of Zeros coming their way, but he saw none. The Japanese didn't know where they had come from, and they wouldn't know where they were heading.

They were in broken clouds by the time they reached the western coast and the Sea of Japan. The navigator studied the coastal islands to get an exact fix on their position, and Rafe throttled back the engines to save fuel for the long run to China.

But where was Danny? Yes, the orders were specific, every crew on its own, once the planes had diverted toward their individual targets; but Rafe and Danny had an understanding. Their targets had been close enough that they should have made the coast at almost the same place at just about the same time, and two planes flying together could provide cover for each other and double their chances of spotting a safe place to land. Linking up was just sound strategy, wasn't it?

But Rafe knew he could not waste the fuel in waiting. Danny should have been here by now, or maybe had already come and gone. Rafe told himself that nobody was a better pilot, and surely Danny'd had the same luck over the target as he had. Sure, the dead gunner was not comforting, but they had caught the Japs by surprise, and surely the other planes had made it too.

Still Rafe felt a sick vacancy in his stomach as his plane cleared the mainland and headed out into the open water, with no sign of any other American planes.

Then he saw it, up ahead, flying easily and steadily at his same altitude—another green bomber.

Rafe caught up to it, and settled in on its wing. Danny looked over and smiled as if Rafe had just walked out to the pickup truck for them to go to a ball-game together. Then Danny saw the flak holes in Rafe's plane and frowned. The bombers carried emergency flashers and Danny used his to signal across in Morse code: *Trouble?*

Red signaled back, *Gunner dead. You?*

Easy came back the reply.

But no one on either plane felt any ease as they steered into the clouds and set their course for the mainland of China, where the Japanese held all the major cities and much of the countryside, but where Chiang Kai-shek's resistance fighters held portions of the countryside and were supposed to turn on homing beacons to guide them to safe landing fields—somewhere, somehow.

The clouds grew thicker, the further west they went.

Occasionally during the first hours of their flight they found breaks in the cloud cover, but by the time the sun went down they could no longer see whether they had sea or land below them.

Danny watched his fuel gauge drift steadily toward empty, and he could not fight off the uneasiness growing within him. They had long ago added the last drops of their spare fuel, and the navigator estimated they had less than a hundred miles of range left in their tanks; that would *almost* get them to the Chinese mainland, he thought, but he could not be sure, since they had been fighting an inconsistent headwind ever since they left the Japanese coast.

Anthony tried not to act nervous either, but he kept thumping the face of the receiver meant to pick up the homing signal from the Chinese. No matter how much he thumped, the receiver remained lifeless.

Night fell, and Red turned and said to Rafe without a trace of stutter, "This really was a suicide mission. I don't know if we're over sea or land."

"We're gonna make it," Rafe said.

"Yeah, we're gonna make it," Red agreed. But it was impossible for Rafe to tell what he really thought, and Rafe knew it was not just the dead gunner that had brought the stillness to Red's core and the distance to his eyes. Red had been a changed man since Pearl Harbor.

Rafe looked across at Danny, his cockpit still visible in the moonlight. He could not see Danny's face, but he knew what was there. They had less than a half hour left to find the coast. They might have less than a half hour left to live.

———

Doolittle's plane was in the same state as theirs, except that he knew he was over land; he had spotted hills through a hole in the clouds before his fuel gauges read dead empty. With no hope of any safe place to land, he climbed until his engines began to sputter, then locked down his controls and gave his crew the order to bail out.

They all went out just as the engines died, and reached the ground safely, with barely a scratch to any of them. Doolittle rounded them up and they hiked to the wreckage of their plane, on a low hill close by. Doolittle wanted to be sure they destroyed everything on the plane that could be of any use to the Japanese. But when they reached the plane he did not look inside—he just sat down dejectedly on one of its broken wings. His copilot moved up and sat down beside him. "Colonel," the copilot said, "what do you think they'll do when we get back to America?"

"I don't know," Doolittle said. "They'll probably put me in Leavenworth Prison." The mission, it seemed to him, had been a tragic failure.

On empty, Danny signaled across. *Going to bail.*

"No!" Rafe said sharply, as he read the flash. "Tell him no!" He grabbed the flasher from Red's hand and signaled back *N-O-N-O.* "Not over water," he said to Red. "Not over water!" he shouted in Danny's direction, as if he could hear.

Rafe had not realized until that moment how terrified he was of going down in the water again. Crazy thoughts flashed through his mind, of the cold he had felt before, then the numbness, and the fear, then the lack of fear, the beckoning comfort of death, with nothing but the hope of Evelyn's love to keep him fighting for life, a hope he no longer had . . .

He grit his teeth and silently screamed those thoughts from his mind. *Do something, Rafe! Do something! God help me do something!*

He saw something below and wondered if it was his imagination. The clouds were thinner, maybe they were breaking up because they were over the coast. He dropped just a few feet in altitude and suddenly saw it clearly—waves breaking against a rocky shoreline.

"Coast! Signal him that we've got coast! Tell him to stay close, I'll lead us down!"

Red snapped the flasher and Rafe put the plane into a descending turn. He hoped the sand was wide enough to land on; if not they could skim through the surf and swim to shore. The clouds were like a low ceiling with holes broken through it, so that moonlight streamed through at intervals; his visibility was not great, but he could clearly make out the frothy surf, the gray sand, and the darker, broken hills rising beyond. The strip of sand looked too narrow and he was afraid that a landing with one wingtip catching sand while the other slid through water would rip the plane apart, so he aimed for the shallow water. Red, sitting on the crate, had no seat harness, so he removed the belt from his pants, passed one end through a slot in the fuselage bracing and fastened the belt tightly around his waist again.

The B-25 handled well, and Rafe still had power in his engines; he brought her into a final downward glide and cut his speed to settle into the surf. It was then that he saw a rock tucked within the surf, a mound of stone as big as an army truck, looming in and out of the water as the waves broke over it. How many of those were there? "Hang on tight!" Rafe yelled to his crew, and decided he must risk the beach. His engines were sputtering, catching, sputtering again as they sucked the last drops of fuel; he would have no second chance. He swung the nose toward the sand, and then he saw them. There were Japanese soldiers on the beach.

His hopes were screaming inside him that maybe these men with rifles and in uniforms with their distinctive caps were Chinese, but Red saw them too and said, "Damn, we got Japs." The maps they had studied back on the *Hornet* had indicated this area of China was controlled neither by the Japanese nor the Chinese partisans; it was a no-man's-land, and they had not gotten lucky.

"We've got a Jap patrol on the beach!" Rafe shouted, as if his voice could carry to the other plane. "Get outta here, Danny! Get outta here!"

The men on the beach looked up as the plane flashed by; Rafe planned to put as much distance as he could between them and his landing spot; maybe he and his crew could get out and make it off the beach and into the hills before the soldiers reached them. His engines sputtered dead and he guided the plane onto the froth at the water's edge.

As the plane contacted the surface, the entire fuselage began to shake, and Rafe battled the controls. He heard the sound of metal ripping and rivets popping. Then a rock the size of a house seemed to fly right into the nose of the plane, and the body of the dead gunner, whom nobody had strapped down, flew into the navigator, ripped him off his seat, and carried him through the front glass of the cockpit. Just before Rafe's head slammed against his control yoke, he thought he caught a glimpse of Danny's plane flashing past, escaping.

The Japanese patrol—a half dozen men armed with rifles and bayonets in hostile territory and surprised by what they just saw—began to move cautiously along the gouged sand toward the demolished plane, several hundred yards up the beach from their encampment.

Rafe's harness had held him in place. He had a bloody gash on his forehead, but he was alive, and conscious. Red's belt had held him too, and his eyes were open, though they were rolling like drunken marbles. Rafe freed himself from his harness, and tore Red loose, yelling, "Come on, Red! We've gotta get into the hills and find the Chinese!"

Red stayed bent at the waist as if the pressure of the belt had nearly cut him in two, but he followed Rafe through the hole ripped in the side of the fuselage, and they tumbled out face first into the shallow surf. The cold water revived their senses and made them more alert. They saw the Japanese patrol, a hundred yards away, raising their weapons and firing. Rafe and Red fell back into the foot-deep water and the bullets flew high into the fuselage. Rafe didn't know if the Japs meant to keep them alive for interrogation or were just shooting high in their excitement, but the shooting did not last long.

Danny's plane came roaring back along the beach, its turret gunner chopping down the Japanese patrol. But as Danny tried to add throttle and turn for another pass, his engines sputtered out. The bomber sank fast, skipped off the water once, then dropped again. His left wingtip caught in the sand and the entire wing snapped off; the fuselage spun into a sideways slip, until the other wingtip caught and the plane spun around in the opposite direction, then hit something solid and flipped upside down.

Rafe and Red got to their feet and ran toward the crash site.

Rafe found Danny face down in the sand, the water lapping at his body. Red staggered through the darkness and found Anthony lying beside the fuselage on the rock the plane had hit before flipping over. As Red lifted him he found the back of Anthony's head was gone. Red laid Anthony back down gently and moved into the wreckage to look for the rest of Danny's crew.

"Danny! DANNY!" Rafe said, rolling him over and trying to wipe the sand from his mouth. It was so dark Rafe could not tell how hurt he was, or where he might be bleeding.

Danny's eyes fluttered open; he saw Rafe and mumbled, "I've made better landings." Danny's hand groped to his chest; Rafe pulled open Danny's shirt and found a V-shaped shard of the fuselage hooked into his side. The shard was the size of a grappling hook, biting into Danny's ribs, and Rafe, in a fit of grief and rage, grabbed the metal with his bare hands and tried to bend it away from Danny's flesh; the sharp metal cut his hands. He pulled his .45 from his jacket and tried to use the leverage of the butt and barrel to pry the metal. When Danny moaned from the pain Rafe tossed the pistol aside and grabbed the shard again with his bare hands, and strained until the metal bent enough for him to pull it from Danny's side, though now in the darkness he could not tell if the new blood at the wound was from Danny or from his own hands.

Danny's eyes squeezed shut, then opened again as he tried to breathe. "You hang on, Danny! You hang on! You're gonna make it!" Rafe said, just before his head snapped forward, crunched from behind by the butt of a rifle. As Rafe sank from his sight, Danny saw more Japanese, four soldiers. Whether they were part of the group he had strafed or were a fresh squad he had no idea, but they were furious and frightened at the same time. As Red emerged from the fuselage carrying the lifeless navigator the soldiers clubbed Red down too, yelling and brandishing their rifles at the flyers on the ground, living and dead.

One of the Japanese was an officer; he was barking orders. He found the captain's insignia on Danny's jacket and began talking even more rapidly. From somewhere they found a twisted tree branch and used it as a yoke, binding Danny's wrists to the wood as if to crucify him, and tying a wire around his neck to pin him back even farther.

Rafe lay on the sand, slipping in and out of consciousness. He was dimly aware that Red had found another flyer alive in the plane, and that both of them were being bound up too. The soldiers rolled Rafe over, shook him, slapped his face, but he remained limp and appeared unconscious. It was easy to do; his head felt huge, his spine locked in pain, his arms numb. He could feel his legs, however, and knew his ankles were wired together. Rafe felt strangely detached, as if he inhabited a dreamlike shadow of himself now, floating above the sand and looking down on everything.

Then Rafe heard Danny choking. And suddenly Rafe was no longer floating and detached, but was a boy again, watching Danny being carried by the neck across the field by his father, the boy's legs kicking the air, his face turning red as he struggled to breathe against the bullying brutality that treated him as if he were nothing. Then Rafe was no longer a boy full of fury, but a man full of pain, being dragged along the sand, pulled by his ankles like a plow through a field. He opened his eyes and saw Danny ahead of him, being half-carried, half-dragged by the neck by two Japanese soldiers. Their officer pulled Red along, hands bound behind him.

The beach was rocky, and maybe it was the smooth hard rocks mixed among the sand that reminded Rafe of the pistol he had tossed aside in the darkness, before the Japanese had gotten to him. Had they looked for the pistol? Why would they, if they had not seen him toss it aside? They seemed in a hurry to get off the sand. Maybe the pistol was still there. Rafe spread his arms out to widen his trail. . . .

And almost immediately his right forearm slid by something metallic and smooth on the black ground. He didn't even have to clutch it, the soldiers towing him slid him along until the pistol came right into his hand. The whole world slowed down. Rafe gripped the .45, slipped off its safety, lifted and swung it forward as if moving through mud, and pointed it at the back of one of the soldiers towing Danny. Rafe pulled the trigger and the soldier's spine split open. As the man dragging Rafe turned around, Rafe shot him in the face.

The officer spun, snatching at the rifle he had slung over his shoulder; at the same time the soldier who had been leading Red along like a mule shoved Red onto his face in the sand and unslung his rifle too.

Rafe's pistol jammed; sand had worked into its slide.

The Japanese officer deliberately aimed his rifle at Rafe's head and was pulling the trigger when Danny slammed him down from behind.

The fourth soldier shot Danny in the gut, then took aim at Rafe's heart . . . but before he could fire, bullets fired from behind him punched through his chest, and he fell like a puppet whose strings had been cut.

The Japanese officer rose in surprise, and was slashed across the shoulder with a farming scythe. Chinese peasant soldiers—there were at least a dozen—hacked him to death, then took a great interest in the American flyers.

Even before they could free his ankles from the wire, Rafe struggled to Danny, moving the Chinese aside. Danny lay on his back, clutching his wound as if to hold on to his life.

"Danny . . ." Rafe said.

Danny's words came in soft spurts. "I'm not . . . I'm not . . . gonna . . . I'm so cold. . . . not gonna make it."

"Yes you are. YES YOU ARE!" Rafe shouted to him.

But Danny was silent. His eyes drifted shut, and in that moment Rafe thought he was gone already. Then Danny's eyes drifted open, finding him. "Do me . . . favor," Danny whispered. "Let somebody else . . . spell my name . . . on the tombstone."

The words caught Rafe off guard; for a moment he almost smiled. Then his eyes filled with grief. "Danny . . . you're my family. You can't leave me like this!"

But Danny did not or could not speak.

"Danny . . . Danny . . . you can't die. You can't. You're gonna be a father."

Did Danny hear? His eyes were closed again. But his head came up; Rafe cradled his head in his arms, and Danny reached up with a hand that trembled, but had the strength to pull Rafe even closer, so that Rafe could hear Danny whisper . . .

"No. You are."

Rafe kept Danny's head nestled in his arms. Danny's eyes were open, but Rafe saw no light there.

"Danny . . . Land of the free . . ." Danny did not answer, and Rafe began to weep. "Land of the free, Danny! Land of the free . . ."

But Danny would never answer him again.

34

When news of the raid spread throughout America, it did not cause wild celebration. As people read the headline DOOLITTLE RAIDERS BOMB TOKYO, something deeper happened than an external demonstration of joy. It was as if each American had been told something he or she had known all along but no one else had seemed willing to believe: that their nation would prevail.

President Roosevelt acknowledged the price the young heroes had paid, and he took delight in their victory. Knowing the Japanese were tormented by the mystery of where the planes had come from and agonized by their resulting sense of vulnerability, he taunted them further, publicly gloating that the planes had taken off from America's new secret base in *Shangri-la*.

But when the headlines announced ALL PLANES LOST, SIX SURVIVE, the mood turned grim.

The early reports were wrong. For an eternity of days, no one knew the fate of the downed flyers. Then little by little, they began to emerge from the Chinese countryside and make their way to help, and home.

Eventually, all but five would make it back to the United States alive. One B-25 crew, knowing they lacked the fuel to reach the Chinese mainland, flew into Siberia instead and were interred by the Russians until the war was over. All the other crews bailed out or crash-landed. Those who made the Chinese mainland were assisted heroically by the Chinese, who later suffered atrocities at the hands of the Japanese military as punishment for their help to the American flyers. Entire villages were wiped out, their inhabitants subjected to tortuous and vile deaths. The savagery of the Japanese against the Chinese during the entire period of World War II ranks alongside the worst of the stupendous cruelties in the dark history of warfare, and though this fact is known it has not been widely acknowledged.

Of the five flyers who died, two were formally executed by the Japanese inside Japan itself, officially condemned as war criminals. How their raid against Tokyo during a declared war could be considered a crime, while the surprise attack against Pearl Harbor could be called a legitimate act of war was never explained by those who conducted the execution.

Jimmy Doolittle was not sent to Leavenworth Prison; he was taken to the White House, where he was awarded the Medal of Honor, and was promoted to the rank of general.

Evelyn was standing among some civilian wives in deathly cold fear as a long-range transport plane landed at the Pearl Harbor airfield and taxied to a stop. When the doors opened Colonel Doolittle was the first to emerge, and those gathered there, both civilian and military, began to applaud politely. He seemed embarrassed by that and waved them to silence. Then several other banged-up flyers emerged from the plane into the sunlight. One wife, overjoyed to see her husband, could not wait for him to get to the bottom of the stairs before she ran crying into his arms. Then Rafe, his arm bandaged and his forehead stitched, stepped from the shadows of the plane. His eyes found Evelyn, and her heart leaped. His did too, but he could not smile; coming through the cargo doors in the plane's belly were several flag-draped coffins. Rafe moved to the one he knew was Danny's, and with the honor guard that had come out to meet them, he escorted his body and those of his other friends away from the plane.

Then Evelyn reached him, and wept in his arms.

When the action is over, and we look back, we understand both more and less. This much is certain: before the Doolittle Raid, America knew nothing but defeat; after it, nothing but victory. Japan realized for the first time that they could lose, and began to pull back; America realized that she would win, and surged forward.

It was a war that changed America. Dorie Miller was the first black American to win the Navy Cross, but he would not be the last. And it was a war that changed the world. Before it, America could watch Hitler storm across the whole of Europe and say it was a local problem; after it, even a civil war in a place as remote as Vietnam would seem to be an American problem. World War II began at Pearl Harbor, and 1177 men still lie entombed in the *Arizona*. America suffered. But America grew stronger. It was not inevitable. The times tried the souls of Americans, and through the trials, Americans overcame.

Out by the crop-dusting landing field in a sun-caressed valley of Tennessee stands a small stone memorial, with an American flag etched in the stone above the name DANIEL WALKER. Engraved below the name is his poem:

> *I soared above the songbirds*
> *And never heard them sing*
> *I lived my life in winter*
> *And then you brought the spring*

A year after Rafe McCawley landed for the last time at Pearl Harbor, he stood beside Evelyn at that monument in the Tennessee heartland. He held a baby boy in his arms; around the child's neck was a medal—Danny's medal, one of a pair that Jimmy Doolittle, in his first official ceremony as a general, had handed to Rafe.

The boy was always comfortable in Rafe's arms, but he squirmed now, restless to walk, and Rafe let him down to the soft summer grass. He took wobbly steps, pointing to the shiny red biplane—Rafe's father's plane, carefully restored. Rafe knelt beside the boy.

"Hey, Danny," Rafe said to him. "You wanna go up?"

The boy had no idea what the man he called daddy was saying. But he smiled, like the first Danny once did, a smile full of wonderment, joy, and life eternal.

Evelyn stood beside Danny's monument—she never thought of it as a grave, so full of life was the son he had brought her—and watched Rafe lead the boy toward the bright plane, and knew she had found that one place on earth that she would always know as home.